ITSUKA

ITSUKA

Joy Kogawa

best wishes
Joy Kogawa

Anchor Books
DOUBLEDAY
NEW YORK LONDON
TORONTO SYDNEY AUCKLAND

AN ANCHOR BOOK
PUBLISHED BY DOUBLEDAY
a division of Bantam Doubleday Dell Publishing Group, Inc.
1540 Broadway, New York, New York 10036

ANCHOR BOOKS, DOUBLEDAY, and the portrayal of an anchor
are trademarks of Doubleday, a division of Bantam Doubleday
Dell Publishing Group, Inc.

Itsuka *was originally published in Canada in 1992*
by Penguin Books Canada Ltd.

The Anchor Books edition is the first edition published
in the United States.

Itsuka *is based in part on some actual events, but all the main characters*
are fictional.

The excerpt appearing on pages 337–43 from the
author's novel *Obasan* is copyright © 1981
by Joy Kogawa.

Book design by Claire Naylon Vaccaro

Library of Congress Cataloging-in-Publication Data

Kogawa, Joy.
Itsuka / Joy Kogawa.
p. cm.
Sequel to: Obasan.
1. Japanese—Canada—Evacuation and relocation, 1942–1945—
Fiction. 2. World War, 1939–1945—Canada—Fiction. I. Title.
PR9199.3.K63I87 1994
813'.54—dc20   93-26076
                                                              CIP

ISBN 0-385-46885-7
Copyright © 1992 by Joy Kogawa

ALL RIGHTS RESERVED
PRINTED IN THE UNITED STATES OF AMERICA
FIRST ANCHOR BOOKS EDITION: January 1994

10 9 8 7 6 5 4 3 2 1

This book is dedicated to the people of the Church of the Holy Trinity in Toronto, especially the Ad Hoc Committee for Japanese Canadian Redress; to the many laborers in the National Association of Japanese Canadians; to all the individuals and organizations who signed up for the National Coalition and those many people across Canada who responded to the Ad Hoc Committee's ad in *The Globe and Mail*.

The author wishes to thank the following people
for their help with this book:
Meg Masters, Gena Gorrell, Ben Fiber,
Sallye Leventhal. Thanks also to Alan Borovoy
for the use of his speech.

1

I'm standing at the bus stop in the splattering rain, waiting for the northbound Bathurst bus, and here, unexpectedly out of the grimy air, is a gift. It's as if I've been in a coma for years, in the debris at the side of the road, and suddenly there's a presence by the roadside, as tangible as an ambulance driver kneeling and doing mouth-to-mouth resuscitation and thumping a fist on my chest to get my heart moving. And my lungs are filling. It's as if I can hear a voice calling my name through the blare and scuffle of traffic, and I want to lift my arms up but I can only take a breath—a deep choking breath. But that's enough. Here. Waiting for the bus. Not moving at all. It's enough to be breathing.

"Thank you." The words come forth unannounced.

There's a promise in the air. I can feel it as surely as I feel the raindrops. I could throw my head back and laugh but the people standing by might say, "Poor crazy thing."

Specifically, what I'm sensing is that it's all right. It's not what people say that matters. What's important is what precedes. It matters to stumble after. In the midst of all the unknown, it matters to trust. It matters in this time of not-yet sight that some skin cells seem sensitized to light.

It may have been something like this in those murky days before there were eyes. Perhaps some of our jelly-bodied ancestors floating on the sea felt the sun beckoning forth feelers. And there they were, our primitive eyes, light-sensitive cells in stamens of flesh quivering across the waters.

What frail creatures we are, yearning to know and desperate for what eludes us. We're a planet of snails with our delicate horns, probing the windy currents of memory and meaning.

Here at the bus stop, there's a whisper in the air—a whisper of a promise in a siren wailing far off in the distance. "Make way! Make way!" it's crying. "Clear the roads in all directions. Clear the lungs, the throat. Clear out the pathways for breath to move through."

Beneath my skin, a rainbow is forming and sending forth its beam of hope. I can feel it precisely. Thank you for this.

It was Van Gogh, I think, who said, "There is a God, not dead, not stuffed, but alive, urging us to love with irresistible force." That's conviction. But in the end, I understand, Van Gogh was overcome by torments.

Rainbows, it seems, come with a history of tears. They follow a deluge of doubts and fears and struggles in which many of us do, in fact, drown. Fears, fears. They come in swarms like mosquitoes at a picnic. They leap upon us like fleas carrying plagues.

Right now I fear most the weight of judgment—the whispers, the sneers, the glances of condescension. I fear too the cunning of the body's inner foes. I fear touch as much as the inability to touch. So, of course, I fear Father Cedric.

I see Father Cedric as a deserter from the ranks of Fear's terrible army. Or a spy. A sort of clerical 007.

The first time I met him was seven years ago, in 1976, the year I moved to Toronto. What a shock everything was that August afternoon when I arrived. I wondered how the birds with their porous bones could fly in the choking smog.

Father Cedric was standing with my aunt at the bottom of the airport arrivals escalator, a wiry dark-haired man, laughing extravagantly and calling out, "Allô!" I'd never heard a French Canadian accent before. He and Aunt Emily were waving wildly as I descended.

"Father Cedric, chaplain of St. John's, meet my one and only niece, Naomi."

Aunt Emily, my mother's younger sister, is completely non-Japanese in her exuberance. She's a militant nisei, a second-generation, made-in-Canada woman of Japanese ancestry. She didn't stop talking from the moment she grabbed my shoulder bag until I fell asleep on the cot in her former study. A stream of consciousness is usually within, but hers is a flood on public land.

"Couldn't get a pin in here yesterday, Nomi," she said as the three of us heaved my trunk into the empty room. She and Father Cedric had just moved her office to a small windowless "rabbit warren" at St. John's College. Her books, papers and dusty stacks of old newsletters were now in their own private archives.

"All my life's junk," she sighed.

"A national treasure," Father Cedric said. "The Japanese Canadian Dead Sea Scrolls."

"You mean *The Nisei News?*" Aunt Emily's chuckle is rich, throaty. There's a density in her voice but, more than that, there's a certain density in her whole being. She exudes an unstoppable quality that makes people defer to her.

The Nisei News was one of Aunt Emily's many efforts to keep people in touch after the war when our community was scattered across the country. In those anxious and lonely times, Aunt Emily's mimeographed letter carried news to her hundreds of isolated friends—one here, one there, in hamlets, cities and farms.

"The dispersed are the disappeared, unless they're connected," she says these days. "If you aren't joined to those you love, your heart shrivels up and blows away in the dust. Whole countries get disappeared that way. It could happen to Canada."

Back in 1976, few people thought that Canada might someday disappear. "But the topsoil's eroding," Aunt Emily would say. "Read the signs. Our roots aren't meshed. A country needs the structures of connectedness."

She wasn't particularly successful in being heard, but "What's success?" she'd ask. "If you're doing what you have to do, that's success enough."

She still looked so "young" then, her short peppery hair a thick mop of health. She was fifty-nine but could have been my age. I'd just made it to forty. No one believed it. Neither did I. As for Father Cedric, he was ageless. He could have been thirty, or sixty, though I now know he's exactly my age. Two months older. And such a jubilantly elfin smile. The laugh lines from his eyes run down the sides of his face, almost touching the laugh lines from his mouth going up. His embrace last Friday was as light and surprising as the touch of soap bubbles. I stumbled over my feet.

The problem is, I can't be direct. My heart beats erratically when I have something to say. The other night at his apartment, I was stammering away like an adolescent. Father Cedric held his head to the side and looked amused. It was unnerving.

Nothing that ever happened back home in southern Alberta prepared me for Toronto and Father Cedric. This city is outer space, and Father Cedric, free-roaming, French Canadian, post-modern priest, is a Buck Rogers from another galaxy. At least in Granton and Cecil there were rules. But here? I didn't even know there was a Toronto rodeo when I was lassoed.

I used to feel so sorry for rodeo calves, roped, strangled and heaving in the dust, their eyes bulging. But then would come the moment of release. The rope would be cut and the legs kick free. It's almost like that, here at the bus stop. How long will it last—this uncanny sense of certainty that is already beginning to elude me?

2

It's early Monday morning and the streetlight outside the window is starting to sputter in its last stand against the morning light. In about another hour the early morning shadow of the chestnut tree will project its moving sketch against the white wall. From down the alley the garbage truck clanks its way past the laundromat. Any second we'll hear the jaws of the garbage cruncher—crunch crunch, burp, gunge. The street is about to start its weekly pre-dawn stomach cramps.

I'm awake and wide-eyed, wondering about the puzzling ways of a freedom-loving priest. He's a man who lives by unknown rules. It's his space, his initiative. When I see him next my questions will clog the drains.

So then, I must phone for the plumber within. He's tunneling under the hair follicles to the broken valve somewhere there, and calling out as he wades, "Hold on. Have faith. You're not alone in this."

But in spite of the messages yesterday at the bus stop and this morning from the ministry of the interior, I know this is aloneness. I'm lying here in this $323-a-month bachelor apartment in Chinatown Toronto, a middle-aged throwback to the reptilian era, and I'm alone alone alone. Alone on a foam-pad bed on a shiny hardwood floor which, quite miraculously, is free of cockroaches.

Until this weekend, I've been more or less content with my quiet life and my solitude. No television. No radio. No Aunt Emily rattling on and on, her hairbrush in her fist, bobby pins in her teeth, drowning out my thoughts from the moment I wake up.

I lived with Aunt Emily in her messy high-rise apartment for my first six years in Toronto. Her constant chattering drove me mad in the end. I longed to be back on the wide-open prairies with the cool breezes at night and the soothing sounds of the frogs and crickets. I finally found my own place.

The other night I fled down Father Cedric's back stairs and out into the late city night, my thongs flap flapping. I ran round the corner to my apartment, fell onto my bed and lay curled up, trying to calm myself, knowing there was not a single person I could call. I certainly wasn't going to wake Aunt Emily at that hour, and anyway, what would I say?

I stared at the walls and the portrait of Naomi Best

hanging above my desk. Maybe if she hadn't been glaring down at me in her intimidating way all my life, I might have turned out differently.

Aunt Emily thinks it's hilarious that I was named after Miss Naomi Best—large-boned English Canadian missionary to Japan. She was a loud woman, severe and authoritative, and when she spoke, she boomed.

"I wonder if Papa thought you'd be like her?" Aunt Emily muses from time to time. It was Grandpa Kato who insisted I be named after his benefactor.

To Aunt Emily, even though I'm now middle-aged, I will always be just a timid leaf in the wind. But I wonder if somewhere inside me there's a booming Miss Best at bay, trying to get out and take charge of wind currents.

In her early dauntless days, Naomi Best, matriarch of the marginalized, was on hand at the docks in Vancouver, greeting the Japanese as they came off the boats. She shepherded them into free classes of English conversation. Christian English conversation. Grandpa Kato, older than her, was one of her series of "houseboys" and she taught him how to pray, how to boil potatoes and how to iron.

I remember certain Sunday afternoons, Stephen, my older brother, in a sailor suit and me in silk and smocking, being trooped off to Miss Best's house for her British Canadian tea parties. There was my beautiful, gentle mother, with her pudgy sister, Aunt Emily, skinny Grandma Kato and my other aunt, Obasan, all elegant in pearls and furs and perfume. Those were our "paradise lost" Vancouver years.

Aunt Emily says I was a silent baby and stared from

the moment I was born. "Your initials should be N.W.N.," she says. "N. Watcher Nakane." I suppose I was still taking the world in when Mother and Grandma disappeared. I was five years old and had just started kindergarten.

"Where's Mama?" I'd ask.

"Japan. She'll be back."

Not long after that, the whole world fell apart as, day after day, people disappeared. In our family, father's brother went first. Then Father was gone. Aunt Emily and Grandpa also vanished. And suddenly one day, Obasan, my brother and I were in the middle of a black-haired throng, milling about at a train station in a ghost town called Slocan. We were separated, and we were concentrated. The displaced Canadians.

In Slocan, we survived. Men built flumes for water from the hills. People planted gardens, built bathhouses and a school. But three years later, and just as suddenly again, we were on trains once more, headed for sugar-beet farms, fruit farms, sawmills—as laborers, servants and factory workers across the country. The government's "Dispersal Policy," Aunt Emily says, was a "smashing success."

Sometimes I'd catch Aunt Emily sighing as she went through old photographs. "Look at us. Dan could have been prime minister," she'd say. Or "Here's Min Kawai. Poor Min. The greatest artist Canada never had." And Obasan would murmur, "Ah ah, Minoru-san."

Minoru Kawai, one of Aunt Emily's friends, was a young artist taken under Miss Best's ample wing. She'd claimed his work belonged in the Metropolitan Museum of Art in New York. Something sad, something mysterious, had happened to him. And there were other half-told stories floating about like mist.

If Naomi Best had been around, she would have helped us, Aunt Emily says. Especially Min. Things would have been different. But Miss Best was called, by God, to Japan.

Before leaving, Miss Best bequeathed her heavy mahogany radio to Father. To Mother she left a handful of lavender seeds in a lavender-colored handkerchief, the powerful fragrance permeating the drawer of the treadle sewing machine. To me, her namesake, came her silver-framed oval portrait. Throughout our travels, when we were, as they say, "evacuated" to the internment camp, the portrait of Miss Best journeyed with us. And later, in Granton, Alberta, "Besto-sensei," in profile, looking more severe than Whistler's mother, hung high up on the wall, her proud Christian nose sniffing the prairie air.

The last photograph I have of Miss Best shows her in Japan, looking increasingly Japanese, her body angled forward humbly, leaning on a walking stick. Even at Death's beckoning, she did not turn back to "the green and pleasant land" of her birth but she stayed with her Japanese orphans.

Obasan clung to memories of Miss Best and happy days in Vancouver. In the beet fields of Alberta, she made pancakes and we'd sit in the dirt and the heat with thermos bottles and pancake "biscuits" and have our Sunday afternoon tea.

When my brother and I were teenagers, we moved from farm shack to town shack. Gone were the long rides in the yellow school bus. We bought a coal stove and lo!—real biscuits on Sundays once more. Obasan unpacked the rest of the apple crates from Slocan and out marched the King George–Queen Elizabeth mugs from their old *Vancouver Daily Province* wrappings. There they reigned on the kitchen shelf among the Melmac cups and saucers, souvenir relics in Obasan's small queendom.

Obasan never once expressed a wish to return to Japan. Both she and Miss Best lived in the country of the heart. They knew whom they loved. They were afflicted with an interchangeable disease. If Miss Best had become an unlikely Japanophile, Obasan was an equally unlikely royalist.

The day King George VI died, no one in Granton mourned more than Obasan. She sat by the radio, head bowed, hands folded in prayer, listening to CJOC Lethbridge. "The king died quietly in his home early this morning. His valet discovered the body at 4 A.M. when he went up to deliver some tea. Death is believed to be due to a blood clot. . . ."

Obasan's royal family clippings were kept in a scrapbook. Beside it were chocolate boxes of old family pictures. Such a spare collection. A few snapshots. A few professional portraits from a studio in Vancouver. Slocan was basically a ghost-town gap. No photos ever came from Mother, who was stranded in Japan and disappeared there. Grandpa was ill in Toronto and died. And I have just one small picture of Father's grave in the mountains of B.C. It all seems so matter-of-fact at times. A grave here. A grave there. Barely visible headstones.

Aunt Emily says that when Canada smashed our lives

apart, it sickened its own soul. A few years after travel restrictions were lifted, she arrived in Granton by train from "out east." She found me still silently staring at the world.

"Where's your power of speech?" she asked, frowning. "Voice box dried up, kid?"

She told Uncle and Obasan, she told anyone who'd listen, that we should be speaking up for our rights. We were Canadians. Our houses had been stolen. All our houses.

A visiting issei, Mr. Makino, admitted, "Government shouldn't to do. Not right thing."

Aunt Emily said that was so and, as far as she was concerned, the Bird Commission had been a complete farce.

I had heard vague words about some ghostly government thing called "the Bird Commission." When I asked Stephen, he growled that I was "too young" and he scorned the "too dumb" issei, the immigrant generation, who understood little English. For Obasan and Uncle, the Bird Commission was another one of those matters that kodomo no tame, for the sake of the children, was better not discussed.

Mr. Makino was afraid the Bird Commission was a trap. We were the birds. The Commission was the cat. It was best to keep still.

Aunt Emily said the Commission, intended to get us fair compensation for the property the government stole from us, was a slap in the face. "Just as well none of you filled out claims." Those who applied got ten cents on the dollar. She said our community should organize and fight to get our homes and farms and stores and churches and restaurants and mines and sawmills and boats and keepsakes returned to us. We should fight for the right to go home. But no one listened.

Obasan said everyone suffers, everyone's life has mistakes. And Uncle, like an old man I heard in Slocan, said, "Itsuka, itsuka." Someday, someday, Emiri-san. There is a time for toil. A time for tears. Someday the time for laughter will come.

3

If I had even a speck of Naomi Best's courage I'd phone Father Cedric. But I don't dare. Maybe he'll call me. He could be sitting by his desk phone this very minute, hands on his high cheekbones, deep smiling eyes looking somewhat perplexed. "Now what is the matter with Naomi Nakane?" he may be thinking. "I didn't know she could be so strange." Or, more likely, he's not thinking about me at all.

If Aunt Emily were here, she'd say, "Talk to him, you fool. Pick up the phone." And before I could stop her, she'd be dialing his number. Thank heavens I'm not living with her anymore.

"Life," Aunt Emily keeps telling me, "is meant to be a hands-on experience. You've got to act. Do things. You've got to be involved, kid." It doesn't seem to matter to her that, at forty-seven, I'm no kid.

She reminds me from time to time that she carried me home from the hospital when I was a week old. Her memory is altogether better than mine, although I do remember the beautiful house we had in Vancouver, the playroom, my dozens of dolls, the living room with the tall gramophone whose wind-up handle I could barely reach, and the velvety curtains, the Indian rugs. And I remember, as a child in Slocan, how I ached, how I longed to go home. I begged Obasan and Uncle to take us back.

"Itsuka," they'd say. Someday. But in 1945, instead of going home, we found ourselves in Granton, Alberta, blowing in the dust of the sugar-beet fields.

When Aunt Emily tells me about the need to get my hands dirty, I think of the mud and the heat and the hoeing, my dirt-blackened fingernails, and, silently, I tell her that I've had more than enough. My childhood was a total "hands-on experience" from spring thinning to harvesttime.

The other night, after running away from Father Cedric, I was lying awake, listening to a lone cricket announcing my idiocy to the world. Chirp chirp chirp chirp. Here lies Naomi, nitwit from Granton.

There were armies of crickets in the beet fields, jumping and crawling along the furrows, their shiny-as-metal black bodies vibrating in the heat. Audible calligraphy. I'd catch them and put them in matchboxes or in one of the many little gift boxes Obasan kept under the bed. And there they would sing through the long twilight night, with the breeping frogs in the slough, the occasional high howl of a coyote.

It's one of those sleepy prairie evenings. The nightly orchestra is tuning up, the eternal crickets stringing the air. I'm twelve years old perhaps. Or thirteen. And here's Stephen bringing a jar of water into the house. And there's a frantic cricket swimming and jumping in it like a frog and—what's this?—a shiny black water snake, thin as a hairpin, curling and coiling along the wall of the jar.

"Hey, where'd you get them, Steef?"

He says he saw the snake coming out of the cricket's behind. I believe him. I believe everything he tells me. After this, I take my captive crickets and plunge them mercilessly into Obasan's tub of rainwater, where they leap frantically, their bodies making small pings against the sides of the galvanized tub.

Eventually I cease these murderous experiments and turn my attention to other creatures. Our cramped little shack is home to an ant farm, a salamander in a bowl, one lame frog I find in a slough and another that I pump out of the cistern. Both frogs disappear, eaten, I suspect, by Poppy, our pure white cat.

Poppy, who has one blue and one yellow eye, is elegant and fastidious and can be forgiven her predatory ways. A cat, after all, is a cat. And cats do kill. But she also, to my great delight, gives birth. And that too is a hands-on experience for me.

One late spring afternoon, Poppy, pregnant and

"ready to pop," as Stephen puts it, is in her safe place on a bundle of rags by the coal pail behind the stove. I'm on an old quilt on the floor. Poppy's sandpaper tongue occasionally sticks on the rags and she shakes her head to get rid of the lint.

"What doing?" Uncle asks, poking the coal in the stove.

Poppy lifts her head nervously, whiskers quivering, tail twitching. I pet her gently, and I can feel a hard round shape, a kitten's head, the size of a large marble, as the fur ripples unevenly over her bumpy belly. She utters a sound like the crabble crabble of Obasan rubbing the soapy clothes on the washboard, then she sits, rolled double in a ball. And suddenly, there it is! A slippery gray sausage creature! Lick lick, pull, lick. Diligently she chews away, removing the filmy sack till she uncovers a dark wet lump with hair-thin toenails, a sturdy wet stick for a tail and a squinched-up face with no eyes and with pinhole nostrils snuffling moistly. While Poppy rests from the licking, out comes the next sausage, just as soundlessly. Carefully, I try to pick up the first baby. It feels like a cold wet thin leather purse full of warm water. I'm afraid I'll puncture it.

In all my decades of life I've never found anything so dear as this one particular gray sausage lump. He purrs within minutes of his birth. I roll him around in the palms of my hands, snuffling his sweet furriness. I know when his twig-stiff umbilical cord drops off and when the first holes begin to poke open in his wet black eyes.

He's irresistible. Even before he begins to see, when his eyes are still pinpricks, he responds to my voice, his head wobbling back and forth as he strains toward me. I warm him in the cup of my hands, and he rolls around languidly, his purr a surprisingly loud rattle.

I keep the kitten, of course. Gabriel, the angel of fur. Obasan and Uncle indulge me. Obasan and Uncle are easily the most indulgent of all people. The Granton snapshots include one of Gaby enduring a doll's hat. And Gaby like an owl sitting on the cistern box. Then there's one of baby Anna Makino wearing a frilly dress and clutching Gaby in her pudgy arms.

When I was about six years old, living in the ghost town of Slocan, I once found a mewing kitten trapped in the pit of an outhouse. I peered into the terrifying depths from which rose a constant convoy of flies and the piercing sickening smell of lye and human excrement. What a torment it was—the helplessness, the need for a savior and for the faint cries to end. I can still hear them.

Our days in Slocan are over but the kitten's voice lingers—in the squeal of an unoiled hinge, in the distant mewl of a seagull. Suddenly in the ordinary day are the disembodied cries of the lost and abandoned in their wretched outhouse dyings.

Aunt Emily tells me that when a Slocan reunion was held in Toronto in 1974, the take-home souvenir was an image of a jaunty outhouse in a puck-shaped plastic paperweight. "We were taken out of the 'benjo,'" she says —benjo is the word for toilet—"but the 'benjo' wasn't taken out of us."

Aunt Emily has a dreadful collection of benjo songs.

> *Fee fie fiddle-i-o,*
> *Strummin' on the old benjo.*

Or

O Susannah
Cry all you want for me,
For I come from British Columbia with
a benjo on my knee.

Uncle is good-natured about Aunt Emily's crazy songs and accompanies her with his spoons tapping merrily on his knees. But as a teenager in Granton, I'm relieved when she goes, taking her singing with her and leaving us to our peace. What matters to me is school and Young People's, the church's youth group, and getting decent grades. At home what matters is to get the dishes done, the homework done, and to feed the cats. All the cats. Our own as well as the occasional stray.

I adore our cats. So do the little girls who come to visit—Lydia Regehr and baby Anna Makino. Whenever a batch of kittens is born, small children arrive like spring flowers sprouting on the kitchen floor beside the stove.

"Oh oh keeka keeka," Baby Anna cries, clapping her dimply hands.

After six weeks or two months, Lydia trots off down the streets with the kittens in a box, looking for adoptive homes. It's a workable system. Crickets and kittens and small visiting children all are part of the ecology of our life. Every Nakane morning dawns and yawns and ticks on past as cheerfully as the cuckoo clock warbling the time away. Above us, watching over us, is Miss Naomi Best, high and oval on the living-room wall. Her God is in his heaven. All's right with their world.

4

All is not right, however, in my brother's world.

Stephen and I are both full-blown teenagers in 1951 when we graduate from the heat of the beet fields to the village of Granton. Stephen, for his part, walks the tightrope of adolescence buffeted by the winds of a fierce emptiness. Though we never speak of it, I know that deep in his heart is a shrine where he worships our missing parents with the intense longing of a lost child.

In that world of the wanderer, his outstretched hands clutch at absences. Out of the silence sifting through his fingers he fashions his cage of music, his violin bow moving across his prison bars, freeing the cries locked within. He is driven, and he is permitted his drivenness, late into the dawn and all day long as he makes and remakes his music—variations on themes from our dead father's scribbled notations. His early compositions are a rage of order, his chaos contained in a precise mathematical passion, his wild energy bowing to Father's delicate and gentle melodies. It's as if he becomes the instrument on which the spirit of our father plays. Never once, no matter what the hour of day or night, do Uncle and Obasan ask Stephen to stop playing his violin or the piano which Uncle buys. Uncle says many things grow in the dark, and if you trample the seedlings there are fewer buds in the day.

His music is not to the liking of all the folks in Granton. There's Hank, the milkman's eldest son, who rides past our house on his horse while taking the cows to and from pasture. He leans over and yodels, and Stephen's multilingual violin moves fluidly from Bach to "Little Brown Jug" to country hoedown.

"Real purty fiddlin' there," Hank calls as the clanking cowbells move rhythmically past.

Then there's Crazy Alex and his mangy old mongrel, Dog. Dog is often seen limping along on three legs, a foreleg raised delicately, like a lady sipping tea. Their usual spot is in front of the Rainbow poolhall/bus stop, where the Greyhound bus makes its brief twice-a-day pause going to and from Seven Springs. He sits on the sidewalk coughing and spitting and waving at the passengers, with Dog anxious by his side. One time Uncle finds Crazy Alex passed out in the middle of the road, and Dog pulling at the semiconnected suspenders, trying to get Alex back on the sidewalk. "Beri good dog," Uncle says admiringly.

Once in a while Crazy Alex comes teetering by our house with Dog limping behind. Dog doesn't take to Stephen's violin. He hangs his head as if he's being punished and blinks his eyes.

In the evenings, sometimes without eating supper, Stephen takes his violin in his homemade wooden case and rides off on his bike or in the truck. His coming and going is never questioned. I imagine him out there alone with the coyotes, baying at the moon.

As for me, I tramp about the prairies never speaking of our days in Vancouver. Somehow I know we will never return to the house where Happiness lived. Once upon a time, there was a peach tree, singing, storytelling. Now the huffing puffing wolf stands over the ruins.

Stephen remains in the rubble. He is quick to anger. He catalogues, categorizes and tries to control the debris. He puts precise labels on every book and photograph. He preserves Father's music on cardboard. His notes are meticulous and detailed. He is smart. His grade ten teacher, Miss Hildebrand, is, two years later, my grade ten teacher as well. One time when I manage 100 percent on a test, she stands over my desk, approval pouring over me like molasses as she says, "My, my, Naomi, you're just like Stephen, aren't you."

"Genius Number Two," the boy behind me says.

Sometimes the little boys shout, "Hey, maestro, get a horse," as Stephen drives past in the pickup. I suspect their kibitzing is more a taunt than admiration. He's not your regular friendly farm lad. But, intense and difficult though he is, I feel a ping of pride when he is onstage.

He begins by facing the piano, as if it's a living being.

And at a precise moment something happens. The piano begins to speak, Stephen's fingers leap and we in the auditorium are trapped, captured in the intimacy of their private, passionate conversation.

Obasan and Uncle never once come to these events. It's understood. They do not belong. The categories are clear. People like Pastor Jim, Hank and especially the Barkers from the farm where we used to work come to school concerts. People like Obasan and Uncle, Crazy Alex, Lydia's roly-poly mother and of course the recent immigrants, the DPs, do not. That is the way of the universe. DP stands for Displaced Person and is as unkind a term as Jap.

Then there are the Hutterites, a mystery to me. They are small flocks of dark birds. You see them standing in their pickup trucks outside the medical clinic. Then suddenly, for weeks, they are not there. Some mornings when I walk down to the post office, I see silent clusters of four or five women and girls in their long black print dresses and kerchiefs, the men in black collarless suits, the married ones bearded and the boys in suspenders and not quite long enough black pants. Once I say "hi" to a little girl who, like most of the others, wears thick glasses, but she doesn't answer back.

Of all these and other categories of Grantonites, it's the Mennonite Brethren group from whom we feel the greatest kindness, and it's Lydia's older sister, Tina Regehr, the blue-eyed blond-haired Mennonite Brethren girl, who is Stephen's first love and nemesis. She wears dresses that have no pleats and her long braided hair is wound up in a wreath. No matter how unshapely her clothes, she is, as Stephen says, "real cute, real smart and real special." The two are the top students in Stephen's class and both of them are on the student council. She is the lead singer in Stephen's musicals, her soprano voice as bright and piercingly clear as the three-toned high-low-high and trill of a meadowlark. Once, after a performance, I catch Stephen flicking what might be a tear from his eye as he stands up from his piano accompaniment and applauds her. She's wearing a borrowed blue taffeta dress that twinkles and swishes with every move, and blue suede shoes, and she is so beautiful I can hardly breathe. The glance that passes between them as they bow and applaud each other is one of the most cloudless memories I have of Stephen and Tina.

Tina and her twin brother, Jake, who is a bit slow, and their younger sister, skinny little Lydia with her pencil-thin braids, live in a small house behind the Mennonite Brethren church. The church is a plain unpainted building a couple of miles outside of Granton. They have a chicken yard behind their house and about fifty Rhode Island Reds. Obasan sends us to buy the brown-shelled eggs with the bright yellow yolks. She says the more yellow the yolks, the better. I perch on the handlebars of Stephen's bike and we ride double, bouncing over the washboard road.

Once during the summer holidays, the church's pump organ breaks down. Some keys are stuck and when you push on the pedals a high squeal comes out. Stephen is called to help Mr. Regehr fix it, and afterward Tina says that thanks to Stephen they now have the mellowest-toned reed organ. She sings "Blessed Assurance" while Stephen alternately pulls out the tremolo and trumpet stops as he accompanies her.

Plump Mrs. Regehr is making Mennonite buns as she often does—munchy fist-size lumps with an extra little lump like a bun hat on top. "You take for Mama yo?" Tina's mother says. People in Granton speak of Uncle and Obasan as our mother and father even though they know they aren't.

Jake, who never wants us to go home, bars the door. "Stay longer, ya? It's early already."

Stephen casts quick glances at Tina.

"Lock open the door, already, Jake," Lydia commands. "We'll come with. Ya?"

And off we go through the long twilight, Lydia and I leading the way, Tina and Stephen dawdling behind, the crickets chirping in the ditches and the dry breezes filled with the clean everywhere faint prairie smell of manure and hay. Jake keeps circling round on Stephen's bike, saying, "Borrow me your bike a little yet, okay?" as they go with us halfway.

5

Granton is a large village, as villages go. Eventually it manages to make it to the status of town.

"Pretty fancy-dancy, eh?" folks say when electric lights appear. For many of them electricity is a "newfangled modern thing," but for us it's nostalgic.

The night after our lights are installed, Lydia and Jake come over and stare in awe at the suddenly bright kitchen with its bare bulb dangling from the low ceiling.

"Can I make out the light?" Lydia asks, and I hand her the pull string.

"In Vancouver we had lamps. We had lights on the walls."

Jake's head bobbles like a jack-in-the-box, as it usually does when he's baffled.

Vancouver, I tell him, was bigger than Granton, which has only one large grocery store, a hardware/dry goods/post office, a meat market, a bank, a Chinese café, the poolhall/bus stop and two garages, one at each end of the constantly dusty two blocks we call Main Street.

"You gots a church in Vancouver?"

"Oh ya." I remember the church with its dark walls and thick pews, and of course our minister, Nakayama-sensei. He's in Coaldale now, a small town like Granton, not far from the city of Lethbridge.

Granton is a town of churches. More churches than trees. More life on Sunday morning than on Saturday night. A fundamentalist fervor threads its way through all the seams of Granton's dark gowns. Even the old and pallid Protestant standbys, the Anglican and United churches, are filled with an evangelical zeal. Close to our house is the Full Gospel Fellowship, which has the largest congregation. The Roman Catholics, we are told, worship idols of Mary, and their mysterious church is a little house near the reservoir.

In summer, we attend every Daily Vacation Bible School in town. DVBS is all more or less the same, with the same children, and Tina teaching in whichever churches it's being held that year. She tells Bible stories using a flannel board on which she places trees and sun and sky made of colored flannel, and the cut-out Jesus and Abraham and so on have flannel glued on their backs to make them stick.

The singing is bouncy, our arms gesturing extravagantly through "The wise man built his house upon a rock" and "This little light of mine." Jake, who has a great voice, sings loudly but gets his words mixed up, especially Calgary and Calvary and cavalry.

> *Mercy there was great and grace was free*
> *Pardon there was multiplied to me*
> *There my burdened soul found liberty*
> *At Cal-ga-ry.*

"Jake's doing a Calg'ry Stampede song already," Lydia teases. "Jake says, 'Our Father chart in heaven, hello be thy name.' "

"Stop it already, Liddy," Tina says crossly. "Don't be so heathen."

Tina says the heathen are, of all people, the most to be pitied, and she has "a burden for their souls." Pastor Jim of the Full Gospel Fellowship tells us the heathen in darkest Africa wear no clothes until God convicts them of their shame. And pagan people in India and China and Japan worship idols of wood and clay.

Obasan has an old clay figure of a Japanese farmer that Jake thinks is a "heathen idol." I put it under the bed, where Gaby keeps knocking it over. Eventually Obasan wraps the farmer in a sheet of newspaper and puts it away with some holey socks.

Pastor Jim is a trumpet-playing soul winner, and a Youth for Christ crusader. When the gospel is preached in all the world, he says, the millennium will arrive. With all our hearts, we want the millennium to arrive.

On Friday nights, through sludge and snow, Tina, Jake, Stephen and I sprint down the wide gravel street to

the liveliest Young People's around. We see movies on
science from the Moody Bible Institute, or go on wiener-
roast outings. Tina, sincere and radiant, is a lovely singing magnet, drawing Granton and district youth for
God's greater glory. With her soft blue eyes gazing past
us, she sings, "I come to the garden alone," compelling
us to come with her to the early morning hush of the
garden where "the dew is still on the roses."

At other times we sit around a campfire down in the
coulees by the river bottom, and Pastor Jim opens his
Bible, thickened by much use. The world, he warns, belongs to Satan. But we belong to God.

"Resist the devil," Pastor Jim says as the unpredictable breezes fan the flames, "and he will flee. Turn to the
Lord, and he'll lift you up."

I usually sit on the log between Tina and Stephen,
who seem to spend a lot of energy trying not to look at
each other. If their eyes do meet, Tina's cheeks flush and
she hunches over her knees, clutching the hard round
toes of her saddle oxfords, as she stares intently at the
fire.

At the end of the evening, Pastor Jim asks us to raise
our hands and make our "decision for the Lord." I'm an
easy believer. I commit mind, soul, body and the air I
breathe to the love of the Man of Love, his God and
their Word. Fervently and sincerely, I vow to be a Christian.

"If you confess with your mouth the Lord Jesus and
believe in your heart," Pastor Jim says, "you shall be
saved."

But the promised peace is not an easy one. I cannot
hold at bay the ravenous spirit of doubt that stalks
through the night. As the grid of the Christian funda-

mentalists' way of life descends, so too do the demons of the flesh.

I encounter the devil's confusing handiwork once during beet-thinning season in late spring. Spring, if you can call it that, is usually a sudden brief slush. After that, you roast or freeze again while the shriveling wind packs your pores with grit and turns your skin into tree bark.

It's unusually warm, this Saturday nausea morning. The stranger has been driving his noisy old car slowly along the edge of the beet field, stopping it, backing it up. He's a fat bald man who has blown into the area with the chinook. No one quite knows who he is. He's been seen standing outside the poolhall reading the Bible out loud to Crazy Alex. But it's also whispered about that he cornered a girl behind the curling rink and fondled her.

"Beware the kingdom of lust," Pastor Jim says, "and be ye not deceived. Satan knows the word of God and trembles."

The stranger is out of the car and standing by the ditch beside the road. He's watching me as I slash the earth with my hoe, once or twice on either side of each beet plant. Stephen, heaving his body to the side, is moving like a crab. He and Uncle are almost at the other end of the field. I gave up long ago trying to keep up with them.

When I reach the end of one row I lean against my hoe to rest. I have my head down and am not looking at the stranger but I can feel him approaching. And then when I turn around, there he is lurching toward me, a five-dollar bill in his thick hand, his eyes so wide they are bulging.

"Hey," he calls out as I stand frozen. "What's your name?"

I turn my eyes from him, not wanting to be rude, not knowing what to do or say. As casually as I can, trying not to look afraid, I step backward. I glance toward Uncle and Stephen, who haven't looked up.

It's while I'm walking toward them, and not looking backward, that the dizziness and the pain roll through me. I double over.

"Uncle!"

I stumble over the clods of earth, faint and retching. "Hey there, hey there," the stranger keeps blurting out.

"Uncle!"

I have soiled myself. I'm mortified. I'm half crawling as I change direction and head for the irrigation ditch bridge. Uncle with his bowlegged rolling gait comes running across the field to where I lie, hiding under the bridge in the mud where the stranger can't see. I remove my underpants gingerly. Without a word, Uncle squats in the mud and the thistles, taking the foul garment as if it were a handkerchief and swishing it in the brown ditch water.

All that afternoon, Uncle stays with me in the clamminess of the dirt cellar at the far end of the field. There's a salamander there, and spiders and sacks of putrid potatoes. Uncle says, as he rubs my back, it's the sun and the bad water, but whether it's that, or the stranger, or something else, I do not know.

Pastor Jim says sickness is caused by Sin. I'm so often sick.

Stephen, mysteriously healthy, survives the world, the flesh and the devil. He goes to the movies in Lethbridge and sees *The Yearling* and *Gone With the Wind* and *Cyrano de Bergerac* and *Ships Ahoy* and many other shows. They are all made by Satan, but Stephen appears to be safe.

The one thing that most upsets him happens in his last year of high school. It's a big blowup he has with Tina over the school campaign run by the wild kids to have dances allowed. Tina campaigns against the campaign. "Keep Granton Godly" is the slogan among her friends and supporters—the quiet and the good who follow the Lord. The ones who vote pro-dance are a small clique of evildoers, reckless and forbidden as Coke and aspirin swallowed during study periods in the washrooms and cloakrooms and out in the patch of weeds behind the west entrance. They're big bad teenagers, mostly from Tina and Stephen's class, loud and laughing and hanging around the poolhall with its jukebox, or roaring down the highway, jammed together in the front seat of the pickup truck that belongs to Cliff, the gang leader.

That fearsome and rowdy gang of five, or sometimes six, want Stephen and Tina to join them. More Tina than Stephen. The girls of the gang are pretty, but no one is as pretty as Tina, who, in spite of her unshapely clothes, is obviously buxom and cuddleable. Stephen, they know, can play boogie and jazz and will always be able to get "his old man's jalopy."

The beginning of the end comes the day that Cliff and his girlfriend, Loretta, roar over in a screech of brakes and dust to ask Stephen to join the campaign.

"Hey, genius," Cliff shouts from his truck window, "whaddya say, eh?"

"Wouldn't you love to dance with Tina?" calls Loretta.

Stephen shrugs and they take that for total support. Their next move is to corner Tina and tell her that Stephen couldn't care less about Pastor Jiminy the crusading cricket and is voting for dances.

Tina gasps and covers her mouth in shock. She tells Stephen she could never, never, never, never even think about such sinfulness. Stephen says dances aren't *that* bad. Tina groans and says she's really sad at his backsliding and she hates Ingrid Bergman (who played Joan of Arc but got pregnant by someone she wasn't married to). She hates her hates her. And Stephen says he can hardly wait to get out of Granton and go to university.

"University! A modernist institution," Pastor Jim tells Uncle when he hears the news. "He should go to Bible school."

Most of the young people at Pastor Jim's go to the Prophetic Bible Institute at Cecil, Alberta, many of them before finishing high school.

Uncle smiles agreeably. Stephen, of course, will do the right thing. And Granton's benevolent sun will continue to shine even if Stephen does decide to go to a modernist institution.

"I'm not going to university," Tina says.

Pastor Jim approves. " 'There is a way which seemeth right unto a man, but the end thereof are the ways of death,' " he says.

The difference between the right narrow road and the wide death road has something to do with the flesh. Whatsoever things are pleasurable are, at the very least, suspicious. "So remember the rule," Pastor Jim says. "If you doubt, don't." And since I doubt almost everything, almost everything is denied. Certainly I doubt what I'm expected to doubt, but I also doubt Pastor Jim.

Secretly, and from afar, I'm dazzled by the bad kids. But they, it is obvious, are not dazzled by me. I'm one of the good, the boring and the limbless. I don't dance, I don't hug, I don't wear lipstick, I don't smoke or drink. I take it all as "the Way the Truth and the Life." It's the way of the Bible Belt, and today the fact remains. The village is still in my middle-aged veins.

6

Sitting as I do these days with Father Cedric and Aunt Emily in *Bridge* magazine's air-conditioned Toronto office, I don't often think of Granton, but when I do I remember the heat and the bluebottle flies, those heavy-bodied little buzzards filling the summer air and frantic around the cowpies. Flies flies—the curled sticky tips of their black thread legs, their brown goggle eyes. They're in everything. Obasan tries to keep them out of the house but it's hopeless. They pillage the world of sleep. In dreams, I rage upon them with my hands, squeezing them with my fingernails, pushing so hard that I cut right into their bodies, but they're utterly indestructible.

Granton in the fifties is policed by a buzzing army of dark-winged gossipers. Piety reigns, her dense gown billowing, her camphor-laden perfume wafting over the scent of alfalfa and the new-mown hay. The odor of the sickroom settles on us all, the faithful, the fallen and the unconvinced.

One day a daring newcomer starts showing movies in the community hall, but the local onward army marching as to war swiftly closes it down. "The devil's own lair is overturned," Pastor Jim says. "Praise God."

I would love to see movies, but I can't unless I go with Stephen to Lethbridge. Stephen is aching to live in a city again. But when we were sent away from Slocan, we could only go to those centers in Canada that would accept us, and most cities, including Lethbridge, emphatically did not want "the Japs."

As a child, I don't understand all this. The adults are silent, whispering the phrase of protection—kodomo no tame—for the sake of the children. But where the hundreds of children from Slocan have gone, I can only guess. A few may be on farms or in villages like Granton —places that have churches, but no movie theaters. Here in the small prairie towns, instead of the evils of Hollywood, we have our one-night-stand evangelists sowing God's word in our hearts.

For these evangelists, whose mandate is to rescue the perishing, there are only two categories of people: the saved and the lost. And those who come from "that Godless nation of Japan" are definitely the lost.

Obasan, Uncle and Mr. and Mrs. Makino are quite unaware that they're eternally damned. Most Sundays

the Makinos, who live seven miles away on a farm, walk
the distance to visit us.

"Kon nichi wa," plump Mrs. Makino calls in her gentle voice as she opens the door and beams at us, her
sweet face round as a manju beancake. From inside her
black woolen handbag come her gifts—a tin of sardines,
an orange, mushrooms from a prairie ditch. Sometimes I
catch Obasan and Mrs. Makino talking quietly of happy
days before the evacuation. And they comfort each other
with low dovelike murmurings. I listen intently when
they speak of my beautiful mother, who had a yasashi
kokoro, a loving tender heart. On those several occasions
when Stephen receives awards for his music, they nod
solemnly and say, "Ah Steebu-chan, Papa wa
yorokonderu yo." Your papa is rejoicing.

At some point, I can't say when, my ache for my parents vanishes into the depths. All I know is that there is
a time when the aching is no longer there, as if it has
fallen through a trapdoor.

The Sunday Makino visits are gifts from another
time, a more gracious, a more kindly day. These are
quiet afternoons, uncluttered by strain, except when Pastor Jim arrives at the back door, the Bible open in his
hands.

"Afternoon," he shouts as he peers through the door.
" 'This is the day which the Lord hath made. Let us
rejoice and be glad in it.' "

Pastor Jim is never quite able to penetrate the sound
barrier behind which the issei move, nodding attentively,
eyes politely downcast.

"Sisters, brothers, are you saved?"

"Thank you," they say, bowing and smiling humbly.

The difficulty Pastor Jim has with the issei seems to

have something to do with a sense of time. For Pastor Jim, the moment is "now." "Now," he says, "is the hour of decision." The past with its sorrows is to be redeemed in the present. Truth is spontaneous. We are to stand straight, look forthrightly in each other's eyes, and the more transparent our feelings, the more we are trusted. But the issei! To them such demonstrations are aggressive, arrogant and, at the least, extremely rude. Pastor Jim, I suppose, must think they are mentally retarded or emotionally dead. I know, however, that they are acutely sensitive and that their feelings are all the more intense for being contained. It isn't that their emotions are denied in the present. It's that they're not being squandered. The moment's joy is being conserved, like everything else, for tomorrow's need. The moment's pain is being attended to in light of time's healing. Itsuka, someday, things will be all right. We can endure. The slow-rolling locomotive of their emotions bears a "made in Japan" label on it.

Pastor Jim, baffled but undaunted, moves on to the English-speaking generation and wins the souls of the Makino sisters, Marion and Suzy. They are both cheerleaders at school. Marion has a terrible crush on Stephen and stands around outside his homeroom after school, but Stephen ignores her. She's nowhere near as pretty as Tina. Narrow slanted Japanese eyes, he says.

After Marion and Suzy are saved, they both turn from their many sinful ways. No more lipstick. No giggling at dirty jokes. With Tina, they become Tina and the Makduo, a singing trio, two trim black-haired altos in black flared skirts and bobby sox with Tina in the middle, her hands folded to her chest as she sways gently.

Pastor Jim declares that the Anglican faith which we

and the Makinos embrace is not biblical. Prayers belong not in prayer books but in the heart. We must be born again. And it isn't right that the Makino baby, Anna, is to be baptized. A non-biblical act. The Makino parents come over several times to discuss the worrisome matter.

Plump Mrs. Makino is forty-six. She didn't know almost up to the birth that she was pregnant. She thought she'd entered menopause and was getting overweight. Uncle says it's a good joke. A grandchild come so soon. Mr. and Mrs. Makino want to name their surprise child Kazuko but Marion and Suzy say they know English ways better. And as we all know, English ways are better.

"Her name will be Anne," say Marion and Suzy, "spelled with an 'e,' like 'Anne of Green Gables.' And no Japanesy name." Like Stephen, they hate everything Japanese. Our horsetail hair. The way we fold paper.

Uncle says it's a shame the baby doesn't have a second name. An extra name is like an extra blanket, a comforting weight at the foot of the bed.

The issei can't pronounce Anne and say "Annu." Nakayama-sensei says "Anna" is easier to say, and that's what is written on the baptism certificate, to the great disgruntlement of the Mak-duo. As it is, the issei all call her "Annu-chan" anyway.

"Babies," Pastor Jim says when he sees Mrs. Makino in town, "should not be baptized. God's Word says that you must believe in your heart and confess with your mouth the Lord Jesus. And *then* be baptized."

"A worry," Mrs. Makino says, relating the incident to Uncle and Obasan.

"Muzukashi," Uncle says. "A difficulty."

Suzy and Marion scold their parents, saying Pastor Jim knows best. Uncle nods his head slightly, wondering if that might be so. It's understood that the matter will be left to the Mak-duo, who will take their directions from Pastor Jim. And nothing will be said to Nakayama-sensei. We will continue to go to Coaldale for Christmas, or funerals, or the frequent farewell parties as families flee the beet fields.

"Anna," Pastor Jim says, "should be rebaptized, God willing, when she makes her decision for the Lord." And several years later, when she reaches "the age of understanding," little Anna Makino is officially, at the age of seven, born again, to the great rejoicing of her sisters and Pastor Jim.

I happen to be there with Tina that memorable Saturday night in June, but Stephen is long gone from Granton's thundering halls of righteousness. He's made his escape to the University of Toronto. I miss him. I miss his music. The standards that Tina and Stephen set are not reached again in Granton school.

Tina eventually goes to Bible School in Winnipeg. That same year, 1954, I take a Temporary License teacher-training course in Calgary, and I return the following year to teach school in Granton. Once in a rare blue moon, Stephen comes roaring home for a few days or so. "Just like Emiri-san," Uncle remarks. He's with us for a brief hello, and then he's gone, leaving Obasan, Uncle and me waving at the edge of the road, our eyes filled with the dust of his departures. Over the years, it becomes a game of musical chairs, with Aunt Emily and Stephen alternately popping in and popping out.

News of Stephen's successes in the world of music comes via the pages of *The Lethbridge Herald*. "Granton's Nakane Wins." Many townsfolk are proud of their own local boy becoming a minor musical celebrity.

But Pastor Jim is unimpressed. " 'Only one life, 'twill soon be past. Only what's done for Christ will last,' " he says. And in Granton, the steadfast singular life of the faithful remains unchanged.

The Saturday night that Anna Makino's salvation is secured, Tina is home from Winnipeg for the summer, full of zeal and eager to hear Brother Leroy Sage, the missionary who is on furlough from Africa.

Saturday nights are when evangelistic crusades, healing services and hymn sings are held in the huge community hall/arena, a dome-shaped metal structure with a wooden sidewalk to the front door. Here Granton's voices may dance though our feet may not.

Brother Leroy's account of his firsthand encounter with Satan in a grass-covered hut is mesmerizing. "Oh yes," he thunders, "don't let anyone lead you astray. Satan is alive and binding the hearts of the heathen to a living hell. I have seen him take a laughing child and, in minutes, murder that precious boy with a sudden sickness. And I have seen Satan flinch and flee at the *name of Jesus!* In that very hut, when the Lord commanded him to be gone, Satan fled, for Satan cannot bear that holy name of the Son of God. Hallelujah!"

"Praise God," Tina whispers.

"But Satan is not just in Africa," Brother Leroy continues. "He's here tonight, hungry as a roaring lion, seeking whom to devour, spreading doubt in this great auditorium. Doubt is the devil's weapon. 'Have faith and doubt not,' saith Holy Scripture. And here tonight, Satan is creeping through the aisles looking for small cracks of doubt so that he can step into your minds. But, praise God, friends, *this,*" he shouts, holding his Bible high over his head, "is God's holy unchanging Word, sharper than a two-edged sword, dividing bone from marrow, and with *God's Word,* we can banish all doubt, my friends. But do you know," and here Brother Leroy holds the Bible to his heart, "men today, in the guise of God's servants, are doing Satan's work, planting doubt into this precious book. Make no mistake. The modernists belong to Satan, my friends. Is there anyone here tonight who doubts that Jesus was born of the Virgin Mary?"

A general murmur rises from the crowd. "No. No." One man stands up and waves his Bible. The woman directly in front of us moans, "Precious Jesus."

"Oh I'm so happy tonight," Brother Leroy continues, "for I know and do not doubt God's Word, that Jesus was born of a virgin. But what do the modernists tell us? They take the word 'virgin' and change it to read 'young woman,' as if God, the All Powerful, who made all things, had no power to bring forth his Only Begotten Son from a virgin's womb. Now isn't that foolish. Oh what a great folly it is to put our trust in man's puny wisdom. What does Holy Scripture tell us? The wisdom of man is folly to God. Yes, dear friends, the Revised Standard Version of the Bible is the handiwork of Satan. Oh yes. Satan is everywhere. In Africa, in that mighty beast, the World Council of Churches, and he is here in Granton. Yes he is. Do you have any drunkards in your midst? Pray for them as they struggle in the grip of Satan's drink. And say all together with me the words that our Lord said. 'Get thee behind me, Satan.' Can you say it with me now?"

"Get thee behind me, Satan," we roar.

"Say it again! Say it till it shakes the very gates of hell! Say it till the power of alcohol is gone forever from Granton!"

"Get thee behind me, Satan!"

I hear a moan behind me as the shout disappears and it's Crazy Alex, holding himself up by the back of my folding chair, gasping the chant over and over.

Tina turns around to grasp his hands. With tears streaming down her face, she repeats the phrase. His eyes are fixed on her with a look of utter anguish. Finally he sits down, heavy with sobs, and Tina puts her already damp handkerchief to his eyes.

"You know what it's like," the evangelist shouts, waving his index finger, "when one little finger is held in a candle flame. You know the pain, the torment. And do you know what it will be like, dear friends, when your entire body is in hell? Not just your finger, but your whole arm, your shoulders, your body, your entire body will burn. And not just for an hour, not just for a day, or a week. No sir. What does God's holy book tell us in Revelations? There is everlasting torment in the lake of fire for those who do not confess that Jesus, the sinless Lamb of God, is Lord."

The rounded ceiling of the windowless hall has a string of light bulbs down the middle. "Will you be a light to lighten the darkness in this sinful world?" he shouts, pointing upward. "If you have never known the joy of the Lord, friends, let this be the night. Let this be your hour of decision. Rise now from your seats all over this great auditorium, wherever you are—you there in the blue jacket, I can see the struggle Satan is waging with you—rise up and come to the Lord."

The hall fills with a chorus of hallelujahs as here and there people rise resolutely, or with heads hanging down. From somewhere, a quartet is singing, "Softly and tenderly Jesus is calling," and as if by a force beyond the room people are pulled trembling to their feet. My heart is beating wildly, as it usually does around this time. A gray-haired woman a few rows in front lifts her arms, crying, "Jesus! Savior!" and suddenly there's little Anna in the aisle with Crazy Alex behind her, walking unsteadily toward the front, through the singing praying moaning crowd.

"God bless you, God bless you," the evangelist is saying to the suddenly born-again believers shivering like newly shorn lambs at the front. I realize with a start that Tina is nudging me to go to the front as well. And without another thought I'm walking arm in arm with Tina down the aisle until we stand on either side of Crazy Alex and Baby Anna, our hands linked behind them.

And that is the beginning of the new life for Baby Anna Makino and Crazy Alex, in the community hall in the summer of 1958, their trembling hands in Tina's and mine. The Makino parents come after a few days to report that Baby Anna is having terrible nightmares and is afraid to come out from under the covers, and that perhaps if we let her have Gaby for a week she might feel better. Uncle and I drive over with Gaby, whose ears seem permanently glued back throughout the drive and whose trust level falls several notches that night.

But if it's the beginning of new nightmares for Baby Anna, it's the release from old nightmares for Crazy Alex. The seed of the fear and love of God falls into his rocky weed-choked life and takes root. The transformation, everyone agrees, is a miracle. Alex, no longer crazy, no longer sits on the sidewalk outside the poolhall. The following Sunday morning, we see a new, clean-shaven, well-dressed Alex walking down the street to the United Church with Tina on one side and heavy Mrs. Alex, his old mother, in a flowery hat on the other. Even Dog looks better. For a while Dog walks around with a red and white handkerchief tied around a splint. Eventually he bites the splint off and starts to walk like a regular dog, which is just as astonishing as the miracle of Alex's sobriety.

As for Gaby, he's returned to us in a potato sack, and emerges with what looks like intense irritation. He licks my ears for a week. I find it mildly disgusting.

7

The years gallop by in a prairie blur. Time, like an accordion, contracts and expands, wheezing out its tunes to which we Grantonites do our daily dance—Hank on his bow legs, Alex on his newly sober ones and Obasan in her slippers, shuffling in her kitchen, to and fro. It's a song of tumbleweeds we all sing, rolling and blowing across the dry land. None of us is quite in step with the others, which seems to worry Pastor Jim but is of no great concern to us or to Hank, our only regular visitor.

Hank is a big-boned bronze-age bachelor, ten years older than me, who yodels his easygoing way past our house every day on his horse. He parts his hair right down the middle of his head, and when on foot he gives the appearance of leading with his pelvis, leaving his arms dangling behind him. A tall ungainly man. But on the back of a horse at the local rodeo, he is airborne, a prancing, wheeling creature. The younger lads outdo him in the speed and bronco contests, but he holds his own with the lasso.

One afternoon, I'm walking along the path of dried cowpies and am overtaken by Hank, his horse snorting beside him, his cows chewing their cuds and lolling their heads mournfully as they clank along.

"Howdy, Hank."

He grunts, thrusting his broad lower jaw forward till his bottom teeth are bared. "Howdy there." He gives his head a quick shake as if to rid himself of insects.

"Problems?"

Hank isn't a great talker. But he knows what's right and what's wrong. Sometimes he'll tell you.

We approach the high ditch bank near our house when he begins to talk, rubbing his forehead with the back of his freckled hand. "Durn city dudes."

I've heard this theme before. It's the Hank-versus-the-city blues. Sometimes it's Hank-versus-the-government. He'll go into a tirade against the unreal people on the six o'clock news. I can't see the point of attacking a tiny black-and-white paper prime minister who looks out at you from the front page of *The Lethbridge Herald*.

It turns out Hank was up to a new ranch with the vet in the afternoon and saw a cow that had bled to death while giving birth to a calf that was too large. "Treatin' cows like they was machines." She was a victim of artificial insemination, a process about which I'm curious but dare not ask.

"I tell ya, that city slicker cowpuncher, I seen him standing right there beside that there pretty cow. And this dude, you know, he had this here black shoe, all shiny like, you know—and he kicks this here little Bessie and I coulda killed him." He lifts his fist helplessly, shaking it at the sky. "And yeah, that calf now. Sure. That's money. But that there li'l cow," Hank spits on the ground and bares his teeth again, "she was just a hunka dead meat."

It's rare to see him actually angry this way. Generally, if there is something to be upset about, he stares at the clouds and rubs his forefinger along his broad jawline.

One thing about Hank, he likes his animals. He likes all animals, even Crazy Alex's dog who has been strutting around recently on all four paws. Hank gives his head a quick no-nonsense shake whenever he sees Alex and Dog and he'll say respectfully, "Man, if that don't beat the band. Mutt's lookin' good, eh?"

Hank's attitude toward me has also changed, ever since I came back from my year of teacher training in Calgary, a "full-growed schoolmarm." I now warrant an adult-to-adult nod instead of the straight flat grin and "Hi, kid." Sometimes I catch him looking at me quizzically as if trying to fathom the change.

I'm not used to Hank's anger and don't know how to respond to it. I scuff the thistles and stare at the ground as his cows continue to mosey along tranquil as milk, flicking the flies off their rumps.

Near our house, Hank stops, looks down at me and suddenly, out of the clear blue stormy air, he grins,

spreads his honest cowboy hands open and says, "Say,
Teach, you wanna go to the movies?"

I'm so startled that I almost trip. Hank? Asking me?
One moment he's cursing the "city dudes" and the next,
he's smiling and asking for a date. Obasan would say
"otenkiya-san"—person of changing moods like the
weather.

"How's about it, eh?"

It's never occurred to me to think of Hank as someone to go out with. He's just always been there, in his
blue jeans and his blue jacket with his gangly walk, delivering the milk since his father got sick several years ago.

"Uh," I say, which is neither yes nor no. My impulse
is to look over my shoulder to see if anyone is in hearing
distance. I'm feeling mildly mortified though I can't
think why I should. I have a fleeting thought about cows
and the difference in size between us. Squash the
thought.

"Think you'd like that?"

"Nh." I've never been adept at the art of conversation.

As things in Granton go, it's almost a marriage proposal. Here I am in my mid-twenties, have never been on
a date, have never danced and have never been kissed.
For all I know, neither has Hank, though I've seen him
at the rodeos being pursued by Anita Jeffrey, the grades
seven and eight teacher. Anita is closer to his age and his
size and is definitely more desperate than I am. She has
shoulder-length dark curly hair, a large vermilion-red
mouth, and she wears her wide-brimmed hat even in the
classroom. Jake Regehr thinks she's beautiful. She's the
only one in Granton I ever see using an umbrella. When-

ever Hank rides past, she waves and he waves back, nodding his respectful nod.

My first date, by the standards of today's world, is completely uneventful. But people like Pastor Jim have standards that can only be met by the dead. He condemns a glance, a notion, a rising blush and all the forbidden sensations that gallop along the nerve ends. And there are still other condemnations that come from the judgment throne in the underground courtroom of thoughts. There are strangers from my childhood, glancing at us with distaste.

Hank is undisturbed by such specters and lopes along the straight and narrow without, it seems, either guile or guilt. He's a genuine respect-your-body, honorable intentions son of the rural route, smiling his wide prairie smile. I like him, of course. Everyone does.

It's hard to know how smart he is. In Granton, the smarter you are, the more you hide it. As we all know, the gopher that rears up on its hind legs is the one that gets snared. Anyone idiotic enough to "talk fancy" gets done in by the swinging lariat of small-town small talk.

He drives into the gravel driveway at 7 P.M. in his blue Chevy and his new cowboy hat. The screen door claps behind me as I go out, no fanfare, Obasan and Uncle being careful not to let on that anything unusual is happening. I'm wearing a pink and white flowery dress with a black cinch belt and we grin our greetings, two suddenly shy old neighbors. We drive off down the empty road, the dogs barking at the wheels, then racing alongside in the clattering gravel spray.

The drive-in is almost empty when we pull in, rolling over the small mounds, past loudspeakers on poles, all heads dangling to the left. Hank leans over to reach through the open window and decapitates the nearest pole. Throughout the movie, I have an insane awareness of his arm resting along the back of the seat, his forefinger stroking the electric-blue furry seat cover.

Once, I remember, Hank tossed a garden snake at Gaby, who was stretched out in the sun on the cistern box. The snake landed with a splat on Gaby's belly. The transformation was instantaneous. Gaby's sleek gray fur came unsprung in a hissing, spitting leap from the box. My reaction to Hank's large hand placed lightly beside my shoulder is not quite as severe, though the non-existent fur on my limbs bristles and an odd reptilian eye opens and blinks through the weedy murk in some ancient slough of my mind.

Nothing happens that is worthy of a camera's attention. But the late-night photographer leaps to the assignment and all night long, in my sleep, I'm in a nightmare of snakes as I walk up the mountain path in Slocan. Hose-like snakes, gray and wet, are here, there, coiled loosely in their unexpectedness. Near the top of the path is a yellow menace, with irregular ovoid markings. Should it decide to strike, its range would easily reach beyond me. Swiftly, before it spots me, I flee down the mountain, past the shell of a house where two children sit in the ruins, having a tea party.

The following week we head for the coulee road and drive through the open-air auditorium of the steep grassy hills, listening to the songs from *Oklahoma!* and the swishing sound of the grass against the car's underbelly. I'm squished against the door at my end of the seat, and Hank's long limbs are spread out at his end. He spends the evening clearing his throat, trying to say something. I don't make the effort and we end up listening to the coyotes howling at the moon.

Over time I become increasingly self-conscious about our after-school strolls along the ditch bank. I begin to see us through the eyes of imaginary onlookers, especially my fellow teachers. It's fatal. No matter how slowly he lopes along, I'm a centipede skittering beside him, struggling with a hundred steps to keep up. It's just too incongruous.

Hank isn't dampened by my offhandedness. One breezy afternoon, he looks down on me from his great height, swallows hard and says, "Been a lotta fellas saying it's time I was getting hitched."

The surprise and the feeling of inappropriateness nudge me in the ribs and make me want to snort. "That right eh?" I manage to say.

"Your folks ever say anything about that to you?"

"Nope. Not really."

"They get along pretty good? Your folks?" The strain of the conversation is showing on his face and his brow is crinkled up in neat farmers' furrows.

"They respect each other."

"Yuh," Hank says. "That's important. Respect." He nods seriously. "You know, li'l Teach, I respect you. Wouldn' never touch you. Not before."

Something inside me roars into revolt. To Hank, "respect" is a term only associated with sex. This certainly is Granton. Words have limited meanings here.

It isn't just that I can't see myself as Hank's wife. It's that I can't see myself as part of Granton at all. I'm a transplant, not a genuine prairie rose. I'm part city slicker, part traitor. Even if I stood still for a hundred years on Main Street, there'd be no Granton roots under my feet.

I write a letter to Stephen and beg him to tell me about Toronto and Montreal. For Stephen, the rootlessness must be even worse. I've managed to be potted in the sticky prairie soil, but he's wandering the world, a cut flower drinking in the fleeting applause of concert tours.

After school the next day, I see Hank through the playroom window, driving into the schoolyard. Anita Jeffrey, who is closer to the window, also sees him, and waves. He grins, tips his hat and waves back. She looks down at me over her shoulder. "I think he's coming to see me," she says. There's a touch of distaste in her voice. It's a sound from childhood. Scorn.

I go back into my classroom and, before I can clean off the blackboard, he's there, standing in the doorway, his cowboy hat in his hands. He comes right up to me and leans over me, his large hands resting on the blackboard, then on my shoulders.

"Naomi, I wanna tell you—you and me, me and you . . ."

Anita sways her hips and tosses her hair back as she goes slowly by the door and looks in.

"We can flow, Naomi. We can fly." His hands move down my arms and he's pleading. "You're tiny like a little bird. I wouldn' hurtcha. No, I wouldn'. But I . . ." He moves closer, breathing thickly.

I duck under his arm and scoot down the hallway, heading for the safety of the staff room. My heart is pounding wildly, and a slightly nauseous dizziness sends me headlong onto the couch. No one, thank goodness, is there. I can feel the tightness in my abdomen, the uproar spreading in waves. I lie still, doubled over in the darkness.

"Something is definitely wrong with you," I whisper to myself.

8

Just as I got up to leave last Friday night, Father Cedric sprang to his feet and stretched out his arms in a wide wingspread. According to him, all living creatures have grace and ease when they're at home. In the air the long-legged birds soar, but on land they flop awkwardly. What we need, he told me, is to find the place where we are most at home.

I feel like Alice in Wonderland when I think of Father Cedric—Alice following a white rabbit as it disappears down into the pupils of his dark eyes. Down at the bottom of the tunnel is Cedric-land, a place of mystery.

Back in the school that day, Hank in his gruff Granton voice had called me a tiny bird. But all summer long he was the bird, a barn swallow, pursuing bugs while I flitted and gerked about in the prairie air.

In 1964, I make my quantum leap, fleeing from Hank and Granton's loving smothering bosom. The town in which I land is on the moon.

Cecil is a hundred and fifty miles northeast of Granton. Most of the way there, except for a thirty-mile stretch of highway, is on a dusty washboard road that is as straight and bumpy and boring as the undanced road of the righteous. I may have abandoned Hank to Anita Jeffrey, but the everlasting fires of Pastor Jim do not abandon me. Three miles from Cecil Consolidated School is the Bible Institute where Pastor Jim's teenagers prepare for a lifetime in the service of the Kingdom of God. And that is where Lydia Regehr, still skinny in 1964, though taller, is also studying so that, like her sister Tina, she may "go into all the world to preach the gospel to every creature."

I spend the next decade in one classroom, where often the only movement outside is a cloud. Some days I sit there in the middle of the treeless prairie and nothing stops my eyes in their sweep over the sleepy world. Occasionally there may be a jet stream, clean and white, cutting open the mesmerizing blue, the only evidence of aggression in the peaceable realm. I watch till the leading dot is clear out of sight, wondering if Stephen is up there, high and distant in his rarefied air. Stephen is so removed from our lives that he's turning into one of those unreachable untouchable unreal people.

Some afternoons after school when the last of the straggling children is gone I stare at the orderly room, the little desks in their neat rows. It's hard to imagine a moment's violence anywhere. I put the attendance register on top of the teachers' manuals, place them in the desk drawer and sit there looking at the trampled brown turf of the empty schoolyard. There's a kind of patient waiting but I cannot say for what. Some charming unlikely prince, perhaps, to break through my gauze of sleep and waken me.

Aunt Emily drops in to see Obasan and Uncle in Granton and berates me for what she refers to as my self-imposed cloister. "You're not getting any younger," she says. But she's twenty years older than me and hardly in a position to counsel me on aging. I've been noticing the subtle changes in her face with each visit, the slightly drooping cheeks, hints of the wrinkled appledoll face to come. We're neither of us getting any younger.

I'm in my twenties and thirties during the quiet Cecil sixties. Lydia and I meet periodically on weekends, generally at the Cecil post office, where we all have mailboxes, and we stand there and talk.

It's risky, I discover, to ask about Bible School. Once we got into a harangue about the theory of evolution, a plot to destroy Christianity. Sometimes she wrinkles her nose and grumbles about the strictness. "Short-sleeve blouses even, when it's so hot already, they don't let you wear."

"What if you did?"

"Dresses like Miss Jeffrey? And lipstick even? For sure they would kick me out."

It's a ridiculous image—bony Lydia in a flouncy Anita
Jeffrey low-cut dress, swaying her non-existent hips. The
other day when no one was looking, she mimicked the
swing and we giggled so hard the tears flowed.

We gossip whenever we can get away with it. Many
people, we keep discovering, are mysteriously managing
to get married. We both feel a million miles away from
the marriage market and have no idea how to get there.
The Makino sisters stumbled upon it together, and
though they have always hated all things Japanese, in the
end they married Japanese Canadians. They both visited
Japan and came back transformed. Mrs. Makino said it
was a miracle. The same change has happened to other
young niseis. Suzy and Marion had a huge double wedding in Taber with all kinds of Japanese food and identical white lace gowns, and beautiful Hisako from the
town of Raymond sang, "When I Grow Too Old to
Dream." It looked as if all the Japanese Canadians from
southern Alberta were in attendance. Marion's husband,
Ken Suzuki, said, "Eat your heart out, Stephen," as he
kissed Marion.

And Tina, Lydia tells me one day, is going to marry a
Mennonite missionary doctor. "They're going to go to
Brazil yet."

"Brazil!"

"Brazil," she repeats, nodding, and her skinny braids
bounce so hard the knots of elastic at the ends make a
patting sound on her blouse.

It feels at once both unimaginable and inevitable.
Tina and Stephen were bound to touch distant lands.
That was destiny. Lydia and I will touch the familiar.
And then there's Jake, who doesn't even get to come
away as far as Cecil.

"I bet Stephen will be mad, ya? For sure he loved Tina."

I shrug. Who knows what Stephen thinks anymore, or where in the bright sky of romance my brother may be. There's usually a letter or two from Aunt Emily every month with a tidbit from the feast of Stephen—a meal from which we, his family, are excluded. Aunt Emily tells us he's in Montreal and on a roller-coaster ride with Claudine, a divorcée he met in Paris. He's too busy hanging on to his hat. "And anyway, some people can't write letters. It's a real disability. Like being born without arms."

I'm not inclined to believe it. Anyone who can buy stamps and address an envelope can answer a letter.

"Have you heard from your aunt?" Lydia asks, poking her right knee. "What does your knee say?"

That's a Lydia joke. I've told her that nisei, which means second-generation Japanese Canadian, is pronounced "knee say" and sansei, third-generation, is "son say."

"And who else is getting married already?"

Lydia hasn't yet heard the latest news. Hank took a bad tumble from a bucking bronco, and when he woke up in the hospital, he found himself in the y'all come wonderful welcome world of Anita Jeffrey.

"You mean, like marriage?" Lydia asks in disbelief.

"Looks like," I say, trying to sound offhand.

"My oh my. Poor Jake," Lydia says. Jake adores Anita Jeffrey. Once when she dropped a parcel, Jake picked it up for her and she kissed him on the forehead, and he said she smelled like heaven.

"Well, Miss Jeffrey, she sure had a hankering for Hank," Lydia snuffles. "She likes horses, ya?"

It was Anita herself who told me about her conquest when I met her one Saturday morning at the Granton grocery store. "We're doing what comes naturally," she said, her large red mouth smiling happily. "White folks marry white folks. That's what my daddy always says."

"Congratulations," I said. I thought I sounded sincere. I tried not to walk away too quickly as I left her showing her ring to everyone in the store.

That night I dreamt of little baby fingertips in the centers of deviled eggs. I opened the fridge and there they were, about a dozen fingernail pupils in the yellow edible eyes, staring out of a gray cookie tray. The aluminum tray was like the one that Obasan used to use in Slocan for checking the rice. She would sprinkle a cupful from the sack onto the tray and our index fingers would shove the foreign stony bits to the edge and out.

I wakened from the dream to find Gaby sitting by the pillow blinking at my eyes. Obasan told me my eyelids tremble sometimes when I'm asleep. I shoved him off the bed and wondered about fried-egg eyes and baby fingernails and not being able to stomach the idea of Hank and Anita together.

"Boy, after she gets married and quits teaching, she'll have to milk the cows. She'll have to throw the horse . . . ," Lydia lifts both arms dramatically, "over the fence some hay." We cackle over her Mennonitism.

Our unseemly behavior is attracting the attention of Erna and Annie, two of Lydia's Bible School friends who are standing behind her and reading their mail. They frown at each other.

"Do you ever get jealous?" I ask in a more subdued vein.

"Not about Miss Jeffrey, that's for sure." Lydia laughs

again, but then she's suddenly serious. "Oh, but Naomi, you wouldn't marry Hank! He isn't even a Christian."

Erna has opened her Bible and is thumbing through it.

"Tina's getting married," Lydia says. "Hank's getting married. Everyone's getting married. But us, not."

Erna steps in front of Lydia and looks up at her through her thick glasses. Erna is stocky and her dark hair is worn, like Tina's, in a braided wreath. But the hairstyle that floated like a halo around Tina is a heavy crown on Erna. From her frown, I guess that she's concerned about our gossip and our laughter, which is malicious perhaps.

" 'For where envying and strife is, there is confusion and every evil work,' James 3:16," Erna says as she holds her Bible open to its red-underlined armament of quotations.

" 'Submit yourselves therefore to God,' " Annie adds, looking over Erna's shoulder.

The mini-sermons are on their way. If we don't take the bait, they may stop casting lines. But Erna and Annie are prepared to make more than one opening move in the back-to-the-Bible battle—a battle to establish risk-free security for the soul in an eternity of the elite. I know the rules inside out. Woe to the one who doubts the word of the Lord that endureth forever. Woe to the one who asks "foolish and unlearned questions . . . knowing that they do gender strifes" (2 Timothy 2:23).

" 'God resisteth the proud and giveth grace to the humble,' " Annie says softly.

The pathway of salvation is lined with slogans and stones. At times, there's a grating sound in the air and the sharp two-edged sword of the word of God clanks like a medieval weapon. It's the way the words are used that sounds the war cry and makes a cudgel of the words of love. There is a spiritual one-upmanship in the call to humility, a ferocious salesmanship. Somewhere in the machinations of the advertiser's faith, in the endeavor to obliterate doubt, the truth that frees lies badly mangled.

Within me is a loathing to engage in their battle—the battle of the saved with the damned. I sniff aggression in the wind, and am off into the tall weeds, quick as a field mouse.

"Have to get back to mark papers," I lie and flee.

I look back to wave to Lydia but the three have their heads bowed in prayer.

9

Fighting is a way of life, Uncle says, for anyone like Aunt Emily, who has a fierce temper. "I've had to be a fighter," she says. "There's been a lot to fight about."

I used to imagine her squabbling with Mother when they were growing up. Mother was the beauty, the favored one, perhaps. There must have been rivalry.

These days Aunt Emily is talking almost constantly about the fight for redress for Japanese Canadians. "It's my last battle," she says, "and I'm going to give it all I've got. Could use your help, Nomi."

"I'm not much use in a war, Aunt Em."

People in the same family can learn such different responses to aggression. Some roll with the punches, some get knocked out, some fight back.

Aunt Emily finds my general mousiness irritating. "Anonymous Nomi, my niece. A nonny Nomi mouse."

Back in the summer of much marrying, the world divides itself into another version of those who fight and those who flee. There are people who have weddings and the rest of us who don't. Tina and her missionary doctor, Hank and Anita, are on life's winning teams. Crazy Alex and I are not. He slips back to battling the bottle. I continue to battle the breeze. As fighters, we are not great.

Being a born quitter has advantages. One meets the creatures from the underground, the moles and earthworms. One hears the gossiping of the grasses and the electronic night music of the bluebell roots. The sounds are decibels below the Bible-battering. My non-combative Uncle and Obasan, whose hands never once strike out in anger, are engaged in small tunnelings. A humble labor.

Obasan rarely leaves her shack, but when she does, she goes over to the Alexes' scraggly little house on Main Street, a loaf of Uncle's almighty "stone bread" swinging like an anchor in her green woven handbag.

"Thank you, my dear," old Mrs. Alex murmurs as she pulls herself to her feet from her doily-covered rocking chair.

On a dusty chest of drawers is a photograph of Mrs. Alex and her two young sons. "There's Alex," she'll say, pointing to the awkward boy standing to her left. "And that's Michael. He was the brighter lad."

Obasan knows enough English to understand that

Michael, the curly-haired infant on his mother's lap, was killed in the war.

"War is a terrible terrible thing, Mrs. Nak. A terrible thing."

Obasan nods sadly. The stories about Michael go on for hours while Obasan washes the dishes and floors.

Crazy Alex and Dog are rarely in, having returned to their usual spot on the sidewalk outside the poolhall. "Consigned to the devil," Pastor Jim says. "A slave to alcohol whom the Son would set free."

People generally know what to do. The postmaster, Mr. Wiebe, drops in with the mail. Hank brings them milk. Behind the Alexes' little house is a crumbling old cistern where they keep their dairy supply in a pail dangling at the end of the long rope.

Uncle is the mainstay of the Alex rescue unit, getting the groceries and fixing the screen and the window on the front door, which Crazy Alex manages to destroy periodically.

"Why, Nak, you've got the knack," old Mrs. Alex says in appreciation. "What a fixer you are."

"Busy is happy," Uncle replies.

One weekend after school, I drive down to Granton from Cecil and arrive to find Dog sitting on our kitchen porch scratching vigorously behind his ears, while Gaby is perched like a vulture on the roof overlooking him. Inside the kitchen entrance on the bootbox is a large pair of old work boots almost twice the size of Uncle's. In the living room, Crazy Alex is sprawled on the couch, his hairy arm across the small table, where there's a Melmac bowl of soup and a plate of Uncle's bread.

"What happened?" I ask.

Obasan nods her silent non-answer.

Over the weekend I learn by the few words and nods, as Uncle and I sit on the porch, that Dog is truly "beri smart." On the previous Tuesday night, Uncle had been awakened by Dog scratching at the door, whining and barking.

"Nanji goro, Uncle? Around what time?"

"Sa. Nanji goro. . . ."

Perhaps it was midnight. It was late, he said. He got up. He followed Dog. Or perhaps he was herded, "like cowboy dog." In his haste, Uncle didn't put his boots on, and he shows me his old slippers, frayed by the gravel road and stitched back together with string. He knew something was wrong with Alex.

The first place he thought to look was by the pool-hall, but no one was around. He next checked the house and found the front door broken again and wide open, which was not too unusual, but neither Mrs. Alex nor Crazy Alex was inside.

Dog in the meantime was off in a southerly direction behind the post office. Mrs. Alex's cane was lying somewhere in the ditch or near the water reservoir. For a moment Uncle worried that Crazy Alex might have fallen into the water, but Dog kept going—"Dog, leg okay"—past the reservoir, across the highway, past the car dump. And then he saw them. Old Mrs. Alex and Crazy Alex were down by the railway station, fallen onto the tracks, and from not too far away came the wavering hoot of the freight train.

Dog's teeth had broken Crazy Alex's suspenders and torn his trouser leg. "Alex too big." Uncle lifted Mrs. Alex to her feet. "Missesu, how can walk so far? No stick." He pulled Crazy Alex off the track and the three of them somehow hobbled along to the school janitor's house nearby, Uncle in his torn slippers, half dragging, half carrying Crazy Alex, with Mrs. Alex leaning and weeping on his other side. It must have taken forever to maneuver their way. Last winter old Uncle was barely able to keep upright himself and had at least two dizzy spells.

As they crossed the highway, Uncle saw a police car. Uncle, who has never broken a single law of this land, dreads the police. Once when he had to show his driver's license, his hands were shaking in his haste to obey. Luckily, he says, no police were in the parked car and he moved along as quickly as he could.

"Missesu okay now. I think so," Uncle says and pats Dog on the head. Dog whacks his tail on the porch like a beaver.

A month or so after this, on a hot August afternoon, I turn into the driveway again and find a clean-shaven Alex sanding some shelves that Uncle has been making for Marion and Ken Suzuki. Dog comes squeezing out from beneath the porch, his tongue hanging out from the heat. His raggedy old red and white polka-dotted handkerchief is once more tied around a splint on his right foreleg.

"Comin' home to the big town, eh?" Alex calls as I bring out the box of corn picked at the Makinos' on the way down.

Dog looks distinctly unhappy, panting, holding up his leg.

"What's with Dog?"

Alex snorts as he slaps his thigh and Dog hops over obediently. "Nuttin' wrong with us fellas," he says as he unties the splint and Dog wags his tail tentatively. "Gotta outsmart him," he says. "Get him so confused he forgets which leg he's supposed to limp on. Not a thing wrong with them hams."

Having regained his dignity, Dog comes up to greet me.

"Say," Alex says, looking suddenly serious, "any chance you'll be moving back home someday?"

"Uh . . ."

"Your folks aren't getting any younger, eh?" He wipes his forehead with the back of his sleeve and takes the box of corn from me.

"Guess not." I swing open the screen door and almost stumble over Obasan, who is squatting inside the porch with her little hand broom, sweeping up the hard chunks of clay and dust.

"O," she says in greeting as I hold out the freshly picked ears of sweet young corn. She wipes her hands on her apron and clutches a bench to pull herself up.

"Good thing Naomi's here, eh?" Alex says loudly in her ear as he stoops and puts the box inside the kitchen. "She oughta come back here. Help out."

"Thank you." Obasan says her all-purpose response. Thank you (you are kind). Thank you (I do not know what you mean).

There's a light groan from the other room, and Uncle's low voice calls. "Naomi-san?"

I go into the cluttered living room followed by Crazy Alex, and find Uncle attempting to rise from the couch. Crazy Alex's head almost touches the low ceiling. He helps Uncle to a sitting position, then picks up the round fan and fans him.

I sit on a mandarin orange box. "Okay, Uncle?"

Uncle grimaces as he straightens himself. He holds

his breath a few seconds before letting out a long noisy sigh. "Sa-a-a." A punctuation sound. A beginning of a thought. Or an ending. I wait for an explanation.

He points to his old pouch where he keeps a grayish wad of crushed mogusa leaves. That's for yaito, the painful skin-burning method of healing. Obasan and Uncle have pockmark scars on shoulders, knees. Is Uncle going to do this "heathen thing" in front of Crazy Alex? He is. Crazy Alex sits on a stool to watch as Uncle pulls off a small piece of mogusa and rolls it lightly into a ball about the size of a grain of rice. He places it on an exact spot, one inch above the back of the wrist, lights a stick of incense, and touches the mogusa. A tiny spark smolders and dies, smolders and dies, creating ash and a pin-thin trail of smoke as it burns its way down to the healing point.

He never does tell me that day in what way he is not well. He will not see a doctor when I suggest it.

When it cools off at night, we drive down to the coulee hills as we do every year around this time. "Umi no yo," he always says, opening his eyes wide as he gazes at the undulating prairie grass. "It's like the sea." Those are the last words I hear my uncle say.

"Umi no yo."

The following month, at the age of eighty-three, Isamu Nakane, my father's older brother, dies. Uncle, who loved music and played the spoons, who learned to tend the earth, but who always and always loved the sea —my kind and infinitely gentle Uncle is gone. Not once did he revisit the ocean and his boats. He lived out his life in a small Alberta town. With his hands, he healed the days. He replenished the soil.

Alex and his mother drive down with us to Coaldale,

and are the only non-Japanese Canadians at the funeral. Nakayama-sensei asks Crazy Alex to say a few words at the end of a hymn and he walks up to stand beside the closed coffin. "Mr. Nakane was Old Nak to me. And he had the knack," he says gruffly. "I owe my life to him."

Stephen plays a medley of tunes on the little reed organ at the back of the church—Bach, "Lead, Kindly Light," "The White Cliffs of Dover." Mrs. Alex weeps and leans on her cane.

For me, this year, a certain circular spinning stops. A cocoon disintegrates. The knowledge of death follows the knowledge of death and gnaws its way through my shell. This is the time of unraveling the tales of distant, lonelier dyings. It's the year I learn that my mother and grandmother were in Nagasaki when the atom bomb fell.

10

"Hope," the minister says softly, "is a great fisherman.
But the fisherman has been reeling in the past. That, my
friends, is a misdirected task. The dead must be permitted their passage to the dead."

Our friend and minister, Nakayama-sensei, has come
to comfort us in our mourning. He sits on the couch
beside Obasan, who is so deaf she cannot hear. In his
hands is a gray cardboard folder hiding an old old secret.

None of us could have guessed when Mother and
Grandma went to Japan in 1941 that they were crossing
the ocean to the world of the lost. As a child I was quiet

and good. I waited for them. I practiced the past and did not weep.

But now in 1972, the waves of her silence reach me at last. "Do not tell the children," the letters say.

"But you are no longer children," Nakayama-sensei says. He holds his bifocal glasses in one hand as he reads, his head nodding up and down.

The rain that falls on our little Granton house that night is a songless rain, a soundless falling. I'm thirty-six years old. I'm five years old. All the questions, the longing, the memories that have vaporized over the silent years, condense in the air and drench the waiting.

There is not an August since that telling that I do not seek my mother's face. For the rest of my days in southern Alberta, I continue the yearly pilgrimages Uncle and I used to make to the coulees, to walk under the night sky and to place our hands on the roots of the timeless prairie grass. There, in the vast stillness, I seek her face. I walk through the walls of my mind and call her name.

These more recent August memorial days, I go with Aunt Emily and Father Cedric to the "Hiroshima and Nagasaki Remembered" service at our old downtown Toronto church that crouches in the shadows of the Eaton Center. I light a white candle for Mother and Aunt Emily offers prayers. Her angry prayers.

"It's racism," she says, "that dropped the bomb on the little yellow people of Japan. It's the same lunacy that locked us up in animal pens. It's still around. It's got to be stopped."

She tells me that, whether I'm aware of it or not, my entire life has been shaped by racism. "Your kindergarten, for example. We started it to make sure all you kids were properly 'Englishized.' You know, they actually took

Stephen and every one of the JC kids out of their classes? Yes, it was segregation. Said they couldn't speak English. What a laugh. Stephen couldn't speak Japanese."

I can hardly remember the kindergarten, but later, the next week, when I'm folding a blue sweater, the memory floods back so suddenly and sharply I can almost smell my mother's perfume. My first kindergarten-going morning. How could I have forgotten? It's my giant step into outer space.

SEPTEMBER 1941.

I'm a pudgy four-year-old being taken by the hand. It's Mama's hand that holds my hand, a lacy handkerchief tucked into her sleeve.

The hall has nothing in it except small red chairs on which mothers sit, clutching purses. In the middle of the big naked space, children stand in a circle, holding hands. A woman is with them, urging the children to sing and clap and swing their arms as she does, and turn about and skip.

This is not for me.

"Come, Naomi," she calls and I'm the last child left, leaning against my mother's knees with my fat hand clutching her blue wool skirt that matches the blue wool dress I wear. Blue is my mother's favorite color.

It's not that Mama pushes me. Nor does she ever frown. She smiles as she whispers to me in secret that everyone is watching me—all the proud mothers who have brave children. And the mothers all smile, knowingly, indulgently, in a faintly teasing, urging way. A big girl, such a big girl, they whisper, nodding. See how Kenji, see how Makoto, see how So-and-so is there in the circle. See, Naomi-chan. See. And it's no longer endurable. I go to the circle with my white hanky in my fist, unwilling to skip, to clap my hands, to puff my cheeks and blow, or to pretend to be happy in this false un-at-home place.

> *January Jolly and February Bold*
> *Two little brothers from the North Wind cold*
> *Mother Winter called them to mind what they*
>   *were told*
> *So January Jolly and February Bold*
> *Blow—blow . . .*

She takes me there and leaves me there, day after bus-riding day, past eyes that Mama avoids, and then one day suddenly she is gone and I never see her ever again.

Aunt Emily's stories are pebbles skipping over my quiet sea. Each one of her stones helps to build the ground on which I seek to stand.

One time she speaks of the day Stephen, the first grandchild, was born. The labor was interminable and, when Mother saw him, she worried that his head was so pointed. "An egghead from birth," Aunt Emily says. An English nurse, who hadn't seen Japanese babies before, was alarmed at the blue patch on his behind, till it was explained to her that blue baby-bottoms were normal.

"He could sing before he could talk. And I was beside myself with jealousy that she had him," Aunt Emily says. "My sister had it all. Beauty. Talent. A husband who adored her. Everything. She'd walk into a room and steal all the glances. I could have stuck pins in her. 'Night and day' people used to say we were. I thought life was so unfair."

When Mother left for Japan, Aunt Emily said, what hurt her the most was that she wasn't given charge of the children. Aunt Emily was so upset.

I assume Obasan was chosen over Aunt Emily because she was more mature. She was rooted in an older world. And as the Second World War descended upon us, she endured. She guided us through the unkind streets, protecting us with her calm matter-of-factness, protecting us while, day after desperate day, the evacuation was under way and our community found itself, a hundred at a time, vanishing into the hills. A widower, given one day's notice, had to leave his wide-eyed babies in the church hall. A blind old woman was found walking down the streets with an envelope of money for her missing son.

Last Sunday, Aunt Emily was rallying some friends from church, telling them the Japanese Canadian community needed redress. She pointed to the high blue ceiling with its pink, white and emerald patterns of flowers and doves that the congregation had painted. "Remember the fun you had doing that?" she asked, and told them of the church on Third Avenue in Vancouver that the congregation had built, plank by plank. "We did everything. Old Mr. Yasui made the garden. We raised funds and bought the font as our memorial to Father Kennedy. Every rafter board, every pew, every embroidered seasonal hanging was bought or built or sewn literally with our own hands and pennies. And you should have seen the place. It was glorious. Glorious! Not a single blessed cent came from the diocese. And yet the

Anglican Church took our building and sold it. There we were, stuck in shacks, using up the last bits of our savings. And not a word to us. Oh those unctuous thieves! I wrote letters a few years ago to ask what they did with the money—and the coldness of the bureaucratic reply! The church, I'm telling you—I accuse the church not just of apathy, but of deliberate malice. It was at the leading edge of hatred. I accuse the church of fomenting racism directly from the pulpits and at the communion rails. I have names to name. Alderman Wilson's clergyman father led the Powell Street riot against us. Decision makers in high places of the church were directly involved in property deals. Directly. Directly in the B.C. Security Commission. I accuse the church today of still having no word of apology to offer us, and I'm telling you I have sought that word through letters and phone calls, but I am told the archbishop would not wish to see 'that woman.' "

Rage rage.

Over the years I have learned to understand some of Aunt Emily's sources of anger. And back in Granton and Cecil, in the years following Uncle's death, I was discovering my own capacity for that unpleasant emotion.

11

Blind alleys, culs-de-sac, no-trespassing signs. What remains for me of the two years following Uncle's death is a desperation of dead ends in my efforts to reach Stephen.

I'm still teaching school at Cecil and go back to see Obasan in Granton about once a month. Her health is deteriorating steadily. At times it feels criminal to leave her alone and I ask her repeatedly to come and stay with me, but she will not. Her house, she says, needs care. So also does she. Her short-term memory bank is almost depleted.

"What reason? Forgotten," she says with a chuckle when she catches herself wondering what she started out to do. After supper one night, she can't remember that she has just eaten. All her old pots are ruined, blackened and burnt. The sturdy old rice pot as well. I take a chisel and hammer to it one Saturday night to try to budge the burnt prunes which are one soldered mass of coal lumps. The next week she searches so persistently for the old pot that I dig it out of the garbage and give it back to her. The kitchen, her queendom, is finally crumbling from her control and turning into a mine field of taps and stove knobs and freezing pipes needing to be constantly checked. It's not a situation that can continue.

I go and sit on the square wooden cistern cover outside the kitchen door and think about what to do. The box is a humble throne in a new springtime of weeds—purple-flowered thistles, crabgrass, a few carrot fronds with rat-tail roots. Uncle's world has become a scratch patch.

The rage within begins its slow emergence that winter as I drive back and forth through the early blizzards and the freezing snow. The night of the freak storm, I'm trapped in a snowdrift for five hours and finally get to Granton at 2 A.M., after inching along in a convoy of cars trailing a snowplow. Obasan is asleep and there is water all over the kitchen floor from a tap that has been left on to keep the pipes from freezing. She forgot to unplug the drain. We need help. I drive her back with me to Cecil. She wants to return the next day.

Two weekends after this, I arrive to find the kitchen sink overflowing again and Obasan asleep in a lukewarm bathtub. I carry, drag, her unresponsive body the few shuffling steps to her bed.

All that wind-reaping Alberta winter, I drive over the squealing snow, from Cecil to Granton, then back to Cecil, stumbling into my unmade bed in the early still-dark morning. Then, groggy at 9 A.M., I sleepwalk into the classroom to face the upturned faces of the children with their thousand unanswerable questions.

One weekend before Christmas I drive home to find there's been a power failure. The furnace is out. The water pipes have burst under the sink and flooded the cupboard. I find Obasan squatting with soggy cardboard cartons of food, jelly powders, salt and cereals piled on a stool while the water seeps over the floor and under the stove to a low spot from where it drips into the dirt cellar below.

It's idiocy working with her in the house that weekend. Hank drops by with the milk and stays to fix the pipes. "This ol' house gettin' ready to meet the saint, eh?" he says, giving his head a quick shake.

"Guess so."

Obasan is salvaging the unsalvageable. Nothing is ever to be discarded. Plastic bleach bottles are wastepaper baskets and plant trays. Mandarin orange boxes are covered stools. Even the hems of her slacks are not cut but are rolled under till they form a heavy clump of cloth at her ankles. There seems to be an inability to let go. Or a sense that usefulness is inherent in all matter. Perhaps it's also a type of tenderness, a treasuring of every tentative little thing. Unlike Pastor Jim, she does not divide the world into the saved and the lost.

The cold she catches that weekend will not let her go and develops into pneumonia.

"She's a very sick lady," the doctor says.

As I drive her to the hospital in Lethbridge, I'm unaware that she has begun her long last haul. I take ten days off and call Aunt Emily, who flies down noisily that week and charges down the hospital corridor with questions as we make our way to Room 212.

Obasan is a small rag-doll shape in the all-white room. In the next bed a barely conscious woman who looks a hundred years old lies gray and heaving in a tent of steam. A breathing machine.

"Kusuri," Obasan says absently in greeting. "Medicine." She gestures around her head and indicates the woman beside her.

Aunt Emily hesitates in her stride, then, leaning over, she cups her mouth to Obasan's ear. "Emily yo," she shouts. "It's Emily here."

"O," Obasan says, shifting her head and staring up. "Emiri-san?" She reaches out and pats Aunt Emily's arm. Obasan's slight smile is that of a small child's faint hope. "Emiri-san?"

A heavyset nurse comes in with a basin and Aunt Emily immediately begins a barrage of more questions. What, she wants to know immediately, are all the facts? Will Obasan be here long? Is there anything serious?

"You'll have to speak to the doctor," the nurse answers in a not unkindly tone.

"You must be able to tell me something," Aunt Emily says impatiently, emphasizing the "something" with a lift of both hands.

The old woman in the next bed lets out a low moan, a sound of utter weariness. The nurse reaches into the steam tent and feels for the old woman's pulse. "We're doing what we can here," she says sharply.

"I'm not being critical. I just need to know," Aunt Emily replies even more sharply.

I'm glad Obasan is deaf and can be spared the distress of their unseemly aggression.

Back home, Aunt Emily's exasperation overflows again when I suggest I might quit teaching to care for Obasan. "And just what do you think you'll do all day?" She waves her arms in the crowded kitchen and her knuckles knock against the flyswatters that hang beside the stove, setting them dancing. "You'll get mind rot. You'll become a TV addict."

The old black and white TV is in a constant twilight zone of flickering shadows and suits Aunt Emily's definition of my life on the prairies. Her solution to all our problems is that Obasan and I should move to Toronto. But I know Obasan cannot be moved from her little house.

"We'll think about it when she's better," I say, though I can't see how our moving to Toronto will help anything. Aunt Emily leaves the next day for a speaking engagement in Vancouver.

The doctor is not optimistic when I speak with him the following week. He says she is no longer capable of living on her own and the best thing would be to place her in a nursing home. It's unthinkable.

I call for Stephen. "It's an emergency. Please ask him to call me." I leave three messages and finally hear from him the following week. He's about to go on tour again, he says, and cannot help.

"But what'll I do?" I ask. "Can't you postpone the tour?"

I can't tell from the low monotone of his voice what he's feeling. "You should listen to the doctor," he says.

"You mean put her in a home? That's murder."

There's a long sigh at the other end. "You can't take

care of her," he says. "I can't. There's nothing I can do. Nothing."

"What do you mean—nothing?" I grip the receiver tightly to my ear and can feel the sand in my throat. "What do you mean?"

After three weeks Obasan is released to my care. I arrange for two neighboring women, plus Hank and a visiting nurse, to check on her. In late winter, I decide she has to come to be with me in Cecil. It's like caring for a baby. I pack her patched underclothes, nemaki, housecoats, sweaters, her chocolate box of photographs, magnifying glass, big-print Bible, her royal family scrapbook.

The penultimate crisis begins in the spring of 1974, a year and a half after Uncle's death. I come home from school to find the apartment door open and Obasan lying on the wet prickly brown grass in the backyard. She's in the hospital for days in a barely responsive state. The old doctor at the Cecil hospital says he doesn't know what's wrong. "At her age, who knows?" he says. After two weeks, the crisis is over. The doctor says she seems to have stabilized and perhaps could go on indefinitely.

She can hardly hear at all now. She's incontinent. Like an infant's, the reflexes of her mouth function when a spoon is placed to her lips. Her lungs have survived another battle. Her mind has all but lost the war. She's moved to a chronic care room where three others are also in a twilight of staring, mouths open, life seeping downhill through the granular bed of sleep.

I begin another barrage of calls to Stephen.

"I have to sell the house. I need you. What should I do with Grandpa's tools? What about your music books?"

His only response is a heavy sigh at the other end of the
long-distance line.

I work feverishly through the following weekends,
digging through the collected memories of the Nakanes
and Katos of Granton, Slocan and Vancouver. Of that
once-upon-a-time clan, all that remains is one aged
aunt, in a small-town prairie hospital, another childless
aunt in Toronto, one successful brother and me, spinster
schoolteacher.

So much happens in a lifetime. Wars come and go.
People die. Families disappear. Even the living grow faint
as memories.

Obasan, of course, has kept everything—Stephen's
first crystal radio, which he made when we were moved
to Granton, and my red, white and blue ball, my Mickey
Mouse, paper dolls, coloring books, broken wax crayons
and pencil stubs. There are some Big Little Books and a
collection of bubble-gum cards. I alternate between frenzied packing, discarding and fits of weeping. Obasan has
spent her lifetime treasuring these things that I am now
throwing away. I tackle the photographs, letters, the portrait of Miss Best, Stephen's homemade musical instru-
ments—the thrumming rubber-band box, the pieces of
elastic as brittle as bits of dried spaghetti—our old boots
—Uncle's, Obasan's, Stephen's, mine—the rice tins in
the cellar full of seeds from Uncle's last harvesting. I'm
an undertaker disemboweling and embalming a still
breathing body, removing heart, limbs, lifeblood, all the
arteries, memories that keep one connected to the world,
transforming this comatose little family into a corpse.
We have entered the garbage-dump stage of life and I'm
rototilling it all—rags, plastic dishes, frayed curtains, a

growing heap of plastic bags. When the garbage collector carts away the mound of black bags, I can feel the muscles and bones, the last connective tissues, strain and snap. The new owners of the house bulldoze it. Our shack of memories disappears. I should not have let that happen. I forgot to take out Uncle's homemade furniture.

Obasan deteriorates slowly. She alternates between wanting to return to her non-existent house and wanting release altogether. She mourns her absence from her house. I mourn her mourning. We never speak of it. She seems to be seeking a sign, some messenger to tell her she is permitted to go.

There are days when I don't know where in her mind she has gone. Days when I think it has to be the end. Days when I think it will never end. Days when I ache for her release, from the morning, noon and night, eating, breathing, defecating body. I blame myself for the murder of her house. I blame Aunt Emily and Stephen for abandoning us. I blame the universe for the scheme of life.

On August 16, 1974, her skin is the color of ashes. She looks as though she has reached the final barrier. But the next day she's back again, waiting in her wheelchair, patient and silent and deaf, her tapered fingers at peace entwined in her lap, then half lifted in some vaguely remembered language of service.

Some nights I leave her convinced she cannot survive till morning, then the next day the crisis is past and she's back, conscious again, her fork dividing the hospital food, taking a portion for herself, then tapping the edge of her plate with her still graceful fingers in a gesture of offering. She cannot survive without offering. Those hands remain, even after decades of drudgery, the delicate precise hands of a koto player, plucking the strings. They are lost now in the snowy world of white sheets. Even in her last days, her hands, confused in the air, still tremble to serve.

I sit beside her, silent as well, not wanting to shout in the hospital. I bring her boiled eggs to peel or peas to unpod. And we are there together, our hands speaking of the kitchen queendom and the past. Our language is gestures, the nodding and shaking of heads, the shrugging of shoulders. A pat on the side of the bed is a request for me to sit. A slight wave means "no." In her cluttered little domain she was once servant and queen. She is now a prisoner, a captive of an orderly, efficient, cold, inevitable ending.

12

One evening I arrive to find Obasan cannot recognize me. The story I piece together is that she went wandering sometime in the middle of the night. She was found around 2 A.M. in a room down the hall, holding her walker and peering at a young man. No one could understand what she was trying to do or say.

There is little mercy in some institutions. You are permitted one mistake. She's tied down in her wheelchair and in her bed.

During a snowfall in early October, she asks if it's Christmas. Her throat, unused to the effort of speech, sounds like a shortwave radio—a brief rasp, her throat clearing static through her dry round mouth.

"Ima Christmasu?" I'm able to make out. "Is it Christmas now?"

I shake my head and put the spoonful of soup to her lips. She moves my arm away, then waves her hand up and down to indicate the snow pelting past the window.

"Ima Christmasu?" she repeats. "Ima Merry Christmasu time?"

She's so insistent, I finally give in and nod agreement. It's Christmas in October. She's content. She repeats the statement once more to solidify the fact. "Ima Merry Christmasu time."

Then, looking intently at my face and tapping my wrist for emphasis, she says loudly, "Steebun wa Merry Christmasu time ni kuru?" She's being as conversational as she can be but it's an excessive plea. An extremity of asking. "Will Stephen come at Merry Christmas time?" She has not once in all her days directly requested anything.

I lie. I say through the nodding of my head that Stephen will arrive. With all my heart I will it to be so—the snow a sign of Christmas and Christmas a time for Stephen's visit.

She lies back against her pillow and settles down. She is content. She has said more than enough.

I have no idea of Obasan's capacity to trust. And even less of Stephen's capacity to stay away. Beethoven, they say, was a deaf musician. No musician could be more deaf than Stephen. My brother has no time to participate in a small prairie dying.

"Steebun wa?"

"Europpa."

It's Stephen from whom I have learned most how not to be. He would not stay. I learned not to leave. He would not submit. I learned not to rage. At least not in the usual ways. It's Stephen who's been entrusted with the family's hopes and dreams and it's he in the end who is needed at the hospital more than me. His absence is unendurable.

Life's final passage is not as neat as it is often portrayed. In movies, there's a last little sigh, a turning of the head, then a fluttering and weeping of mourners. But my dear aunt's departure is an indecisive journey. She attempts to leave, attempts to stay. She keeps stepping back from the gate.

I call and call Stephen for her sake. I travel down all the avenues, the tunnels, all the paths I can imagine in my toward-him way, seeking the right time, the right word to reach him.

"She needs you, Stephen."

I write. I phone. I try approaching through friends, through strangers. I beg. I weep. Once I scream.

Stephen. Stephen.

Where into the wide world is he compelled to flee? I search throughout the cities of the world, calling for him in concert halls, in hotels. I run from echo to echo, looking for him, the one who leaves, the seeker of garlands. What demon sends me clawing through the night to my brother, my mother, my loved ones in their caves in their graves in the valley of dry bones singing the songs of childhood?

Stephen, I seek you diligently, and find a world of shovels overturning a soil full of dreams, half-dreams and sand, in a land of shadows. You seek to fashion a house of music where love can always live. But in all that labor, you only unearth for us our longing, our hands, mine and Obasan's, clutching at absences.

Most of the time when I call, he is in another country.

"Allô, Naomi? I'm soree. Ee is not 'eer. Yes, I will tell 'eem you called."

Each time I think I cannot forgive him. But I do, over and over until gradually I reach out less, and then finally not at all.

"I can't come right now."

"When then?"

"I just can't right now. Don't lay your guilt trip on me."

During this year, a new heaviness forms and starts to grow. A harder, more solid shape. Anger. I begin to want him to know the hurt. I can feel the want. Then even that gives way. When my love for him is bludgeoned, a solid emptiness takes shape. A dry weeping, a form of gangrene, sets in.

What I feel some days is that unless that hard hollow is surgically removed, it will grow and overtake my very life. Maybe it's already done so. Perhaps if I had borne children I would have had no time to construct this deformity which I still bear. I'm reminded of a gory article Aunt Emily was reading in which a woman from San Francisco was poisoned from inside by an incompletely aborted fetus. There's a surgeon needed. There's a time for scalpels.

"The truth," Aunt Emily says, sounding uncomfortably like Pastor Jim and quoting a higher source than herself, "the truth will make you free. If you know what Stephen's truths are, you'll stop blaming him."

Aunt Emily is a minor surgeon of the soul, but her

operations on me have not been successful. She herself bears no Stephen-shaped scars.

"Trouble with you, Nomi," she said once, glaring up at me over her reading glasses, "trouble is, you're too much of an accountant. One up for you, you wrote him a letter. One down for him, he never replied. Life's not like that."

I know she's right. It's not the accountant who makes the world go round. She must have sent me fifty letters to my one or two replies. Her answer to problems is to be busy. It works for her.

"Find someone else to help," she writes one time from Mexico. "Call Mrs. Makino. Or ask a stranger. Every tenth stranger is an angel. And don't worry if you don't believe in angels. Just rely on them."

The advice is useless. No kindly, well-intentioned friend, stranger or available angel can fill in for Stephen, absent stepson, absent brother. I can feel the shape of our memories together evaporating from that huge room in my heart where he used to live.

Sometimes I sit by Obasan's bedside and plead with her spirit to release us both. Sometimes I rage at the skies. She is waiting, I believe, to say goodbye to Stephen. She is waiting for him to finish his tours. It seems at times that she can will herself to wait forever and she will outlast us all.

When Stephen was in high school, he tried to make a metronome out of a toy electric motor, but its tick was erratic. I think of it sometimes, watching the uneven pulse in Obasan's neck, her life in limbo, marking time, waiting for Death to arrive, to release her finally from the interminable toil and bondage of breath.

"Merry Christmasu ni . . ." It feels like the water-drip torture, her mouth forming the same words, over and over, night unto night. I can hardly see the point of the barely awake, breathing, heaving effort. Where into the scheme of things does this joylessness fit?

Nakayama-sensei visits us several times. He cups his hands to her ear and sings hymns so loudly that some old men in the corridor come by and stand at the doorway, listening. "Good day," they nod. At times I think I see Obasan's mouth moving as if she's trying to sing along.

"Toh   toki   waga   toh   mo . . ." My precious friend . . .

The spring day Stephen returns to Montreal from his European tour, she sits up in bed for the first time in months and requests food. She drinks some soup. All day, she is alert, agitated, intent.

"Steebun. Rippa. Rippa," she says once clearly. "Stephen. Wonderful. Wonderful."

I try to stand in.

The phone call at 5 A.M. the next morning says she died at 3:30. I lie in bed and find her spirit everywhere—in the arrangements of the flowers above my head—one yellow blossoming and two green buds. It's as if she's telling me that death is the flowering and that we, the living, are not yet in bloom.

Her last act of service was to wait for Stephen in order to praise him. An extreme and extravagant gesture. In the end, he did not hear. Obasan, who devoted all her days to our remnant family and especially to Stephen, did not deserve that long last loneliness.

13

The year that Obasan dies, 1975, I look in the mirror and see an old-maid orphan, a barren speck of dust. Aunt Emily's bimonthly phone call is the kite string, the long-distance umbilical cord, that keeps me connected to a mothering earth.

"We're going on a trip, Nomi me gnome," she announces at Christmas. "Put in your notice. You're quitting last week in June."

"But—"

"No 'buts.' You're quitting. That's it." I can see her flying down to tie me up and cart me off.

In the end it isn't so much her vehemence that up-roots me from my flowerpot as my own drooping limbs. She has everything planned. A job. A room in her apartment where she intends me to live.

"But first," she says, "we're going to Japan. We'll visit your mother's grave. We owe that to her. After that we'll spend a week in the one place in the world that feels the way home ought to feel. You'll love Hawaii."

She arrives before the school term is over, sends a heap of my stuff to the Salvation Army, and the afternoon that school is out, we set off in a rented car. A teary goodbye from Alex and his mother, ten-minute stops at the Makinos' and the Regehrs', one last wave to Granton's Main Street and we're on our way, over the prairies, and through the Rockies on highways that Uncle and Father built. Aunt Emily points out a spot near Revelstoke where a friend died in a road-building accident.

After two days we enter the magic of Vancouver, the lost city of my childhood with its wonderful Stanley Park. Then the next morning, I'm giddy with excitement as we board a plane. It's my first flight. My first time out of Canada.

A swift streak of rain and we enter a vast nothingness. The world outside is a blank sheet of paper—not a cloud lump, not a star. It's white and deeper white from every angle. After a few moments, except for the buzzing of the plane, I'd swear we're not moving at all, suspended like a giant hummingbird. Or is it a giant mosquito? Any moment a flyswatter could swipe through the clouds.

Aunt Emily is scribbling notes. She's writing an article for *Bridge,* "the multicultural voice from St. John's

College." *Bridge,* according to Aunt Emily, is a verb, "taking you from one side to otherness."

"We were flung to the winds, not to disappear, but to learn about injustice," she says. "Injustice is the chasm *Bridge* has to cross."

Every time she speaks I have to release my ears from the squealing symphonic music coming through the plastic stethoscope plugged into the armrest.

We're sifting through the white mist now and come into a bright world, Mother's deep royal blue, while far below, between clouds that lie thick as meringue, is the blue-white speckled expanse of the Pacific Ocean.

"Whether we like it or not, Nomi," she says, "Japanese Canadians are east-west bridges. We span the gap. It's our fate and our calling—to be hyphens—to be diplomats."

"Diplomats, eh," I say noncommittally. It's hardly a category that fits either of us.

Aunt Emily says that on this trip, she intends to look for some of the four thousand that Canada exiled to Japan in a final rampage at the end of the war. She wants to find Min Kawai.

"Our Michelangelo-ko," she says softly and there's a desperate look of tenderness in her eyes as she stares into space. "You wouldn't believe what a spectacular artist he was, Nomi." From her description it seems Min Kawai may have always been unstable—a bit too bright, a bit too sensitive. His mother indulged him, she says. It isn't likely that he emerged from the womb round and brown and placid. Even when he was a small child his drawings were odd and arresting. She remembers one he gave her of a translucent bird.

"Birds birds birds," she says. "His notebooks were full
of birds with Japanese eyes."

He was barely twenty when the police caught him
leaving Sandon, the sunless ghost-town internment
camp. He was imprisoned for a year. His family couldn't
stand the shame. Like most Japanese Canadians, they
disappeared. Aunt Emily thought they might be somewhere on the prairies. And Min, she heard, had suffered
a breakdown. As far as she knows all Japanese Canadian
mental patients were shipped en bloc to Japan.

After a scrunched-up day/night of small-tray eating and
fitful dozing we descend and land with a bump and an
alarming roar. Thank heavens, the earth once more.

Mr. and Mrs. Omoto, friends of Aunt Emily, are at
the airport.

"My sister's daughter," Aunt Emily says, introducing
me.

"Ah. Ah. How do you do?" They bow, smile, nod and
simultaneously organize a handshake, their precise
hands neatly slicing the air.

All around the crowded bustling airport are clusters
of black-haired, neatly dressed Japanese—the men in
dark business suits, some children in navy-blue school
uniforms, pigeon-toed, bobbing like gophers, breathless,
polite. Everything surprises me, especially the smallness
of everyone. I'm so used to looking up at the world that
now I feel I'm suddenly in a world of midgets. But very
alert midgets. There's an antlike kind of electricity. A
skinny man close by is saying, "Nh, nh, aha aha aha," in
quick little attentive gasps and nodding with each eager

sound. I think of the phrase I used to give my grade three class when they were practicing their penmanship. "The quick brown fox jumped over the lazy dog."

There's an odd sense of having flown backward into a Lilliputian dream world. Images from infancy come filtering through the channels of memory—a gently angled head denoting playfulness to a small child, the instant-as-thought hands and the ready offer to carry things. There's an attention to detail. Emotional detail.

This is the country of my ancestors, where tenderness and toughness coexist in the same instant and sensitivity is an institution. The air is full of paradox. The female announcer is speaking over the loudspeaker in the completely non-aggressive voice of a child and I remember the studied humility of the issei, every breeze bending them along the necessary paths of protocol and propriety.

Aunt Emily in Japan, this land of silk, is an eastern version of English tweed. She's more eccentric than diplomatic. I wonder if we Canadian cousins will be accepted here. Mr. Omoto produces the week's itinerary and Aunt Emily immediately starts making changes, pouring sand into the well-oiled Japanese world of schedules. As usual, Aunt Emily is no Emily Post.

"We must visit my sister's grave first."

"Ah, ah," Mr. and Mrs. Omoto say in unison, nodding urgent agreement.

"But first," Aunt Emily says, lifting her finger, "western-style toiletto, please."

Mr. and Mrs. Omoto direct us, walking in front and behind, smiling all the way to an airport washroom, then out to a perfectly polished car with white doilies on the headrests. We drive down the crowded highway in the

steamy haze and maze, and enter the bustling Tokyo trot
—a never-ending race of small cars, small trucks, bi-
cycles, carts. From the slow clanking cowbells of southern Alberta to Japan's crawling, zapping traffic in one fell
swoop. It's a dizzying distance.

We spend our first night in a ryokan where the toilet
is flat on the floor and separate plastic bathroom slippers
are kept inside the sliding bathroom door. Our plain
tatami-mat room is supplied with buckwheat husk pillows, futons and sheets that feel like cardboard. Before
supper, Aunt Emily and I sink into a deep hot bath and I
am taking Japan in through my nostrils—the fragrance
of the tatami, the pungent odor of latrines, the moist
wood and water smells of the bath.

The next day we come to the halls of the private hospital in mountains south of Tokyo, Miss Best's once-
upon-a-time orphanage. My mother's secret place. This
is where I yearned to be through all the days of my
searching childhood, a place of bamboo trees and tea
bushes where Mother and Grandma ended their days in
hiding, hoarding to themselves the story of the
hibakusha, the survivors of the atom bomb. Here on this
time-heavy soil, they breathed and died, connected to us
by dream alone.

I'm sleepwalking as we turn off the crowded street
and enter a densely treed yard with a white stuccoed
building at the back. The doors are open. We remove
shoes, put on slippers. At the end of a short hall, above
the archway to a chapel, is stern-faced Naomi Best in a
photograph identical to the one I have. So this is where
she lived and toiled and loved and died—this English
Canadian foreigner in a foreign land. In a group portrait
hanging in the hall, she is seated on a bench in front of

her orphanage, leaning forward on a cane. I have an urge
to stand at attention and salute her. This regal austere
woman. My mother's collaborator in silence.

Is it the rock that compels the rain? Is it inviolacy
that births the rage to know? Aunt Emily pursued her
sister with a torrent of letters. She spent hours feverishly
fitting together the patchwork picture, seeking clues,
seeking the person-to-person word.

After the war, in 1949, Nakayama-sensei visited Japan. The only news he brought back was that Miss Best,
now feeble, and her orphanage had survived. The house
where Mother had stayed had been destroyed in the B-
29 bombings. Obasan and Uncle were shocked to see
from the slides how old and bent "Besto-sensei" had become. I remember our sending parcels and parcels of
food to the orphanage that year.

But as for Mother and Grandma, it was only a picture of shadows that finally emerged. Aunt Emily sifted
through the rubble heap of postwar Japan and came to
the silence that was Mother's final will. Mother covered
her trail with leaves and commanded the mist. She
would not be followed.

Yet not all the footprints disappeared. A letter from
Grandma said they were in Nagasaki when the bomb
fell. Mother was disfigured. The flesh melted from her
beautiful face. She preferred to have her children think
she had perished. One of Miss Best's helpers wrote of
the arrival at the orphanage late one night of two Japanese Canadian women from Nagasaki. One was English-
speaking. Her head was covered in a shawl. They would
not give their names.

Aunt Emily immediately cabled for more information, sent pictures and simultaneously applied to the Ca-

nadian government for help. Fruitless efforts, all. The next communication said the women were no longer there.

Not long after, a barely legible letter from Miss Best came saying the women had recently died. Finally there was word from a missionary couple that their names had been found in the graveyard where Miss Best was buried.

We know so little of their last days, except that they lived within a well of silence, a grave before the grave. A haunted place. Mother hid herself from view. She scuttled through the night. By not communicating, she believed, she spared her children pain. A strange faith.

There is in life, I have learned, a speech that will not be hidden, a word that will be heard. This day in Japan, I hear Mother in the sounds of footsteps, in the swishing of the broom outside, in the light laugh of a little boy. I sense her in the touch of my hand as I lean against the wall and in the sudden twirl of a cool breeze in the stifling hall and in one perfectly round white stone on the stand where the visitors' book lies. When I pick up the pen to sign my name, my hand shakes so much that the N ends up looking like a V. I can't finish my signature. That's Mama's fault. Mr. Omoto notices but looks away quickly so I will not be embarrassed, and walks outside with his hands behind his back.

At the high hillside grave overlooking a highway, Mr. and Mrs. Omoto and Aunt Emily talk softly. They tell me to take my time while I wander among the broken headstones. I lean against a maple tree which I'm told must have been planted in 1954 by a young Canadian missionary couple.

Perhaps it's the weight of centuries of belief that descends upon me in the late morning mist. I kneel by the maple tree and know. We're, all of us, dead and alive. We the dead and we the living are here among the trees, the colored snails, the moss, the singing insects. We're everywhere here in the sound of distant traffic, in the long-haired grass, in the filtered sunlit haze. In this short visit, on this hot muggy day, within this one hour at Mama's grave, I meet the one I need to meet.

Nakayama-sensei has often said that it is not necessary for people to clamor and shout for their voices to be heard. He says there is time enough and listening enough. "We will all hear what must be heard."

I think of his words from time to time throughout the rest of our whirlwind two weeks in Japan, and then as we go on to Hawaii. "Too much the world intrudes upon our listening. But patience," Nakayama-sensei used to say. "You will be told what you are made ready to hear."

14

A group of Aunt Emily's outspoken nisei friends are at the airport to meet us. A whole gang of Aunt Emilys. What a shock! I'm introduced as another "kotonk"—a jocular term for Japanese Americans from the mainland. They say our heads are made of wood and make a kotonk sound.

Hawaii's niseis, Aunt Emily says, are as unbent as freestanding trees. Unlike us crippled bonsai in Canada, they've retained community here.

The extravagant moist air on this island is thick with

the sweet scent of fruit and flowers and there are ferns and fringe trees, fronds, fat grass, skinny velvety moss grass, trees with fan-shaped leaves as high as a house. Mynah birds chatter in trees. Little gray-brown robin-size doves with turquoise beaks go bob-bobbing along the floors of indoor-outdoor restaurants. On the streets, in the stores, we blend into a collage of races. We're both tanning quickly and beginning to look like the "locals." If belongingness was all that mattered in life, Aunt Emily says, she'd move to Hawaii in a flash.

I've never been anywhere that felt so comfortable. Japan was strangely familiar, but too intense, too unrelaxed. In Hawaii the open friendly smiles signal ease and I discover, wonder of wonders, that our ethnicity here is an advantage. Bank tellers know how to spell our names, the clothes in department stores actually fit, food counters have take-out sushi lunches. Imagine being able to eat Japanese food and speak English.

We've been staying by the ocean on the small island of Kauai, in a little beach house. Through slatted glass windows we can hear the sea, the watery explosions frothing on the shore. On the bamboo night table is a fragrant eucalyptus branch with its skewer of gray-green baby-tongue leaves, resting on a bowl of papayas, huge oranges, mangoes, bananas. Our two white leis hang limply over the edge. In a little dish there's a raw root vegetable that looks like potato but is surprisingly sweet. In Hawaii so much is surprisingly sweet—even the language. "Mahalo," the people say. "Thank you."

It's early morning, the third day of our week in Aunt Emily's "nisei paradise." I'm sinking down and down through the slipstream of sleep, down through the rolling weight of ocean rhythms, to where the deep-sea dream sweeper is sweeping dreams. Bubbles from the deep. Drift, drift. I'm ebbing away in the dream, shrinking and shrinking and . . .

shrinking. . . .

I am three tiny women in an inch-high library in a miniature world . . . and a man . . . stands there . . . behind the library stacks. I barely catch a glimpse of him. He is a man who loves. He loves. He is no one recognizable. Shall I stay in his tiny world, or go on to oblivion?

I choose to venture on. The other two women stay behind. I am leaving the room where love lurks.

The instant I look down, I know it's happening. I've passed the boundary. My limbs—legs—arms—are gone. There's nothing left to see or touch, yet I find myself plummeting, further, into the infinitesimal.

Somewhere in this no longer physical, no longer visible world is the moment of discovery. What I know is that I am without a body, but I am not, I am not without consciousness. There's a quality of knowing that is completely unchanged as I slide down the stream of deeper disappearing, and during some pre-dawn of speech I'm aware of music, of song. Then, at the very heart of the listening, in that one moment as I attend fully the mind's singing, in the speed and stillness of dark light, I become, and I am, the song. I am Song itself. Then again in a seamless shift, I'm past sound, into thought. I'm a single waft of thought and I know that I, the thought and the person, am one, indivisibly, consciously and utterly myself.

This is what torpedoes its way through the seaweed and debris of the drifting dream. The awareness roars through the back of my head into the wedge-shaped space between sleep and waking and explodes full-blown into morning. I am suffused with heat and a heart-pounding certainty. There is no death. There is no disappearance, no finality in the drift downstream. Annihilation is not possible. Individual consciousness cannot be extinguished.

So that's what death is.

". . . Mama . . . ," I whisper and feel the shock of speech, the jolt back to the body, the cumbersome tongue—primitive tools for primitive communication.

Aunt Emily is starting to stir in the other cot.

"You awake, Nomi? Ol' Nonny Mouse?"

I turn my back to her and return to the authority of the dream. I see Mother's face, her eyes gently oblique, and I know without a stammer of a doubt that she is present, a conscious being as real and palpably alive as I am. Father is alive, and Uncle and Obasan. They live not just as memory, but as thought itself, within every fragmentary wave of remembering. I can touch them and hold them as surely as I feel the pink flowery pillow hugging my cheek.

I lie still, and my mind is filled with an exquisite melody of Father's that Stephen played as a cycle of variations. The simple theme would keep diminishing till his hands finally lifted off the keyboard. But then they would come down again barely audibly for more tentative notes. Echoes. And echoes. A song without end.

It occurs to me later in the week, as I lie in the warmth at the beach, that the dream was the final signpost in my steadfast journey toward Mother. All my waiting life I kept my heart turned toward her and away from the tiny choices of love offered in the inch-high rooms of possibilities. I sought her and only her, tumbling downstream, back and back till I reached her grave and I sought her in dream beyond the grave, in the stream that circles forever and in the song that does not vanish. Love, it seems to me, must be at the end of the journey without end.

I walk on the sand, in the light spray that falls from passing clouds, wondering if we humans are, after all, doomed to love. We are driven by our hunger for knowledge though we hardly know why. We seek the ultimate building blocks of matter, or the ultimate building blocks of consciousness. But in the end, as the wave breaks, as we waken from our lives, will we not find that what we have sought is the face of love?

It's a lazy week. Even the dog that comes sniffing by is languid in the sun. I listen to the uneven sound of the waves, to the silence between the waves, the crash, the echoes rolling, the white clap, then the boom like a roar of thunder or a jet streaking across the sky. Each wave is as unique as each human life.

Last Friday night, a full seven years since our visit to Hawaii, I suddenly remembered the dream again and I told it to Father Cedric. He reminded me of Uncle, sitting quietly and nodding. Uncle used to say, "No one knows the ways of the universe. No one knows."

We were sitting on the floor in his apartment, facing each other. Finally he leaned forward and smiled. "A dream of the Incredible Shrinking Woman," he mused.

I was mildly embarrassed that I had talked so much.

"Dreams are brave," he added. "It isn't easy for them to break into this little world." His eyes were just a crinkle away from laughter as he lapsed into one of his quizzical stares. "Humans are, what did you say? Doomed? To love?"

I shrugged.

Over the years, though the imprint of the dream remains, Time has been busy scouring the shine off the sureness. It's the power of the conviction that now seems strange—that from something so ephemeral there should have been such certainty. Such bone-deep knowing.

"So that's what death is," I'd thought. But that was, as I've said, a long time ago.

15

It's three years ago. Or, to count from the other direction, four years since I moved to Toronto. Four years since Aunt Emily and I gasped our way over the hill. "You aren't forty and I'm not sixty," she said with chagrin and disbelief.

Perhaps it's because I'm middle-aged that I haven't found it easy adjusting to this frenzied city. How long does it take, I wonder, to get used to the place? Maybe my roots are in Granton after all.

Aunt Emily's various friends drop in from time to

time, ascending the elevator to her eagle-nest Eglinton Avenue apartment. Father Cedric is a not infrequent visitor. Usually the two of them sit together in the cramped kitchen, drinking tea, munching rice crackers and talking politics. Occasionally I hear Aunt Emily's laughter like a gunshot blast, accompanied by the rollicking chortle which is Father Cedric's laugh.

He's a somewhat bemused and whimsical man, coming and going with light footsteps—a sort of Peter Pan character, careful of shadows. When he leaves, he closes the door softly behind him. Once when Aunt Emily was being critical of me, he grinned, put his hands over my ears and said, "Hear no evil."

Living with my aunt has been, to say the least, trying at times. This morning she comes bolting into my room, her long flannel nightie flouncing about as she looks for her keys. Delicate she is definitely not. In her rushing about she knocks over my last remaining King George-Queen Elizabeth mug. It almost breaks my heart. "Good grief, Nomi," she says, as if it's my fault. She never apologizes for anything.

Her keys are in the medicine cabinet. "Hah," she says as she grabs them from me. I'm sure she needs to get herself better organized, and she should have her desk and work space back.

"Oh stop being so thoughtful," she says irritably when I suggest I could find a place of my own. "You certainly are your mother's daughter."

"How do you mean?"

"Always worrying about me. Always doing things for me. That's just what she was like. Cleaning my desk. Fixing my dresses. Fixing my hair. I'd say to her, 'Forget it, Sis. I look like this. I'm an ugly duckling. I'm not you.'"

Poor Aunt Emily. She was born and remains a tank-shaped bird, hefty and headstrong and weighted down by the thick glasses that gobble up her gumdrop nose.

I do my best to stay out of her way, reading or writing in my room, her former den, with its view of rooftops and as much sky as one can hope to see in smoggy Toronto. Or I stand on the balcony perched in space.

Toronto, it seems to me, is an enormous ant colony. Far below are the constant traffic and the tiny ant people carrying their crumbs, their antennae waving their complex signals. It's confounding how it all works. Sirens yowl their throbbing wails, an accident brings an ambulance, a traffic jam brings police, and fires bring little red trucks with firemen ants and their toothpick ladders. It's all marvelous and efficient and chilling to my middle-aged Cecilized soul.

"Naomi Watcher Nakane," Aunt Emily will say as I stand and stare, "you're turning into a statue. The world is for living in, not for staring at."

But what else can one do in a world of ants? That giant factory of a school, Carson Junior High, crawls with struggling student ants tunneling back and forth from class to class, where we teacher ants sit woodenly, marking papers, marking time.

I tell Aunt Emily I find Toronto to be too impersonal and she says my problem is that I don't take risks. I'm as predictable as the clock on the wall. "I swear I look at you instead of my watch sometimes." She may well love me but she finds me unspeakably boring.

I suppose she's right that I'm not a risk taker. That

must be why I haven't made a single friend. I'm comfortable, though, with Eugenia, Aunt Emily's gray-haired colleague from *Bridge*. Eugenia and Aunt Emily are great pals, laughing easily about the ways of the world. The two of them marching down the street are a Mutt and Jeff routine—Eugenia Agnes Stong, thin and tall, and Aunt Emily, an aging bulldog always slightly ahead of her.

On Sundays, Eugenia, Aunt Emily, Father Cedric and I go to their old "watering hole," an Anglican church right splat in the middle of Toronto's cathedrals of commerce on Bay Street. "We should call this place 'the Church of the Trojan Horse,'" Aunt Emily says. "If we get our strategy right we could capture Bay Street."

"Who needs it," Eugenia says.

Eugenia believes in the currency of prayer, and sometimes I attend a prayer and meditation group with her on Wednesday nights that is relaxing to the point of sleep. One time Father Cedric slept through an entire evening, his hand flopped open beside my foot.

On Sundays it's a different matter. The church is jumping with its odd collection of priestly folks, defrocked or disgruntled clergy, an ex-Jesuit, a bartender priest, a politician priest, an academic priest, professors, gays, street people. Often there's no sermon. The church is as far removed from Pastor Jim's as midnight is from noon. The hands of the clock may point in the same direction but the light is different.

"It sounds like a backslider's church to me," Lydia writes. She thinks Anglicans are born-again backsliders, slipping downhill from their place of ease to a place of ease.

Aunt Emily thinks fundamentalists, whether from the

Bible Belt or the money belt ("praise the lode"), are ter-
rorists at heart. "But everybody's a fundamentalist about
something. What are you? A fundamentalist mouse?"
She says I'm terminally passive and she hauls me off
with her to meetings or potlucks or whatever. I feel like
the cardboard box in her backseat, taken along in case I
might be useful.

Tonight I'm sitting on the couch, tired, half asleep
and halfheartedly watching TV, when Aunt Emily comes
home, marches right over and turns the TV off.

"Up up," she barks like some sergeant major. She
takes me by the hand without dropping her briefcase and
I'm being dragged off again. "You need to meet people,"
she says, and so perhaps I do, but I don't appreciate
this.

"Tell you what, Nome," she says, "we'll take in a Toronto JC League meeting. It's about your speed." And
we're on our way to the Japanese Canadian Cultural
Centre at the city's thinner edges. As soon as we look
into the upstairs room, I know we're intruders. The half-
dozen or so people, mostly middle-aged men, sitting
around a table glance at us suspiciously.

"Don't worry," Aunt Emily whispers. "I won't create a
riot. I promise."

How she has the nerve to barge in, I do not know. I'd
dearly love to turn around and leave, but she's hooked
her arm in mine and she's pulling me in.

The League is a chronic itch Aunt Emily has to
scratch every so often. Back in the late forties, she
helped found the National Japanese Canadian League,
the umbrella organization for all the local leagues across
the country. She had big dreams then. "Human rights is
our responsibility," she said. But the will to action was

killed over time and the League deteriorated into a social club.

"It's dead dead dead," she says. "It's a dancing corpse."

She's nevertheless a lifetime member of the Toronto League, and she knows League people right across Canada.

As a child, I was not the least interested in southern Alberta's League, although I went once with the Mak-duo to the League picnic at Henderson Park in Lethbridge. Stephen came to get me in the pickup and Marion kept walking past him, her nose in the air, trying to snub him. Then there was the League talent show where Stephen won the Outstanding Talent award. And when the Mak-duo had their big double wedding, the reception was in the Taber League hall.

This committee meeting discussing grants from the Department of Multiculturalism looks decidedly dull except for a quite striking-looking woman who's in charge. She'd be younger than me, though it's hard to say. Fashionably dressed in a soft gray leather suit. She looks startled, wide eyes blinking as we walk in.

No pause for introductions. I sit down as invisibly as I can, pushing my chair back softly from the table as the dustball of a discussion rolls its way around the room. How long will this be? Curse Aunt Emily. May I never be dragged to another meeting by her again. If I'm to be consigned to my role as watcher, I'd rather be back in Granton, sitting by the slough, watching frogs and water spiders splishing and skating about.

What slow-moving creatures in this human slough. A couple of sleepy bullfrogs breep their tunes and the pretty dragonfly, dragonlady skims along on her gauzy wings. Miss Nikki Kagami—angular face, eyes made large by thick mascara, dancing now here, now there.

One extremely short, bucktoothed man and a thick-set man in a business suit are discussing their proposal for free bowling for a senior citizens' group. All eyes are seeking their leader's reaction. She nods approval. She's satisfied and the room is satisfied with her. Aunt Emily rests her forehead in the heel of her palm and her foot taps irritably. Her reading glasses are almost falling off the tip of her nose as she leans forward. She's getting set to leap in. So much for her promise to be quiet.

"Has anyone asked the issei what they need?" She stabs the table with the eraser end of her pencil.

Nikki Kagami frowns. Almost imperceptibly, the others are also frowning. The room has one mind. "You can't ask the issei anything," Nikki Kagami says. Then she chuckles lightly. "They don't have a clue." Almost inaudible titters accompany her little laugh.

This is not Aunt Emily's element. She's the zoo's kangaroo, hopping about in the hippopotamus pool. Occasionally a submerged head rises out of the mud, nostrils quivering. A whoosh of wet words. A thin man gives a small speech on the need to project a positive image. Then down under again for another think. No haste. No deadlines. No struggle for the meaning of life. Aunt Emily is getting ready to jump in again, pouch full of thoughts. I duck.

It's proving to be a murky evening. The fallout of her frustration settles over the room.

On the way home, Aunt Emily grumbles about the "ridiculous Toronto League" that held an election this year and voted Nikki Kagami in as president. "What a fairy godmother she's getting to be, waving her magic wand around for her club. What an abuse of federal funds! Bowling once a week for their cronies?"

She's so irritated she's forgotten to shift out of second gear and the car's motor is whining away painfully. "This is the way the feds do things. They fatten up a chosen few."

It's nerve-racking driving with Aunt Emily. A wonder she hasn't had any accidents. Thank heavens she's finally shifted gears.

When we get home, I tell her I'm thinking of going back to Granton. "What!" she says and blinks and feels my forehead. "Are you out of your mind?"

"Well, I have friends there at least. . . ."

"Enough," she growls. She makes a few phone calls and the next morning, before I've finished breakfast, she shouts, "To horse!" yanks me out of my slippers and we're on our way to *Bridge* magazine's office at St. John's College.

We take the subway south, then head west. Walking with Aunt Emily is like training for a race. I follow her breathlessly till we come to the four-story weathered brick building set back from the street by wide stone steps.

"Don't know why I never thought of it before," Aunt Emily announces to Eugenia Stong as we enter the ground-level office through a side door. "You need the help, don't you?"

"Right," Eugenia says agreeably and without a moment's pause, as if it's the most natural thing in the world that she should suddenly have a new assistant.

Father Cedric waves at me from his office at the front. "Allô, Naomi. Allô. Welcome. Welcome."

16

There's a crack in the off-white painted ceiling above my bed. It extends from the corner for about two feet, then ends in a short sharp "correct" sign, a rather large check mark, thin and black as pencil lead.

It's quite quite correct, I'm thinking, that I should be here in my own space. Quietness at last. It was Eugenia's urging that finally got me moved out from under "that overwhelming aunt of yours."

"You mean I should leave my niece in peace?" Aunt Emily was quite miffed at first.

Eugenia thinks high-rise living causes thinning of the blood and she told Aunt Emily I would probably survive my "big city jitters" better if I could see the whites of people's eyes and walk to work. She says if I'd stayed another year at Carson Junior High I'd have mutated into an ant. "Lucky you quit in time." Eugenia helped me find this studio apartment in a low-rise around the corner and down a back alley from the office.

"It's a house for a mouse," Aunt Emily said, poking the tiny ice cubes out of the tiny tray of the tiny fridge.

Mouse house or dollhouse, I'm content with mini-kitchen, closet bathroom, ceiling crack and all. It's clean and orderly and I love it. Miss Best looks down from her place above my desk. Aunt Emily's Mexican gift, a multicolored pottery sun, is a small ping of gladness grinning on the opposite wall. The miniature alarm clock sits on a bamboo stand beside the Japanese paper lantern and my low-lying foam-pad bed. It's a floor-level room, compact and spare. In the early morning, the shadow of the hanging vine is a Japanese ink sketch on the wall, barely touching the shadow of the chestnut tree.

"You could paint a mural over that," Aunt Emily said, pointing out the ceiling crack. "Make your own little Sistine Chapel. Cherubs maybe? Trumpets? Or how about God flinging that rippling arm of his across the sky?"

People these days don't paint pictures on ceilings, though I think we should, especially in hospitals or dental offices. I consider myself lucky to have my check mark to ponder—a flaw in my sky through which an angel might peek. Or where dreams might break through.

Angels and dreams are on the lookout for ways to enter our world. Safely, if possible. Perhaps dreams are stronger than we think they are. Some are persistent as dandelions—those powerful plants with their green dragon wings leafing themselves wherever they can, in hostile lawns or through cracks in sidewalks. It's a lucky dream that doesn't get trampled to death.

Maybe Father Cedric was right when he said that dreams were brave. If by any wild chance something real starts to happen— Ah, it doesn't bear thinking about. He's a priest, a counselor, a professional helper of people in distress. I should put him out of my woolly mind.

Could try to get back to sleep. Haven't had a decent rest since Friday night. Father Cedric is probably still in bed. Or maybe he's up doing yoga, greeting the dawn— the very same dawn that's greeting me less than one block away.

It's been over a year since I moved here. Much as I love Aunt Emily, it's a relief being in charge of my life again. No more Japanese Canadian meetings. Not a single one. Each time she's asked, I've been able to say, "Not tonight," or "I'd rather not," or "Not this time, Aunt Em." I've sound-proofed myself. The moment I hear the mention of a meeting, I tune out.

Eugenia says Aunt Emily is a fluke of nature. "People over sixty are supposed to slow down," she told her.

The thing about Aunt Emily is her unshakable conviction that she can do anything. And more often than not she'll do it all, like the little red hen planting and harvesting the wheat, carrying the sack to the miller and baking the bread.

"You're an inexhaustible fiend, Emily," Eugenia said once. "If you want us alive, you'll have to ease up."

When I lived with Aunt Emily I used to feel like a piece of driftwood at the edge of her whirlpool, twirling in circles for no good reason. "Hurry up, Naomi. Why aren't you ready?"

Some weekends I'd waken in the darkness wondering why I'd left the prairies. I'd go out to escape her nagging voice and find myself on the streets walking aimlessly in the world of the life-bludgeoned. People seemed almost violently empty, deactivated by loneliness or dread. All those glazed stares. There was a dullness in the air, as if the taste buds of the soul had gone dead.

"Must be getting old," I muttered one day.

"Old!" Aunt Emily said with a snort. "You haven't even been born yet."

She was right, I thought. I'd hardly lived and here I was ready for Time's compost heap.

Being alone in this apartment has restored my peace and my sense of self, but the *Bridge* office is also a haven. I love Eugenia's quietly refined ways, her efficient, unfrenzied busyness. Several months ago I realized in the midst of my typing that Aunt Emily was nagging me in a very loud voice and I'd not heard a word.

"Good for you," Eugenia said when I confessed. "She should realize that megaphones make us deaf."

And then there is Father Cedric, who is generally attentive to Aunt Emily, but if something strikes him as incongruous he can hardly hide his infectious grin and there we suddenly find ourselves, floating along on his bubbles of mirth. But it's Morty Mukai, *Bridge* magazine's young new editor, who is the main reason I'm safely out of Aunt Emily's path of fire.

Aunt Emily and Morty are two of a kind, both from the land of Oz, arguing at full tilt, howling at each other's gruesome witticisms. They could be mother and son.

"Let's go, Short Mort," Aunt Emily will say, slapping him on the back.

I like Morty. He's a fast talker. Gets things done. He's one of your more unlikely-looking English professors as he darts about in his sweatshirt and sneakers and his wispy Fu Manchu beard, which is sometimes pointy, sometimes chopped. His hair is a thick black brush cut perpetually at attention. When he's not upstairs in his classes, he's usually with Eugenia and me in the large central room where we have the photocopier, couch and worktable. Most afternoons, he's rummaging through the mail, twirling on the swivel chair at the long worktable.

The other day he was guffawing his way through an orange-colored book called *Oriental Missions in British Columbia.* "Oi Cedric. Says here that Chinese women have dark necks and only their faces are light-skinned." He swung around to face Eugenia. "What do you think of that, Miss Stong?"

Eugenia shook her head blandly and kept typing.

Morty slammed the book shut. "Okay, just let some of us non-whites write the facts, folks. We'll give you a subtle little army of put-downs that get into your head before you know it." He growled and stomped into his back room, where he hunkered down like a small bear, his chunky legs swinging.

Morty's office is completely impregnable when he brings his two large, not overly intelligent English sheepdogs to work. "My children," he says ruefully. They're all he has left from his tumultuous four-year marriage to a fiery redheaded Irish Canadian. Eugenia has tripped over the dogs more than once and now insists he keep them tied to his desk. Once he brought them over to my apart-

ment and they flopped all over my cushions. I kept finding dog hairs for days, in my cereal bowl, in my books.

Morty has taken over from Aunt Emily as chief nag
in my life. "Hey, Naomi, what're you doing tonight?" he
will ask as he bounces out the door. I congratulate myself that I've resisted being dragged off to meetings by
either of those two perpetual-motion machines. They've
been going on and on for months about redress meetings.

"Redress? What's that?" I asked once.

"Well, it's not about putting your clothes back on,"
Morty quipped, a bit sarcastically. "And it's not about
one Nikki Kagami getting a nice chunk of change."

Nikki Kagami, it seems, is no longer simply after
bowling grants. She now wants twenty-five million dollars for our internment, our stolen properties, our dispersal, our exile.

"Twenty-five million dollars? Million?" What a huge
sum of money, I thought.

"Sure it's a lot for one person," Aunt Emily said, "but,
my stars, how many of us do you think there are? We
were a people once and we had a life. Everything was
entrusted, everything was stolen, and everything's been
covered up ever since. Now tell me—are we going to
collaborate in another cover-up? Tell me how twenty-five
million to Nikki translates to people in Kapuskasing and
Hundred Mile House and White River and Golden and
Grimsby and Black Harbour and Nipigon and Creston?"

Across the country, Aunt Emily says, the word is
spreading and alarm bells are going off. Some people are
waking up and blinking. Others gasp. A group in Vancouver hasn't stopped roaring since the first report. Who,
they want to know, is Nikki Kagami?

The way Aunt Emily and Morty carry on, redress is an evangelistic crusade. It's Pastor Jim they need, not me. Crusades need crusaders. In my opinion, the redress effort is rather inconsequential if you consider what's going on in the world. Famines. Tortures. Genocides. Our history is barely a ripple in a rain puddle. They'd like to make waves, perhaps. Rock some paper boats.

"How can you not be interested?" Morty asked me in exasperation.

"It doesn't seem all that important. . . ."

"Not important! I can't believe you'd say that!"

Morty was born and raised on a beet farm in Manitoba and he says he was fed his mother's pain in her breast milk. Every day she'd come in from the mind-numbing labor in the beet fields, wailing about "the evacuation" or how magical life had once been, and how she missed their friends and Stanley Park and she wanted the family's heirlooms back and she didn't get to finish university and her life was ruined, ruined.

"She had *faith* in democracy. She *believed* in Canada."

Morty is as zealous as anyone I ever met from Cecil's Prophetic Bible Institute. "People like you, Naomi, they really disappeared you good," he said. "Come to a meeting of our Democracy group. Get undisappeared, for a change."

Morty's a strong-fisted dreamer, fit and ready to blast through ceilings. As for me, I'm not inclined to thrust my green limbs through sidewalks.

The little clock tells me it's time to get up. The sunlight has become a swash of light on the wall. Later it will touch the tatami-type rug and beam itself onto the round glass eating table.

I don't know how I'll face Father Cedric today. What a fool I made of myself. Still, there was yesterday when I was standing in the rain at the Bathurst bus stop and there was that strange, that inexplicable surge of confidence and aliveness. It was like a dam bursting. An attack of breath.

17

"Ah," Father Cedric says. "Ah, Naomi."

Friday, three nights ago, was the first time I'd been to his living quarters. It was late. Past eleven when the phone rang.

"Naomi? Are you busy? Do you . . . ?" There's a pause and his voice lowers almost to a whisper. "Do you have time?"

"Um . . ."

"If it's too late . . ."

"No, it's okay."

The familiar lilt is back in his voice. "You're not too busy? You're not sleeping?"

I am in fact just getting ready for bed and the bottom of my hair is wet from the bath, but I pull on my Indian-style wraparound skirt and loose white linen top and step out into the not too clean hallway with its cracked marble floor.

Eugenia was right about ground-level living. It's more human here. This section of town is more human as well. Unlike the perfect mannequins that pose in their perfect window displays where Aunt Emily lives, the people of this district have history in their faces.

"No denying that," Morty says. "Lots of reality going on round here."

Even at this hour, as I trot down the alley in my plastic thongs, I pass a half-dozen stories. Two men with gray stained aprons cart crates of vegetables through the sawdust-strewn back entrance of a restaurant. A young woman, large with pregnancy, sits on a bench at the bus stop beside a white-haired man. She calls him Daddy and is asking for money. Then there's Greta, the bag lady, with her enormous bags piled high on a shopping cart, making her slow swaying way down the late-night street.

I walk down the west side of St. John's College along the narrow sidewalk to the side door of the apartment building, then up the dimly lit concrete stairs to the third floor.

His door is open. He's in a gray jogging suit and leaning back at his desk under a stained-glass window which I hadn't noticed from the outside. His dark curly hair, receding at the temples, is unruly around his ears, as if he's been lying down.

He holds out his arms and springs up, his body lithe, athletic. He indicates the couch as he sits down again, folding one leg under himself.

I have no idea why he called. I slip off my thongs. An oval mirror hangs between the couch and desk and I catch a glimpse of my bland matter-of-factness. Obasan taught me well to conceal my inner face. There is no bewilderment evident. No curiosity.

I sit on the couch, tucking my bare feet to the side, and he smiles the disarmingly clear, uncomplicated smile which shows his slightly crooked front teeth. He seems softer tonight, his dancing eyes a little subdued.

The room is cozy, warm-colored. There's a plain woven rug and the couch has brownish pillows. I had imagined his walls lined with books, but there are no bookshelves at all. A curved driftwood shape, part crucifix, part bird in flight, hangs opposite the door above a worn armchair.

"Emily was here just now. Crying, crying."

"Aunt Emily? Crying?" I've never once seen her in tears. Not at Uncle's funeral. Not at Obasan's. Weeping is not a part of the aunt I know.

It happened after work tonight, he says. They were walking along College Street when she stopped short. A little old man was crossing the street against a red light. The old man stared at her, she frowned back and the old man kept on staring. She walked right in front of the streetcar toward him. Father Cedric says he couldn't believe it. The cars were honking, one motorist was cursing, waving his arms. And still Aunt Emily and the old man stood there like zombies gaping at each other.

"I had to run into that traffic and get them out of there."

It was Min Kawai, the artist of Aunt Emily's youth. All these years, she's been wondering about him. And here, right around the corner from us, he's been coming and going, in and out, as a patient at the Clarke Institute of Psychiatry.

He's living down the street these days with the fleas and sleaze at Gary's Hideaway, in a room he can leave at any time. A permanent getaway.

Aunt Emily was shaking after the encounter. She came up here to Father Cedric's apartment and wept. She told him that every wounded Japanese Canadian deserved healing, and every able-bodied one of us should be rallied to locate every single Min Kawai. This was our last chance. If we didn't wake now, we'd sleep forever.

"Speak to Nomi," she begged. "She doesn't hear anything I say. Redress matters so much. So much."

"Tell me," he asks after a moment, "what do you think of the redress movement?"

I'm uncomfortably aware that I don't know anything at all about it. I'm afraid I'm being rude by not answering.

Father Cedric sighs and stretches his arms wide. He slides forward onto the floor, pulling his legs into the lotus position. Then he tilts his head to the side and looks up at me.

I stare at the floor. "I'm not really part of the community," I say hesitantly. It's my guess that we don't really have a community at all. After all, as Aunt Emily puts it, we were all "deformed by the Dispersal Policy" and grew up striving to be "the only Jap in town." "No, I don't speak Japanese," we'd say proudly.

"You don't know any of your people?"

Something inside me cringes whenever I hear the phrase "your people." It tells me I belong to a "people" that don't belong.

He looks thoughtful, then pats the floor in front of him, gesturing to me to sit. The floor for some reason is more comfortable than the couch. We are three stories above the ground, but I feel closer to earth and more at home here.

Many people, he says, including himself, have no communities. "My mother said we lacked 'appartenance.' We weren't Quebeckers. We knew that for sure."

He tells me he was born in northern Ontario. He glances at me hesitantly as he tells me he was not the child of a normal union. His father, a parish priest, was sent away discreetly. His mother was a young novitiate. He looks suddenly vulnerable, his eyebrows raised in inquiry as he waits for my reaction.

"You were the only child?"

"I think so."

I nod and show no surprise. There is, after all, no such thing as an illegitimate child.

His mother, he says, was swarthy and small. Her name was Cecilia. "She was so quiet. Even more quiet than you, maybe." Her thick black hair was in one long braid to her waist. She was, he believes, the great-grand-daughter of a Métis woman.

"And your father?"

He reaches behind him to a rattle resting on a small pile of round stones. A native artifact? Maybe. Maybe not. A talisman perhaps. A carved bird's head is at the end of a stick, and thongs with a pebble at each end dangle below a fist-size drum.

"Have you seen one like this before?"

It's vaguely familiar. It reminds me of a tiny red cardboard rattle, part of the costume of a Japanese doll I once had. Instead of stones, beads hung at the ends of two threads. The doll had a hole in its porcelain fist for the toothpick-thin stem.

"My father sent this to my mother. It's a Japanese Haida rattle."

"Japanese Haida?"

He smiles at my curiosity.

Before Cedric was born, his father was sent far away to work among the Haida of northern B.C. He was not to communicate with his young lover, Cedric's mother, but occasionally he did. That rattle was the only gift he ever sent.

"My mother loved him. Always. This rattle told her sad stories about children who lose their fathers. It was made by a man who left his child."

Back in the early 1900s, Japanese miners and fishermen had settled on the Queen Charlotte Islands. At the time of the Japanese Canadian roundup in 1942, a few of the men fled to the more remote islands and were sheltered by the Haida. Father Cedric's father visited them and brought them news about the war.

The isseis and their protectors ate the same food— seaweed, herring roe, young ferns, berries. The sun and sea joined them. Children were born. Moon-faced children. Babies with Japanese eyes. And there were dark-skinned children on the islands as well—offspring of slaves in flight from the south. One of the issei fathers carved this rattle for his child. He carved toys and bowls and long-handled spoons. Then he left for Japan.

Father Cedric places the rattle on the floor between us and looks up at the stained-glass window. The street-light shines through the bright warm colors. When Father Cedric speaks seriously, he angles his head and addresses a space above him. The more serious he is, the softer his voice becomes. "So many stories in the world, Naomi. My mother, before she died, said, 'Life is a gift, Cedric. Breath is a gift. I thank God for the breath of life.'" He repeats the phrase slowly. "The breath," he whispers and inhales deeply, ". . . of life."

"Tell me, Naomi," he asks after a while, "what is for you the breath of life?"

I chew my bottom lip and stare blankly. The breath of life?

If he were to ask Aunt Emily the question, her mind would race through her file of puns. The meaning of life. The bread of life. What would she say? Give us this day our daily breath? I shake my head.

"For Emily," he says as if reading my mind, "redress is her breath, don't you think? For me, breath means 'yes.'"

"Yes?"

"Yes."

I'm not certain how long we sit in the stillness of the room. It may be ten minutes or more. The eastbound streetcar makes its rumbling squeal as it goes past. His breathing is slow and deep. I think about the Japanese Haida child and about the child Cedric, about his parents and my parents and about families that are destroyed by various decrees. Then the image of my mother comes to me—her long black hair, her oval face, her yasashi kokoro. I tell him, haltingly, about the high hillside grave and my dream in Hawaii. He nods as he listens. I can't think when I have spoken so freely.

After this we chat lightly. I am beginning to feel that it's late and I should leave when he stretches out his arms, palms out, as though beckoning to an infant.

18

It's altogether inappropriate. My reaction. The slight

choking sensation. The frozen flight in my limbs. The

terror is ridiculous but so palpable I cannot stop the

trembling of the invisible violence within.

I can feel, too, though I dare not look up, that he is

as instantly perplexed and bewildered as I am. His touch,

I know, was intended as a light, perhaps brotherly em-

brace. A "good night and thank you for coming tonight."

A "see you later" kiss.

I'm not making a single sound, but I can feel Father

Cedric listening with such a sudden intentness that a

wordless speech is being dredged forth. A tiny rebel cry. His arms move away and his hands cup the air around my face. It's as though he's infusing my hiding with a loud invasive listening. There's a kind of hearing in his fingers that penetrates my stillness and pulls forth sounds.

"Father . . ." A whisper. A tiny breath. A small animal cry. And then the insanity. Decades of undisturbed dust in a stampede of wings.

I'm paralyzed.

There are birds, flushed into the open air, pulled into the windstream of jumbo jets. There's a reptilian roar of plane engines and some somewhere leafless tree on some too sudden mountainside.

"Naomi . . . Naomi . . ."

I gasp and flee. I run down the steps, out into the nearly empty street and down the alley. All the way back to my apartment, the air is shaking with guffaws.

Within me, the night is wide-eyed. It's like the time I asked Tina about her body and she fixed her beautiful blue eyes on the floor as if down there, beneath our feet, was some vile thing too heinous to mention, and I did not dare to speak to her again of whatever it was that mysteriously surged within.

I'm thinking the phone may ring when I get in, but the only sounds are the humming of the fridge and the brief growling bark of the temperamental Pekinese next door, announcing that he's heard my late-night footsteps.

Such spinsterly absurdity. What must he think of my ludicrous behavior? But what of his? The swift glide of his arm around my waist as we rose was a motion as smooth and windswept as a seagull soaring in the open air. But I could no more fly with him than a tree could uproot itself and dance.

I close the door softly behind me and collapse onto my foam bed. The tiny clock's hands glow the time. One-twenty. I'm too embarrassed even to turn on the light. I crawl under the covers with my clothes on, as I did the night of a huge snowstorm when I shared a bed with Tina and Lydia under their enormous down-filled quilt.

I've always known that on an emotional quotient chart I'd score somewhere between a cactus and a chimpanzee. Hank obviously found that out and gave up on his throat-clearing efforts toward me.

The fraction of a moment's first hug remains with me, the tiny electrical shock of Father Cedric's light touch on the nape of my neck. It's all been magnified by my absurd collapse. I bury my face in the pillow and eventually fall asleep.

It's five-thirty when I waken with a familiar dizzying shudder. I push my fingers against my ears.

Bees.

Or the high whine of telephone wires on a prairie highway in midsummer. There's a ringing jangling hum of insects in my head. Tension. The old stress response. The buzz of the heat bugs from the fields—the beet fields—the magnetic fields. My compass is berserk.

Think peace, I command myself, think stillness, sweet peaceable sleep. Think somewhere outside the city —maybe a bonfire at night by a lake, no insects.

And Father Cedric in a sleeping bag beside me?

The sudden nauseous pain extends from somewhere around my navel and across the abdomen. I bend double and attempt to ride the tide, my mind reeling backward as it does in its efforts to find the source, the cause, the spark. It's like being a researcher in the middle of a forest fire looking for the incriminating cigarette butt.

Who knows what the psychogenesis of an illness may be? There are so many mysteries in the past—so many unknowns and forbidden rooms. According to Aunt Emily, I was fat and funny and healthy and never cried as a baby. I have no memory of that. She says I became sickly after Mother disappeared.

My abominable abdomen. Something vast as childhood lies hidden in the belly's wars. There's a rage whose name has been forgotten.

In Granton I grew wan and thin as a sickle moon. Perhaps it's the fear of hell that was the hook in the night skies from which my adolescence hung limp and clammy in the prairie weather.

"Let go and let God," Pastor Jim used to say. The problem, I think, is not so much to release as to be released.

Pastor Jim's message of hell probably spread within me a fear of life. Fears still fall like sparks onto tinder. Tinder turns to flame. Flames leap along the fuse to the cache of TNT—a ton of damnation in the body's vaults. It's half a lifetime later and still the old fears.

Pastor Jim's God was a devouring fire feasting on us, his fundamentalist flock. The Bible Belt was so tight it squeezed us in half at the waist, dividing us into two hemispheres. And there we were, God's half-creatures from the anti-liberalist, anti-modernist, God-have-mercy-on-us churches, praying to be whole.

Praying has never once helped me in the middle of an attack. All I know is that when the retching ends, the spasms stop, the waves recede and it's over.

The pain has always been the same—a solid force coming up through the otherworld. There's nothing I know that can stop it. Back in Cecil, the doctor said it was tension and stress and I should get rest.

Roll and roll with it, I always tell myself. Breathe deep. Over the top like a surfer. Eventually the wave will break. Eventually.

I crawl along the floor to the bathroom, my wraparound skirt trailing behind me.

"Oba! Uncle!"

Saturday before dawn and I'm in those wretched Cecil nights, when I screamed for Stephen till the body emptied itself and flapped like laundry in the midnight wind.

Illness is a body at war, the soldiers so confused they keep out friends and welcome foes. There are, there must be, messengers in the mine fields, zigzagging through the battlegrounds, carrying the word from headquarters that the war is called off. Yet from out of unexpected night an attack begins. The officers at the front lines carry on with old orders.

I should shut down the munitions factory of my mind. To impute meaning to everything or to nothing is the same impudence.

I make it back to bed as night seeps into the walls and the morning light spreads. No sunrise. Another long Toronto day in the forever prairie field by the irrigation ditch—a bubbly slide along the muddy bank. I take the phone off the hook and sleep till noon.

When I waken, it's gone. Survival again. The all-clear signal, and sunshine across the floor. I've had another minor victory in the history of minor wars.

I look out the window and feel only relief. No anxieties. No tormenting embarrassments. A plump black squirrel jumps across the branches of the chestnut tree and over the rooftop of the building next door, his furry tail a twitching treble clef behind him. It's enough to be out of the battle zone. It's another reprieve.

19

Eight o'clock Sunday morning and Aunt Emily is on the

line, sounding throaty as if she's just wakened.

"The Makino obasan wants to see you."

"Who?"

"Mrs. Makino. The Granton Makino."

Obasan's old friend, Mrs. Makino, is here? Mrs.

Makino of the sardine gifts and the very late pregnancy?

I remember our surprise when she gave birth to Baby

Anna. I've sometimes thought of her as my own

childbearing years flew past. What is kindly Mrs.

Makino, the patient mother of the Mak-duo, doing in

Toronto? I can only picture her in the cornfields or with Obasan in the kitchen in Granton.

Aunt Emily's early morning noises remind me of hogs snuffling. "Thought you'd be surprised. She moved here last week to be with Anna."

"Baby Anna's in Toronto?"

Baby Anna, it appears, has survived, thrived and become a sansei lawyer. The pudgy child sitting with kittens on the floor is married to a Toronto journalist.

"And Mr. Makino? Is Ojisan here too?"

Aunt Emily sighs. "You've got a lot of catching up to do."

Makino ojisan, she tells me, is gone. She names others.

Japanese Canadians, she says, are an endangered species. Some study she read somewhere shows that more niseis are dying of stress diseases than any other group. "And it's clearly not a question of what we eat. Believe me," she says, "we do not live by diet alone."

Aunt Emily reminds me of those flypaper coils Obasan had dangling in the kitchen. Any nisei-related notion that flits by gets stuck in her mind and buzzes there for all to see—a nisei honored, a nisei disgraced—she's a walking trap for nisei news. She says a study should be done on the many older nisei like herself who never married. It would show how deeply they've obeyed the order to disappear.

We've had a cultural lobotomy, she says, and have lost the ancient ways. There's a button in the brain that signals when to die and there's a universal law—if you honor your mothers and fathers, the button stays on hold. "It makes sense, doesn't it?" she asks. "Look at Japan. Centuries of parent pandering and they're the lon-

gest-living people in the world." She does go on and on.
She's going to become one of those non-stop talkers who
are only quiet when they're asleep.

I tell her I'll meet her at Baby Anna's home, which
she says is "establishment brick."

A few rain showers are washing away the smog and I
find myself walking most of the way, my thoughts bouncing from Granton and the Mak-duo and Hank to my idiotic Friday night flight. And so what and so what, I tell
myself glumly as I slap along in my thongs.

It's while standing in the rain, waiting for the Bathurst bus, that I find myself breathing deeply as if my
lungs have just been pried open. The breath of life.
"What is the breath of life for you, Naomi?" I didn't have
an answer for him on Friday, but right now I can feel
myself being called to breath. Called.

The splatter of raindrops trickles sensuously down
my face and onto my tongue. And here's proof. I'm not a
natural-born prude, not a cactus. Only a plant with
leaves can welcome rain.

It seems to me, as I think about it now, that Father
Cedric's hug was an accidental falling of a spark, and
that a tiny flame leapt and spat, darting panic along
some ancient fuse.

The sky is dramatically dark and bright, one thick
cloud roiling past with its load. In this moment, I feel a
fusion of elements—earth, breath, fire and water—entering my pores and conceiving life in my dusty limbs. The
breath of life has never felt so instant. Noon-hour shadows bounce underfoot. I have stepped into a Van Gogh
painting with light streaking through the air. A coiling
visceral light.

I catch the bus just before the hill and am so absorbed I forget my stop and have to walk back through streets glistening with autumn flowers in the landscaped yards. More Van Goghs. I spot Aunt Emily's little red car first, and then, on the other side of the street, I see the group in the paved driveway beside the sunny house—square two-story solid brick, leaded glass windows, skylights. A mansion.

A fairly tall woman, by Japanese standards, leans against a van beside pumpkin-faced Mrs. Makino, her plump little body bent forward, her hair thin and white. Both her hands hold the round ivory handles of her familiar black wool handbag. Dear Mrs. Makino, with her crinkly kindly eyes.

Aunt Emily is her usual intense self, talking animatedly with a lanky dark-haired man.

Mrs. Makino seems smaller than the last time I saw her, weeping at her door when I dropped in to say goodbye. Her heavy glasses kept falling off her nose and finally she let them dangle there and she could no longer see that I was waving while she wiped her eyes with a corner of her apron.

"Maa, Naomi-san," Mrs. Makino murmurs and bows as I come up to her. "Nagai koto . . . such a long time. . . ."

The barely recognizable sophisticate slaps her forehead and her mouth falls open. "Wow," she groans, "what an old woman you've become, Naomi Nakane."

"Why, thank you, Baby Anna," I say with chagrin. "I didn't recognize you either." Anna is as elegant as a model, heavy ebony bracelet on wrist, hand on hipbone, dark glasses holding down her exuberant hair.

Her handsome husband, Brian Cooperman, is a jour-

nalist with *The Globe and Mail*. His handshake is warm
and his gaze inquiring as we are introduced.

"We've been in Toronto a whole year, Ms. Makino,"
he says, stepping back from Baby Anna with mock aston-
ishment, his thick eyebrows arched, "and we haven't met
Emily's niece before?"

"I know, I know," Anna says. "But you know how
busy . . ."

Brian lifts his hands and his eyes to the sky.

It's the way things are in Toronto. People are mad
with busyness. Anna is a fledgling lawyer. She works all
the time, Brian says, but these days, with community
activity, life is out of control.

I can hardly believe that this professional woman is
Anna Makino from Granton. She's a taller, more stylish
version of her sisters, the Mak-duo. The fat baby I once
knew is nowhere evident. She's more handsome than
pretty, large cheekbones, sharp, slanted eyes. And she's
completely western in her body language. Not a coy bone
anywhere. There's the slightest look of defiance in the
way she flings her head. And here she is with husband,
career, house and garden, and all the symptoms of happily ever after.

Some people walk with such confidence, boldly down
the winding pathways of their fairy tales right through to
the clearing and the sunset. My walk, by contrast, is a
stroll along a stretch of sand. Pebbles. Sea and sky. Min-
imal vegetation. It's a life that's more uneventful than
most people could dream possible.

Anna, Brian, Aunt Emily and Morty have been meeting all year with other Japanese Canadians, they tell me.
Last week even Father Cedric got involved.

Mrs. Makino is standing by, polite and smiling in the way of the issei. A leprechaun. I nod my sympathies, telling Mrs. Makino I didn't know that Mr. Makino had died, and she says, "Nh, nh," appreciatively, handing me a familiar tabloid, *The New Canadian*. She points out the obituary in the English section.

Back in Granton, these papers were stacked on shelves, under beds. "So ka. Mo shinda no ka," Uncle would say as he held his glasses at the tip of his nose and read the vertical script. So then, one has died now, has one? This faithful sentinel still calls out its lonely news —a flickering light gone out in Chatham, another in Vernon, one in Granton. Three deaths in this issue.

"Everyone someday dies," Obasan would say.

Marion, Mrs. Makino says, is here too, in a Toronto suburb. "Mississauga. Nice house." The last I saw Marion and Suzy, the Mak-duo, was at their big double wedding.

Aunt Emily has opened the side door of the van and is hailing us to get on board. They've been standing around, she says, waiting for me so that they could set out on a round of "hospital hopping" in their "granny van," as Anna puts it. Brace Lodge first, then Chesterview.

Brian is solicitous, almost lifting Mrs. Makino up the high step and into the back seat. She sits with her short legs dangling as he fastens her seat belt. "Sun kew, sun kew," she says, nodding her thanks while he gives her a culture-clashing goodbye peck on the cheeks.

Brian has to get down to the paper. "But we'll see you Thursday night," he says, shaking my hand. "You'll have to come and meet our Gaby."

"Your Gaby?"

"Our cat," Anna says. "And Thursday night, why not come with Cedric, after work? We need all the help we can get, Naomi."

I climb in beside Mrs. Makino feeling as if all the buses in all the world have been going by all my life and I'd better get on now, before it's too late.

20

For as long as I can remember, Aunt Emily has been "bringing memories" to issei in nursing homes. "When you're old," she says, "that's what you want the most. Connections."

"Plus food," Anna adds. "Did we bring enough today?"

Aunt Emily laughs. Last Sunday, a crotchety old man followed them down the hall, waving his cane. He was starved for Japanese food. "What a pig," Aunt Emily chuckles. "Old toothless, the ruthless. Lost his false teeth but grabbed all the sushi."

The old man is desperate to leave the bum-bye-oh-rye-house (the by-and-by-all-right-house). He thinks he's in a hospital.

"Just one issei in Chesterview," Anna says. "One in Brace Lodge."

"Where have all the issei gone . . . ," Aunt Emily sings out on cue, as Anna turns the key and the van jerks forward, "long time passing. . . ."

She's off again with her terrible mix of puns and songs. Last week at the office, she spilled coffee all over the plans for the annual general meeting, and while I was wiping up the mess she was singing, "Oh God, our help in AGMs past." It's enough to put your teeth on edge.

We're setting off raucously, Anna and Aunt Emily singing, the Volkswagen motor roaring. First we're going to visit Mr. Kagamihara, an old friend that Mrs. Makino hasn't seen in a long time. She tells me he was such a humorous man. One time, in Vancouver, he came for dinner carrying a piece of lumber and said, "Ita daki masu—I carry lumber." But the phrase also means. "I receive this food." She holds her handkerchief over her mouth and laughs.

Mr. Kagamihara, Aunt Emily turns around to shout to me, is Nikki Kagami's uncle. "Did you ever meet Nikki?"

I remind her of the meeting at the cultural center where Aunt Emily blew up.

"That was her," Aunt Emily says. "Nikki Kagami—Noriko Kagamihara."

"Fashion designer?" I ask. I've seen her label, "Design by Nikki," on blouses at a store in the fashionable Yorkville area.

"The queen of redress, the bane of our lives," Anna replies aggressively.

It's curious how Nikki Kagami's name elicits irritation, exasperation, even anger. At work, Morty and Aunt Emily spend a lot of time talking about her.

We're zigzagging through the city, and finally pull up to a low-rise, a nondescript concrete block stuck on the pavement.

Inside, the place smells of age—aged bodies, old clothes, stale air, medication. Men and women move haltingly, limbs shaking, eyes vacant. Some people sleep in wheelchairs, their heads dangling like wilted flowers. A row of seats against the wall is partly filled with prickly-faced men being shaved by a woman with a basin and a razor. One man, white brows lifted high, watches us intently.

"Hello, hello," Aunt Emily calls out as we troop past. A flicker of attention registers and one woman clutching her walker, her face open as a newborn infant's, tries to respond. This is a hidden garden full of transplants and cuttings, fading blossoms.

In a far corner of a windowless dining hall an issei man is slumped in a wheelchair at a long table, and at the other end is a Caucasian man, also in a wheelchair, hands shaking, fingers sliding mashed potatoes onto his fork. A woman in a brown uniform pushes a cart full of dishes and stops long enough to give him a mouthful, then she pulls his plate away. He reaches in the air with his fork. She pulls off his bib, tugs the fork from his fist. His mouth is open, protesting. We walk quickly past.

"Hello, Ojisan." Aunt Emily waves. Hello, Uncle.

Mrs. Makino, dabbing her eyes with her sleeve, makes bobbing bows as she approaches. Such decorousness. The dance of humility and peace.

The man seems barely conscious. "O," he says as if he's just wakened. He attempts to bow from the wheelchair in which he is strapped. "O-o-o," he says when he sees the rest of us. He is tiny and thin in a brown wool sweater. A purplish discoloration covers half his face. The name "Kagami" is written on the back of his wheelchair.

"Ojisan," Aunt Emily says loudly in his ear. I catch a whiff of urine and see the dribbled food stains on his baggy pants. He gazes at her with a mouth-open stare, his top teeth fallen from his gums. Part of a bun is clasped in one hand. Jagged prayer lines are in his forehead.

Mrs. Makino bows and touches his hands tentatively, as she stands beside her old friend. "Ma-ki-no." She cups her mouth in her hands.

The old man leans back and peers up.

"Ma-ki-no," Mrs. Makino repeats.

"O." He seems not to recognize her. He turns back to Aunt Emily and whispers a torrent of soft rapid sounds, then he turns again to Mrs. Makino and offers his half-eaten bun—offers and offers in the way of the issei. Like my obasan in Cecil, he will offer all the way to the end of the road.

The old man whispers that he is now in "such a place," "konna tokoro ni." Then he bows his head and is silent. He will be no bother to anyone. He wishes all to be smooth and at peace.

Mrs. Makino, nodding all the time and dabbing her

eyes, takes a tape recorder from her handbag and hands
it to Anna.

"Gohan tabeta, Ojisan?" Aunt Emily asks. "Have you
eaten, Uncle?"

"Eh, eh," the old man replies.

"Did you tell the doctor about your . . . ?" She pats
his throat.

"Eh, eh."

"No, no, Ojisan, did you tell him?"

He lowers his head in a humble bow and raises his
hand, waving it rapidly back and forth in the gesture that
means no.

"They'll die before they admit there's anything
wrong," Aunt Emily says in exasperation.

How well I know the issei, who will never ever complain. It's their code of honor requiring them to gaman,
to endure without flinching, that makes them the silent
people of Canadian nursing homes. From their early
childhood in Meiji Japan, they witnessed the poverty of
fellow villagers who suffered in silence, for the love of
parents, for the honor of ancestors, for the sake of the
whole.

Anna presses a button on the recorder and the re-
winding tape hurtles along till it stops with a click. The
familiar rich voice of Nakayama-sensei comes through
the black box. A flood of nostalgia. Here he is again. He
was with us in our Vancouver years, at picnics in Stanley
Park, then in the crowded halls of the mountain internment camp of Slocan. Later, out on the wind-flung
prairies, he rode his bike from Coaldale to help us on the
sugar-beet farm—round-eyed, round-faced plump little
minister in his black suit and his glasses and with his
portable communion kit. He is here now, disembodied in

a box on a dining-hall table, calling out the old rallying call. Hold to the faith. We are together. God is love.

It's his lifelong message, coming via his dwindling network of friends. They bring these tapes, one to one, or to a few here or there in their care facilities, in hospitals where they sit or lie and listen or sleep, remembering and forgetting the days of their British Columbian youth.

The ojisan leans forward, straining to hear, his eyes wide, a smile of recognition beginning to form.

This is where the issei have gone. Into their last days —one by one. They wait alone at home or with family or in these permanent places of transition, their final internment centers, holding their tickets to a distant land. In wheelchairs and beds, with their day-long stares, they wait for the hour of their call.

And who is it, then, who comes to the station to bid them farewell? A voice in a machine, a familiar hymn, a memory of a dream.

"Arigato, arigato." It's the constant habitual word of the issei. "Thank you. Thank you." He whispers his chant as the prayers end and the minister's voice rings forth, still strong and powerful—the old familiar hymn.

> . . . *warera mo*
> *ai sen*
> *ai naru*
> *Kami yo.* . . .

> . . . *we also*
> *shall love*
> *O God*
> *who art love.* . . .

The old man is straining to see. Is Nakayama-sensei here? He looks at each of us and reaches out his hand to Mrs. Makino.

"Wakatta no. Ara! Wakatta no," Mrs. Makino whispers. He recognizes. Ara! He understands.

His rasping voice follows the words of the hymn as a bright smile spreads across his face. His eyes are alive and present.

"I haven't seen him like this in years." Aunt Emily lifts the tape recorder from the table and turns up the volume.

"Whatever the suffering"—Nakayama-sensei's voice emphasizes the "whatever"—"the God that is Love does not discard. Look. That chair. That bed. Love sits. Love sleeps."

21

Monday morning. Father Cedric is away according to the all-purpose calendar on the wall. I haven't heard from him at all since Friday night.

The only thing that is real between us is the question mark. The shape of a single footprint. Mine. Between all my questions are still more questions I'll never ask. The absurdity of it all. I stride along, imagining what will happen if I'm ever in his arms again. Then crunch. Halt! Seabirds swoop down to block the way.

Aunt Emily is in the middle of a call from Mrs. Makino. Normally she uses the worktable piled high with Morty's papers, but she prefers Father Cedric's office. "Brighter here," she says. His big front window faces College Street. Our space is next and at the end is Morty's claustrophobic room like a caboose.

Aunt Emily is speaking in Japanese. "Nomi?" Her hand cups the mouthpiece as she leans over to peer through the door. "Ojisan died. Mr. Kagami."

"What? But we just saw him yesterday."

Eugenia glances at me inquiringly. "Friend of the family?"

"Sort of. Everyone is, I guess."

Aunt Emily shuffles in and sighs as she lowers herself onto the chair at the overflowing table. "Wasn't he alert? I should have known. I've seen it before—that aliveness just before the end." She lays down her head over a pile of papers. "He hadn't recognized anyone for years. Years!"

Perhaps Kagamihara-ojisan during all that time was waiting for some kind of release, a visit from a son or from Nakayama-sensei. I'm convinced, having watched Obasan day after day waiting for Stephen, that one sometimes needs strength in order to go, one last dip in the river where blessings flow—to drink of the waters or to give or receive a final word, a gift, a benediction.

Morty emerges from his cubbyhole, scratching his thin little beard. "Another funeral?"

"Mr. Kagami. Nikki's uncle."

"Give her my love," Morty says and rolls his eyes.

"Don't be unkind, Morty," Aunt Emily says. "Aren't you coming to the funeral?"

He shrugs. "Never knew him."

"That's the trouble with you sanseis. You don't have the connections."

. . .

It's Tuesday noon. Aunt Emily picks me up first before getting Mrs. Makino. She has a white sympathy card and the koden, the traditional gift of money, is a check made out to the cultural center, as requested by the family. I can remember how it was when I was young—that business of giving and giving. You never went anywhere without a gift. To funerals you took money and food. Funerals were festive occasions—sushi, manju—and always some adults bending down, saying how big the children had grown.

The service this afternoon is at a funeral home. At the moment, we're stuck in the traffic hiccupping along on Bathurst Street following a streetcar. The driver is helping a blind man get on.

"Did Cedric tell you I ran into Min Kawai?" In all these years, Aunt Emily says, she never dreamt that her childhood friend was in Toronto. She was sure he'd been trapped in the exile to Japan of the mentally ill. "I probably passed him a dozen times on the street." She shudders and both hands grip the steering wheel tightly. "He's so medicated now, the light's gone out of his eyes."

We pick up Mrs. Makino and arrive at the funeral barely on time. The organ is playing "Nearer My God to Thee." The place is almost full. Mostly old people. A table at the entrance seats two thin white-haired men accepting the cards and the koden, their eyes politely downcast, serious unsmiling faces. I'm surprised that we are welcomed in English by the usher, who looks old enough to be an issei but is obviously Canadian-born. "Hi, Em," he whispers, and nods to me, bows to Mrs.

Makino. I follow Aunt Emily and Mrs. Makino down the aisle to the open coffin at the front.

There he lies, Kagamihara-ojisan, in brown paint makeup and gray suit, so presentable at last and so not here. No more urine stains, no teeth falling out, the mouth properly closed. Aunt Emily bows. I bow. We turn and bow to the family—niseis, sanseis, strangers all. They acknowledge our greetings. Mrs. Makino lingers, wiping her eyes as she bows deeply before an old woman and clutches her hands.

"That's Nikki Kagami's mother," Aunt Emily whispers as we make our way back down the aisle to our seats.

To think we just visited Ojisan in his nursing home on Sunday. One little sparrow sits on the line. He flies away. Then there are none. And here and there on the long trans-Canada wire, in Revelstoke, or Thunder Bay, or Kenora, another small bird sits alone, then flits and disappears, leaving a small empty bird-shaped space in the watching air.

We stand to sing a hymn and I'm back in Slocan, back in a childhood that seems to me to have never been. The Japanese characters in the hymnbook are familiar squiggles. Everything is familiar—the bowlegged women, the bullnecked men. One difference now is that most of these older people are not isseis singing in Japanese, but English-speaking niseis.

"You see people at funerals," Aunt Emily whispers. "That's all we are now. A culture of funerals."

It's hidden and shadowy here, the last stand of Canada's issei, invisible to the politician's naked eye. Small ghost riders of the skies. They've gathered together from who knows which directions, to say goodbye to their brother ghost, and when it's over they'll disappear as soundlessly as they've arrived and you will not see them again, in shopping mall or subway or theater or any other public place, until the next funeral. And what they think as they sit here, and whether they are lonely, they will never say. They are too humble to declare themselves. I can see it in their discreet eyes. Like Obasan, like Uncle, they are people who are proud to be humble.

How short we all are. Normally at any public event my view of the room is someone's broad back, but here at this short people's gathering, I can see clear up to the front of the church where wreaths surround the coffin. A youthful unsmiling photo of the dead man sits on a triangular stand above the coffin, which has now been closed.

I feel I should know every stranger here by name—all these ojisans and obasans, isseis, niseis, sanseis, threaded together through history, language, geography and the will, perhaps, to disappear. If I could touch the heartstrings of this quiet room there would be somber tones resonating. Every single face is one I know and do not know. Perhaps there are schoolmates here with whom I played in Slocan, or who came to visit us in Vancouver. This is almost a reunion, but I do not imagine that I will learn anyone's name. No one will come up and ask who I am. That is not the way we are—we quiet ones. Apart from a very few Aunt Emilys, the most quiet of us all are older Japanese Canadians. I can imagine Aunt Emily roaring and stomping on my skull if she could read my thoughts. "Out, out, damn stereotype," she would say.

Nikki Kagami moves like a model as she mounts the steps to the pulpit. There is something quite elegant and magnetic about her. How is it, I wonder, that this one woman warrants so much criticism from Morty and Aunt Emily and now, I've learned, even Anna. "She tries to turn out all the bright young lights so her own dim light can shine," Anna said the other day.

Nikki Kagami's eulogy is unexceptional. A colorless recitation of her uncle's life—where he was born, where he lived. Next an old man speaks in Japanese. He praises his dead friend because he never complained, because he paid the price for harmony in a world of discord. He did not add to the din. He was obedient to the command to be meek, but he did not in the end, I am thinking, inherit the earth.

The minister, a recent immigrant from Japan, clears his throat and speaks in halting English as the eulogies end. We are all sitting politely, our quiet hearts ticking the funeral away.

This is a hall of flightlessness. I imagine most of the people here are like Obasan and Uncle and me, folks left behind by the Stephens who have flown far away. We who remain are penguins with folded wings, formal and flat-footed. We've evolved for submerging but not for the air. Perhaps it's only the dead who fully escape the "bounds of earth."

Ah, Ojisan.

22

Red sumac moist morning and the coolness of the autumn deep blue sky. A few leaves are curled like mittens and gloves of small children flung about on the kindergarten floor—all the colors, the whisperings, the children invisible, hidden in trees.

We are here, he and I, driving through these bright woods along the Muskoka River, a falling of water in the Laurentian Shield. There are no pebbles to show the way home, no signposts to tell which way to go. We glide in the swish of this bright leaf light. Legato. I feel no weight.

He's chatting lightly as if nothing unusual ever happened between us. There's a story, he says, that his mother told, of a dryad from the northern woods. Before disappearing into a well, the dryad offered three riddles about the meaning of life. These were the riddle of morning, the riddle of noon and the riddle of love. The answer to the riddle of morning was wonder. Definition was not the place to begin. And laughter was the solution to the riddle of noon. But the third was a silent falling. The dryad went on to the dawn through the stars reflected in the well's dark waters. She was a tree nymph, a wood sprite and a breath of mercy. When we drink from her well, we extinguish the night.

I'm listening intently, searching for clues, wondering if he will speak directly of last Friday, wondering about the unexpectedness of that moment when he was no longer quite who he was. And when I tried to move, the room was a forest of arms and I did not know whether a predator or a woodsman held that absurd uncontrollable trembling.

When he called me early this morning to suggest this little trip, I was hesitant, feeling the sudden pull of some leash taut around my throat. I could barely say yes.

It was before 8 A.M. and cooler than I expected. I had to dash back in for warmer clothes, pulling on knee socks under my jeans and digging out the blue winter ski jacket from the back of the closet. He was waiting in his car in the parking lot behind *Bridge,* his heavy Mexican sweater flung onto the backseat. The Japanese Haida rattle drum was on the dashboard.

He's been telling me again about his mother and her silent ways. "The animals that make no sound," he says,

"—the rabbits, the deer—they feel as much as the ones that cry out."

Theirs were daily struggles from morning to night. They moved from place to place. His mother left the church, but to the end of her days, she prayed.

We pull off the straight northward route and onto a winding road lined with trees, some of which are already sun-colored, red, russet and yellow. Then we turn northward again up another road and onto a curving dirt trail, past two bridges, till we come to a place where the track disappears over flat rounded rock and clumps of bushes.

He brings the car to a stop beneath a large tree. "The place of my great-great-grandmother," he says lightly. He picks up the rattle from the dashboard and taps his cheeks. "You see these high cheekbones? They come from here. When I go back in my mind, it isn't to France. It's here. I begin here."

Such a specific sense of place he has—this bright woodland of boulders and trees. My uncle, I know, also had a strong sense of place. He was the old man of the sea, banished to the flatlands with its oceans of prairie grass.

This solid ocean undulates at a different pace. The rock, red-veined, lunges out of the earth, lurching upward in a slowness of stone. I feel the touch here, not so much of history as of prehistory. The granular lines are a map of time.

He twirls the rattle and the pebbles on the drum skin sound soft as acorns falling. Thud thud. The little bird head looks back and forth. Yesterday, tomorrow, yesterday, tomorrow. It could be a canary. Definitely not a fierce bird of prey. The "thunderbird," I've heard, was the prime bird of all creation and the communicator between earth and heaven. This is a rattle of a lesser bird. He places the precious object firmly in my hand.

"For you, Naomi. Maybe it will help us to communicate?" His fingers tap my hand lightly as he speaks. "And Friday night?"

A flush of heat touches the back of my neck.

He goes to a tree and looks up into the bright yellow canopy. He is released, he tells me, from the political by the personal and the primitive. His mother's gift to him was a capacity to sense sentience. The sense of the Presence, he says, is the most primitive sense, more precious than all the other senses.

"Naomi, I like that you don't talk so much. That means to me many things." He reaches out his hand and we walk.

The coolness in the air is touched with an appetite as small and sharp as the tiny chipmunks darting up the trees. It's the breath of his ancestors that comes of this air. A soft-footed breeze. They breathed here where we are, and infused their lungs with these living seasons.

What is the breath of life for me? It is this. To be here where the lone bird calls in the forest's noontime. To see the startling red of the sumac stand on the slope, the leaves the feathers of exotic birds. Northern flamingos.

We walk in the woods, among the widesprung milkweed pods. Along the water's edge, there are clusters of brown furry-tipped bulrushes stuck in the earth like giant birthday candles. Occasionally he sprints ahead through the pathless forest, then waits for me to catch up. He is watching everything. I am watching another

watcher but I do not know what he sees. The air is full of
eyes, and I am extravagant with imagining.

This is the closest I have ever been to the prince's
ball. In this my autumn season, I am opening the book
of an untimely tale. Somewhere in the air are Cinderella's slippers, and on earth, soft moccasins are dancing.

The sun grows so warm, we spread our jackets on a
rock and lie on our backs under the bright bright light of
the sky and the fiery trees. It's a fairy-tale afternoon. And
what woods these are, Father Cedric, I do not know. I
am walking along the pathways of my mind where there
are cliffs, where there are many detour signs. And there,
over the walls of old legends with their dark woods and
ancient altars, comes Eden's winged serpent, green and
coiling, down and down to the forest floor.

A curtain of leaves shields us as we glide farther and
farther from the forest's edge. What wings there are on
the serpentine forms that roam along these ancient
stones. Flying reptiles. Amphibious birds. The scent of
fur is on the touch of the hands that circle my face.
Nothing will ever be the same again. There are as many
dreams in the forest as there are shadows in the trees.

23

Cinderella Cinderella lost in the midnight transportation finds herself in a cloud of fairy dust and where's this we're heading for, sir? Somewhere ahead, a bus driver drones, "So you want to get back to your safe old story? Well well, so you want to get back."

The driver is gaunt and brittle as glass. He races through the night while Cinderella sits at the end of the pumpkin-coach bus. She's a shadow in search of her flesh, and the clock chimes on and on past thirteen o'clock.

Where are we going?

I'm not really voicing the question, though I need to know I need to know. My ballroom gown has vanished and I'm in my soot-covered yellow and black chimney-sweep rags. I'm not in charge. And instantly everything is elsewhere and I'm standing alone in some something road. How long does this last?

Eventually and eerily, out of nowhere comes my rescuer, a fairy godmother, a one-dimensional cardboard silhouette. She hovers around me. She wears a black clerical gown. She opens her mouth and her long tongue is sharp and red, red and sharp as a flattened carrot.

"Kill!" orders a ghostly voice, a disembodied everywhere voice. "Kill the wicked stepmother, whose tongue is sharp and red. Kill the wicked red-tongued witch." But there is no wicked witch in sight. There's only a fairy godmother in the long black garb of a priest—a cardboard savior with a long red tongue.

Cinderella is bewildered on the nowhere road. She is helpless to murder. "But there is no wicked stepmother," she cries at last. "Fairy Godmother, it's *your* tongue that's sharp! It's you! It's you! It's *your* tongue that's red!"

The shudder of waking stabs the dream to a halt. Whoosh. Sudden morning.

Up from the sleeping edge and fumble into familiar. Warm pillow. Ah. Familiar foam-pad bed and old spotted banana smell from round glass table. What time is it doesn't matter idiot dream life. It's pre-dawn time. Early Sunday. And I have a voice within me, urging me to kill.

Low rumble of city traffic through the gray light. No noise in the alley. The rattle drum by my pillow. And Father Cedric, the autumn sun, the cool rock—and—
and
here—right here—in the middle of my body beneath

my ribs, the familiar pain. If I lie on my side—dizzy pain
—if I lie on my front—is the nausea on its way? Is it?
Breathe deep, Naomi, don't
fight
the body. If the attack comes, then let it come. Coast
into the wave. Release the night. Fight nothing. Let the
thoughts rise.

There I was yesterday walking with him, the fairy
godmother priest, through the forest of my adolescence,
with the wild beast pawprints along the trail, the scent,
the spoor. I tripped. I fell into his arms. I fell into the
circle of demons dancing.

Let the pain roll down. Let it roll. I have tasted the
forest's noonday light. I have walked among the wood
nymphs in the autumn leaves. I have fled the songless
streets willingly, gladly, on my spinsterly feet.

Your feet, he said, are soft and perfect as babies' feet.
He thought high heels were like foot binding. His
mother hated heels and stockings and called them traps.
You don't wear them, he said. No. Nor glass slippers, I
said.

My whole body has been a foot binding all my life.
How have I breathed through the layers of rules and propriety, through my fears—
    breathe now—breathe deep—
my fears of what people might say. Someone saw us
standing there in my doorway after we came back last
night, the silly dog next door yapping.

I've always needed structure. If rules are yanked away
I'll collapse. I'll disintegrate into a pile of dust, like an
ancient Egyptian mummy exposed to the air. What does
it mean? His hands. His arms.

The driver of the Cinderella transport is asking for

order. According to Aunt Emily, a structure is only a skeleton. Only? She doesn't worry about rules because she takes her own almighty bones for granted.

"So you want to get back to your safe old story," the driver asked in his dull monotone.

I'm sick of my safe old dead-end tale. Give me a crossroads where the beginning of an altogether new story touches a turning point in the old.

The dream was suggesting that I choose the familiar. That I pull in the reins if my horses threaten to bolt. But why should they be contained forever? In this gray morning, in this whatever hour, I choose. Let the horses bolt. Let them run. The plot line of the old fairy tale does not contain a license to kill. Nor is it needed in the story of my life. I'm too old for murder and there's death enough in the world as it is. "Happily" is the word, is it not? And "ever after"?

What comes to mind now in this still early morning is the driftwood crucifix bird on Father Cedric's wall, and a wire-mesh Christ on a wire-mesh cross he has on his desk, the outstretched arms gathering the wind. The way of the wind, he said, is the way of the dance.

Last night, he stood in the hall outside my door, respectful, waiting for I know not what. He brushed my cheek with the back of his hand. Strange how like the wind touch can be. Completely unpredictable. In the forest, I was wrapped in storm. In the hallway, the winds were calm. A few raindrops fell. There was a gentle mid-air refusal to fly. A swift grief of the mind.

"Good night, my sister."

"Good night, Fa . . . Goodnight, Cedric."

The dim light at the end of the hall formed a bouncing haze around him as he walked away. I closed the door and curled up with my thoughts. And all night long they roamed here and there, looking for a story in which to belong.

And behold now, the pain, the nausea, is creeping away and my body is calming. Is growing calm.

24

Day dreams, night dreams, slip through sliding doors,

slip past softly, seeking little toeholds in the waking day.

"If you have time, Naomi . . ."

"She's slipping," we used to say when Anita Jeffrey's

slip showed under her flouncy skirts. Slips aren't meant

to be seen, but sometimes they show. Eugenia, I'm sure,

notices. I look up from my desk to catch Father Cedric

watching me and he looks away a little sheepishly.

I must stop thinking of him as "Father" Cedric. I've

been calling him Rick or Cedric as the others do, but in

my mind he's always been a priest.

He tells me, Cedric tells me, that the clarity of the heart directs us and when we embrace—lo!—the amino acids of trust are being formed.

"You have so many thoughts," he whispers. "I can hear them in my arms."

He's my black-robed fairy godmother. His words fall through the air. He flies to meet me in his clerical gown and alters the clock. He has told me without telling me that the destination is unknown.

"It's better, yes?—where there is no path?" he says.

Perhaps one of these mornings I will wake up and fly, unless I discover that, after all, I'm an amputee and have no limbs. In the meantime, I see him at work almost every day.

It's Tuesday afternoon. Father Cedric's door is closed tight. Here I am again, still thinking of him as "Father" Cedric. He's Cedric. And his door has just been closed by Dr. Stinson.

Dr. Clive Stinson, vice-president of St. John's, fellow of the Royal Military Academy and consultant to the Multicultural Directorate, was in our middle office a minute ago and talking down to Morty, as if to a schoolboy. "Morton, you do know that *Bridge* is a multicultural magazine." Mul-ti-cul-tural, he said, making four words out of one.

Dr. Stinson doesn't drop by very often, but when he does, I'm instantly aware of our disorder. Once he came to the office in the middle of a terrible storm, striding through the sleet without a sideways glance, head erect, a one-man marching drill. He's a professional stranger, always tense. I can see him shattering into a thousand shards.

"He's never been hugged. That's what's wrong with Stinson," Morty mutters.

"Well, yes, he is a little stiff," Eugenia whispers back.

"Stiff!" Morty croaks. "Imagine him without a shirt and tie. I mean, picture it. Boxer shorts. See? Impossible. Do you think he sleeps in a three-piece suit?"

Eugenia shakes her head. "Don't be rude, professor."

Morty himself dresses so outlandishly, it's impossible to imagine him in business clothes. Today he's sporting an oversized black and white tee shirt with the Japanese characters "de-mo-ku-ra-shi-ii" across the chest.

"Want one of these?" Morty asks. "Come out to our Democracy group meeting and I'll give you one free. All JCs should wear them. Democracy is the only real armor we've got against the demagogues—the Stinson-Nikki combo."

Dr. Stinson and Nikki Kagami apparently met one day at a multicultural bash, Morty says. Lights flashed. Hearts glowed. And a trickle of funds began flowing through—a book project here, a little folk dancing there. "It's terrific for her. She likes being liked. But now," Morty says, yanking at his skinny beard, "now we're not talking small grants. We're into millions of dollars of JC compensation. Who does she think she is? Do you know what she did, eh?"

"Well—uh—"

"She appointed herself head of a defunct League committee. Just like that!" He snaps his fingers. "Then ran off to Ottawa on all four paws. She's got no man-

date. She represents no one and she's not accountable to
the community. It worries the hell out of me."

Dr. Stinson was looking more severe than usual
when he came in this morning. He and Morty were head
to chest in fierce conversation.

"We live in the most benign country in the world,
Morton," Dr. Stinson said. "We don't need any rabble-
rousing here."

"I'm just writing about racism," Morty replied, slam-
ming his fist into his hand. "Do you want to call it something else?"

"We don't see eye to eye on these matters, I'm
afraid."

"No. And I'm telling you Nikki Kagami has no business—"

"She's an appropriate spokesperson as far as I'm concerned."

There's a certain cheerless deliberateness about Dr.
Stinson. Morty calls him "Rigor Mortis." He has long
stick legs and an unblinking straight-ahead stare that
makes me think of a stork. Morty automatically crosses
his arms whenever Dr. Stinson visits us, "the *Bridge*
team"—a term Dr. Stinson finds offensive. "After all, you
aren't a card-playing club," he says.

He seems to have a great capacity to spread mir-
thlessness about him. When he smiles, it's as if he wills
it in response to a higher command. His mouth turns up
obediently but his eyes remain fixed and piercing. He's
alternately haughty and humble in his relations with us
and when he speaks, his words come out well chewed.

"How do you do," he enunciated when we were introduced, and he looked down at me sideways.

I imagine that every one of Dr. Stinson's teeth is a

neatly executed root-canal job—permanently anchored but without sensation. Better than false teeth, one might say, though why should I be so unkind.

"If we had an active National JC League, Nikki's nonsense wouldn't be tolerated," Morty says, glowering. He's sitting at the long worktable, which looks like a volcanic eruption these days, but he insists it's a stable mountain range. On the right side is a stack of the latest *Bridge* magazines, with Morty's capsule history inside.

In 1942, 22,000 Japanese Canadians, most Canadian-born or naturalized citizens, were branded enemies of Canada.

This is what happened under the War Measures Act:

—We were rounded up and forcibly uprooted from our homes

—We were fingerprinted and made to carry ID cards

—Families were broken up

—We were imprisoned without trial

   —in animal stalls at Hastings Park in Vancouver

   —in hastily built internment camps

   —in prisoner-of-war camps

—We were forced to labor on road gangs

—All that belonged to us was seized and sold and the money was taken to pay for our imprisonment

—After the Second World War, 4,000 of us were exiled and deported

—The rest of us were dispersed across Canada, east of the Rockies

These war crimes and acts of racism by the Canadian Government—actions opposed by senior officials within both the Department of National Defense and the Royal Canadian Mounted Police —have never been officially acknowledged, nor have the victims been compensated.

Morty was patching the magazine together right up to the deadline. There were a few glaring typos as usual. Our magazine has often been in late labor, but miraculously we get it to the printers precisely on schedule every time.

It didn't occur to me that this special Japanese Canadian issue might meet with the disapproval of Dr. Stinson. As a fellow of the Royal Military Academy, he has a special interest in the history of the Second World War.

"You and Emily may be well intentioned, I'm sure," he told Morty, "but in this matter, you're both misguided. I can understand your personal bias, Morton, but please remember, *Bridge* magazine is not your personal newsletter."

In the midst of this, Cedric came to Morty's defense, saying it was time the Japanese Canadian story was better known.

"Yes indeed," Dr. Stinson said. "But from what point of view, Cedric? What point of view? Surely not that of a young firebrand like Morton."

25

THURSDAY NIGHT.

There's a scene of carnage on Anna Makino's dining-room floor. Paper carcasses lie in a paper graveyard. At the oak dining table, Anna and Brian are a pair of Bobbsey Twins in their floppy new "Democracy" tee shirts. They're stalking through a pile of newspapers, wielding their lethal scissors, cutting out articles for the meeting tonight. Every time a stray piece falls to the floor, their gray cat, Gaby, torpedoes it. It's uncanny how much he resembles Gaby the first. Aunt Emily is laying the clippings out side by side. Paper trophies. Woe to the cat if he leaps on the table.

Cedric and I walked up after work, munching sandwiches, tossing our crusts to pigeons and seagulls.

"Emily has hundreds of friends," he said. "Enemies too, uh?"

Over the years I've seen her cronies come and go—a sociologist, a filmmaker, a few professors. I never got to know any of them.

I have only a few friends in the world and even fewer enemies, although my childhood was filled with a kind of dread. I'd be skipping down the path through the woods in Slocan, and there, startling as a snake, was the enemy. I was the enemy. A creature to look at in swift sideways glances.

"You'll meet some good folks tonight," he said, taking my hand and swinging my arm merrily. It's hard to imagine this lighthearted man having enemies. He's trusting and open. He doesn't, for example, have blinds on his office windows. There's enough darkness without them, he says. Come to think of it, there are no curtains in his apartment, either, though I don't know about his bedroom, which, of course, I've never seen.

"It's a miracle. Finally Emily's Nonny Mouse coming to a meeting." We were waiting for a streetlight to change and I thought he was about to give me a bear hug, but he didn't. A happy bear he is, I thought, and well acquainted with the ways of mice.

Here at Anna's house, a mouse doesn't have a chance, thanks to the much-indulged Gaby. His keepers, Brian and Anna, are a fanatical cat couple—attack-cat cartoons on the fridge door, a shower curtain of mul-

ticultural cats and a toilet-paper roll held up by two porcelain cat paws. On the living-room mantelpiece is a
large black statue of Bast, the Lower Egyptian cat deity,
surveying the messy paper world. "The bureau-cat," Aunt
Emily calls it. "Lord of the files."

It's been a long time since I've been in a real house—
not since the happy days in Vancouver. Granton's shacks
hardly count. The strange sadness I felt when I first
walked in here hasn't altogether gone. Is this envy? Or
grief? It's an echo of an old longing I felt as a child when
I wanted and wanted to go home. I should be glad for
Anna. Where on earth is my generosity of spirit? I could
think of the old man we saw sleeping on the sidewalk. A
redress movement for homeless people would make
more sense than ours. But on the other hand, we were
forced into homelessness ourselves.

They're expecting about two dozen people later tonight—Japanese Canadians who are disturbed and excited by news reports that Nikki Kagami is trying to get
twenty-five million dollars on behalf of us all.

"Her meetings are closed, her talks are secret. It
drives us nuts," Anna says. She makes a paper wad and
tosses it aggressively at the wicker wastebasket. Gaby
leaps to the challenge, charging his paper victim over the
hardwood floor. Pounce pounce and he's captured Aunt
Emily's jiggling foot.

"Here, Gaby! Scat! You wagamama!"

Anna laughs. Wagamama is the term for selfish indi-
vidualism. Obasan would probably say that redress was
wagamama. After all and after all, Canada was a wonderful country.

I'm sitting in a wing chair by the fireplace, eating a

jelly doughnut, and Cedric is on the floor beside me, grinning and pinching my baby toe, when the doorbell bongs.

"Bet that's Oliver," Anna groans as she gets up and glances through the front window. "It's him all right."

Brian rubs his hand rapidly through his hair and grumbles as he goes to answer the insistent ding-dong, ding-dong.

Ollie Oliver, Anna says, is an old war vet, tipsy at times, who lives with his daughter next door. He's the neighborhood handyman, painting porches, trimming bushes. He'll talk endlessly about his war days to anyone who'll listen. He's been objecting to "all the Japs coming and going in the neighborhood," and drops by, especially when he's drunk, to complain. Last week he made the mistake of telling Aunt Emily she should go back to her own country. Poor unsuspecting Ollie Oliver.

The heavy front door opens to a rugged old man in a baseball cap, red bomber jacket and work boots. Ollie Oliver reminds me of Crazy Alex as he stands there swaying, one foot in the doorway, one hand on Brian's shoulder to steady himself.

"Sorry, Oliver." Brian blocks him from entering the vestibule. "Sorry, old man."

"Forty thousand Canadian kids died and did'n get a puking cent." He shakes his finger in Brian's face, his words slurring. "Know how many Chinee got murdered in the Rape 'a Nanking?"

Here, out of nowhere, out of the clear blue autumn air, comes this horrible stab of memories. It's been so long since I felt the sudden chill of that slithering shadow underfoot. I can remember, as a child in Slocan, hearing about the war and the sickening atrocities—the

beheadings, the barbaric slave camps—the totally unthinkable evil called the Yellow Peril. How I prayed that
we would win the war. I prayed, walking home from the
Orange Hall at night where the war movies raged. I
prayed for Mother and I prayed for our soldiers as Ollie's
daughter must also have done. And here's Ollie to this
day, in his own liquid way, seeking surcease.

The old man lurches back and forth. "Y'ever been a
guinea pig in th'r stinkin' labs?"

"Hold it, Ollie!" Brian's voice sounds almost resigned.
"Can't you get it into your thick head? The Japanese
army is not hiding out in my house. There are no enemies here. No en-e-mies! Got that?"

"Not worth it, Brian," Anna cries out.

"War gets people so confused they'll put dynamite in
their own boots," Aunt Emily says. "That's what Canada
did. We've been crippled ever since."

Anna sounds fed up as she says Oliver can go on and
on for hours with his litany of atrocities in Manchukuo,
Singapore—

From the window I can see Ollie Oliver's square
white house, the cedar-hedge fence beautifully trimmed.
Anna says he's lived there for thirty-seven years and his
living room is as static as his mind, with faded pictures
of war buddies on the dusty mantelpiece. "It's a museum," she says. A Union Jack is tacked up over a case
full of regimental badges and shell cases. A bust of
Churchill sits on a table with books about the war. Ollie
Oliver's doily-covered heart is still back with the Allies in
"their finest hour."

"Once a Jap, always a Jap," Anna mimics, wagging
her head from side to side. "The mos' treacherous breed
'n earth. Made Belsen look like a kindergarten party.

They kept Korea under rule for thirty-five years. Sent emissaries to Washington to sign a non-aggression pact, then . . ."

"Then they bombed Pearl Harbor." Aunt Emily has taken off her glasses and pinches the two red spots by her bridgeless nose where the pads rest. She does that when her head hurts.

"I could just scream!" Anna says. "He always always brings up Pearl Harbor. Pearl Harbor! Pearl Harbor! That's his justification. It's like screaming at the Jews that they killed Jesus."

Pearl Harbor. Belsen. Nagasaki. Calvary. How loyal we all are to our many holy ghosts. The dead stand with their feet in doorways, asking not to be forgotten.

Brian pushes Ollie Oliver out the door and returns to the dining room waving his arms. "Great neighborhood, eh? He holds you personally responsible," he says, wagging his finger at Aunt Emily.

"We are personally responsible," Aunt Emily says.

"What?"

"We aren't the enemy. You were right to say so, Brian, and it's our responsibility to keep saying it till we drop."

It's hard to think a time will come when Aunt Emily will drop. Not at the rate she's going. I imagine that, when the day arrives, she'll ram through the barrier with the gas pedal down to the floor and the horn blaring. "Make way. Here comes a Canadian." She'll probably go on shouting that from beyond the grave.

26

Boots stomping on Anna and Brian's front porch as the doorbell bongs its mellow two tones again, and there stands a man against the rainy night, a ghost from the past, his wide crooked horsey smile on his oversized jaw.

"Uncle Dan?"

He peers at me, then over to Aunt Emily, who laughs her rich throaty wonderful laugh.

"I don't believe it," he says, squinting at me, his hands cupping his eyes. "You're just like your mother. Isn't she, Em? I'd know you anywhere."

I'd know him too—instantly—that broad generous

grin on his older and now lined but infinitely recognizable face. His once thick black hair is wispy and gray. He's smaller than the laughing man who towered over Stephen and me. I have a picture of Uncle Dan with his arm on Father's shoulder when they were university students and lithe and laughing. He wasn't a blood uncle but all familiar men were "uncles."

"So you got tired of being out there in Alberta, 'blowin' in the wind'?" He chuckles a vaguely familiar rumbling sound.

"Dan. Such a long time." It's like an ache in a phantom limb. I can't remember when I saw him last but it would have been in Vancouver—Uncle Dan with his wide happy smile, his pockets full of English toffees wrapped in colorful cellophane. I used to climb up into the wicker chair in the music room to wave goodbye. It's an amputated lifetime ago.

"I didn't know you were in Toronto, Dan."

Aunt Emily wags her finger at me. "See what happens when you don't pay attention? I told you he moved here. I told you Anna was here too."

So much for soundproofed walls. If you cut out the traffic noise you also don't hear the bird songs.

Back in the fifties, Aunt Emily wrote to us that Dan was fighting the good fight in the courts. "He's the most battle-scarred Canadian around," she said. He fought as a young man for the franchise. Then in the forties, patriotic citizen Dan fought for the right to fight for his country. He fought against Japan in the Intelligence Corps. He fought against the exile of Japanese Canadians. And then there was the land grab.

Dan's father and other issei pioneers cleared the Fraser Valley with horses and their bare hands, and their strawberries were large and luscious. The burgeoning berry industry, lands, equipment—all were taken by the government and turned over to returning war veterans. White war veterans. Men like Ollie Oliver. Dan fought for his farm. He lost. Then he became ill.

But tonight he's here and he's staring at me with delight. "Did you know I used to watch over you when you were this small?" There's an inch between his thumb and forefinger. "You looked like your mom right from the start. All of us fellas were in love with your mom, you know."

"Didn't I tell you." Aunt Emily rolls her eyes.

"But the kid sister here," Dan's eyes twinkle and he gives Aunt Emily a squeeze. "She won the spelling contest."

"Sure, sure."

"And the essay contest."

"Then you came up from the valley and ran off with the scholastic award."

Dan and Aunt Emily were competitors and colleagues and young collaborators. In Toronto in the late forties, they founded the National Japanese Canadian League to "comfort and serve" a completely disheartened and scattered people. And now, this year, they've come home to the familiar old cause of their youth. Justice for Japanese Canadians.

In spite of his joking manner, Dan has a commanding air about him. His speech is deliberate and articulate, his sentences punctuated. He's a born leader. The rest of us are a motley crew, sitting on stools, on the floor, on the couch—ranging in age from four months to the eighties. Morty in his tee shirt came bounding up the steps not long after Oliver left. Next came Aunt Emily's filmmaker friend, also in a tee shirt, and the sociologist from out of town. There's a baby-faced nisei Mickey Rooney standing behind a striking professional woman of about thirty, prim and orderly in a business suit in the wing chair. A couple with a sweet infant sit in the middle of an armload of baby paraphernalia. An academic is greeting Dan with a clipped wave and a quick nod. Over by the window is a man with a face like a skull. And there's a rather rotund youth who has a nervous smile. It's a stereotypical mannerism—the ever-ready smile. Mrs. Makino is bobbing at the doorway as another couple arrives.

All the chairs from the dining room have been gathered and there's still not enough seating as the door opens and—surprise, surprise—here's Anna's older sister, Marion, with her husband, Ken Suzuki. How skinny she is!

"Marion of the Mak-duo?" It must be ten years since I've seen her.

Marion does a little jump and cries, "Oh! Heavens! Naomi!" She flaps her dainty hands like wings as she comes rushing over. Her hair is tied back in a severe Granton bun and she's grown so thin she's almost gaunt. But Ken is pudgy. He has the beginning of hound-dog jowls.

"Howdy." Ken pumps my hand and flashes a good old prairie grin. "Long time no see." He says he misses the smell of manure and he'll always be a westerner, cheering for the Calgary Stampeders and the Edmonton Eskimos.

"Oh, but Kembo," Marion says, "Anne's here. Mother's here. Naomi's here."

It's funny hearing Marion call her husband "Kembo" —Marion, who didn't want Anna to have a "Japanesey name."

Ken says, yeah, lots of Japanese Canadians are in Toronto, but that includes "that Kagami woman," and he tosses his head in contempt.

From all the conversations I've overheard tonight, there is a festering indignation here toward Nikki Kagami's exclusiveness. The Democracy group, which started as an ad hoc gathering of friends, was formed about a year ago to pressure Nikki for information. Was Government going to give her twenty-five million dollars? How had she come to that figure? Was there going to be a review of the War Measures Act? Nikki refused to elaborate. She said things were well in hand. She knew the people in the Department of Multiculturalism. There was no need, no need at all, for anyone to get excited.

Anna wafts through the general hubbub handing out papers, as the young couple, their baby, diaper bag, bottle and teddy all slide in a heap to the floor to make room for Marion and Ken. Brian is introducing me as "Naomi from *Bridge*," telling everyone that I'm Emily's niece. "Oh, you're Stephen Nakane's sister," Sumi, a plump white-haired woman, says. She's round as a dumpling and looks as if she's been happy all her life.

Cedric and I are on the floor beside the fireplace, our elbows sharing a footstool. Some people, I realize with a tiny glow, are seeing us as a couple. "Rick and Naomi from *Bridge*."

Marion comes and pokes me in the side, peeking at Cedric curiously. "What's with you two?" she whispers.

I whisper back that we work in the same place. He's a

priest. It doesn't tell her much but there certainly isn't much to tell. "Shh. No. He's not my boyfriend."

People are still arriving. So many Japanese faces! The clippings are being passed from hand to hand and people turn to one another, reading and exclaiming. "Nikki Kagami bypassing National Japanese Canadian League." "Groundwork inadequate, claims Edmonton sociologist."

Nikki Kagami apparently has announced that a conference is to be held in Toronto this fall to which the Minister of Multiculturalism is coming, and that redress is going to be resolved.

"What a lot of nerve! She can't resolve redress by herself."

"It's not nervy," Morty says. "It's lawless."

This gathering is quite unlike any I've ever seen—not like meetings at Cecil Consolidated or Carson Junior High or church or Pastor Jim's Young People's. It's the antithesis of Nikki Kagami's sleepy cultural center meeting. A bystander is likely to be dug out of the grass and pecked to bits. If anything, they remind me of Tina's fervent fundamentalist friends, intent on "keeping Granton Godly."

The issue is compensation—whether there should be a lump group sum, as Nikki Kagami wants, or individual payments, or no compensation at all. "Please. Let's not equate our suffering with money," one woman said.

I wouldn't dare to admit it right now, but I'm not a true believer in redress. I'm not a true believer in anything much. There was, I'm afraid, a misnaming at my birth. I'm the Ruth of the biblical tale, not her mother-in-law, Naomi. "Whither thou goest I will go," Ruth said, "and where thou lodgest I will lodge. Thy people shall be my people. . . ." I may not know what I believe but I know whom I follow. I'm here mostly because Cedric is. And Anna, I suppose. And though I hate to admit it, I'm not unaffected by the AC/DC dynamo called Emily Kato. My guess is that Aunt Emily, Dan, Morty and Anna are the main magnets here, and the rest of us are iron filings. We are drawn not only by their energy but by something else as well. There's some faint stirring inside, of curiosity or sympathy or memory. I hardly know what to call it.

Dan is calling the meeting to order. On the agenda tonight is some startling news. Nikki Kagami ("God bless her banana heart," Morty says) has caved in to western pressure. The national League president and other community representatives are flying to Toronto for a weekend at the Garland Hotel to discuss Nikki's proposed conference. It's the first time ever that national delegates will be discussing redress.

"About time! About time!" the rotund young man says. "We're all going to observe, aren't we?"

"That's pushing it a bit," the prim woman says. Her position is that Nikki Kagami is our best-known person in Ottawa. She's therefore indispensable.

"You're worried about pushiness?" Morty cries. "Nikki's waltzing around solo in Ottawa and you're worried about pushiness?"

I'm definitely not going, I'm thinking, remembering the discomfort I felt at the cultural center meeting.

The hubbub is being punctuated by the baby's wails as she resists the pacifier her young mother prods into her mouth.

The one thing that unites this group is a passionate belief that Japanese Canadians everywhere should have a voice in redress. And that can only happen, they say, if we have a strong grass roots national organization.

I can hardly remember ever thinking about "Japanese Canadians everywhere." I do know that, once upon a long time ago, Japanese Canadians were the only people I ever saw, except for maybe a missionary or two. Then we moved to Granton and—poof! A vanishing trick.

Dan has his hand up for attention when the doorbell goes again and a leathery-faced, somewhat troll-like man stands shuffling in the hall, his eyes downcast.

Aunt Emily jumps up from the couch and claps her hands together. "You made it! Great! Come in, come in!"

People pause to look at the newcomer.

"Son-of-a-gun," Dan says, frowning and pushing himself up off his footstool with one hand, the other outstretched. "Is that Minno? Min Kawai? I'll be damned. Haven't seen you in forty years."

Well, well. So this inelegant little man is Aunt Emily's old friend Min Kawai. He certainly is not the way I pictured "the greatest artist Canada never had." It's ridiculous, I know, but I saw him as wearing a navy-blue beret.

This is a night of little reunions, as Sumi also approaches, her moon face beaming. "Well, I'll be . . ."

Is there a magician at work, I wonder, bringing Japanese Canadians back?

Mrs. Makino is peering uncertainly. Min Kawai's head bobs in greeting and he scrunches against the wall to take off his boots. Mrs. Makino advances a few steps, eyes wide. Then, "Ara!"—the cry of surprise. In her amazement, she isn't bowing. She reaches out her wrinkled hands and touches his sleeve. "Minoru-san? Minoru-san? Honto desu ka?" Is it true? Is it really you?

The younger people are only mildly interested in the latest arrival, the prim young woman frowning with disapproval. This street person with unkempt hair does not look as if he belongs with the rest of us. Even Gaby has doubts. He's treating Min's boots with considerable respect, one paw lifted high as if to strike.

27

"Bridge leaper." Cedric looks at Aunt Emily incredulously. Aunt Emily scoffs. She's through with office politics. She's quitting. She's been thinking about it for half a year and she's made her decision.

My little room is full with Aunt Emily, Cedric and Min Kawai sprawled out on the cushions and foam-pad mats. Aunt Emily groans as she sticks her legs out flat. This floor-level sitting isn't easy for her any more.

We've just come from the meeting at Anna's place. Min was ill at ease all night, not looking around. Aunt Emily caught him leaving and she jumped to her feet, offering a ride. We left together. She ended up inviting everyone to my room, even though it's late. "Oh, c'mon," she urged, holding the side door open, and Min bumped himself up the stairs in his shambly brown jacket like a Fred Flintstone cartoon, his eyes on his boots.

It's Cedric's first time inside my room and his face lit up as he took everything in—the one picture, one plant, one lamp on the floor. "It's you," he said. Min's eyes were less intrusive, but he did notice the portrait of Miss Best.

"My reluctant niece, my long-lost pal—both showing up at the same meeting," Aunt Emily says. "It's a sign. And the League meeting next month? Redress is on the move, Rick. It's time to march with the troops. I can't cross the river if I'm stuck on a bridge."

I remember her telling me that a bridge was a place to traverse, not a place to linger. She would not, she vowed, ever become a bridge-dweller. "It's the way to turn into dead wood. And you know what trouble dead wood can cause," she said, "especially for traffic on a stormy night." But Aunt Emily is hardly dead wood.

Cedric's eyebrows are arched in disbelief. "But you can't quit! Writing is your calling!"

"What's a calling?" Aunt Emily asks. "I've been waking up in the middle of the night this whole month, and it's not the pen that's calling me." She gazes up at the ceiling and quotes an old Jewish dictum that says that when the laws of God are in conflict with the well-being of people, the well-being of people shall prevail. The Sabbath can be violated to tend to the sick. The writing can wait. People cannot. Words are made of ether. Her kinsfolk are made of flesh.

Cedric follows her gaze and we're all looking at the

check-mark crack in the corner. "So someone is calling, 'Samuel, Samuel,' " he whispers.

Min shifts uncomfortably. There's flight in his eyes. This room is not a safe place. Cedric's whisper is not safe. I know the story of the boy Samuel being called by God, but Min may have never heard it. His eyes dart nervously here, there.

"It's you, Min," Aunt Emily says, tapping his arm.

He's startled by the touch. "Who? Me?" He blinks rapidly. It's the first time I've heard him speak. His deep baritone voice seems incongruous in his small body.

"It's you, Michelangelo-ko, and the old gang. You all wake me up."

Min's darting eyes crinkle and his radio broadcaster's voice jumps in a nervous chuckle. He jerks a stiff arm in my direction. "Yeah, yeah," he says. "And your dad was Beethoven."

Aunt Emily turns to Cedric. "I'm not jumping off the bridge, Rick. I've found the one to my backyard. And what a lot of work there is."

If, as Uncle used to say, "busy is happy," there was a happy crew at work tonight in the community's backyard. When we left Anna's house, people were splayed out on cushions among boxes of filing cards, paper clips, staplers, demolished phone directories.

"Japanese Canadian League, here we come!" Anna cried.

The Democracy group is committed to the building up of the country-wide organization, the National Japanese Canadian League. To that end, they're creating a mailing list of Japanese Canadians in Toronto, to try to pull them together.

"What the JCL needs," Anna said, "is people, people, people. Love to the people!"

Morty was helping Brian set up makeshift tables out of planks of wood spread across the backs of chairs. "The times they're a-changing, Nikki," he said. "The people are on the march." Anna settled down with a postal-code book, saying that it was the most exhilarating work she'd ever done. "We're an endangered species," she added. "But look! All these lost children we're finding in their caves."

I was going through the Anglican church directory and finding a few names of kids I knew in Slocan. Kenji was there. And one of my teachers. And Sho, the tough boy who used to beat up Stephen. It was like the day when I first came to Anna's house and raindrops were plopping onto my face. Something wet and unexpected was seeping up out of childhood and tingling through the dry rootlets of my memories. A whiff of the mountain air. A climb up to the bluff and a view of rows and rows of tiny houses with thin trails of smoke. And the public bath. Looking around at the niseis, I could imagine us as children in the baths—the steam and the wet wood and the washcloths rolled tight and hard as fists.

The niseis seem to be innately organized. In the midst of the paper chaos, they understand what needs to be done—the cross-checking for duplication, the alphabetical ordering, the phoning to get apartment numbers and to check ambiguous names. "Richard Baba? You're not Japanese Canadian? Sorry." Or "T. Baba? T. for Tsutomu? Aha!"

The mailing list is in four sections—A to K, L to N, O to S and T to Z. To date, they have over four thousand names. I could feel the passion beneath the banter. It was contagious. Each name mattered. Each life.

"Everyone here going to the Garland Hotel?" Morty asked. "Right? Anyone not interested in what's going on?"

"I'll go if you go," Marion said to me. "C'mon. Let's see who's coming from Alberta."

No one had asked Min. He kept staring at the floor, though once he looked quickly at me, and quickly away.

Here in my room, he seems almost to be conversing with the portrait of Miss Best. What could she be saying to the talented artist whose work belonged in the Metropolitan Museum of Art? What would she say to us about the redress movement?

Cedric, his hands folded together, listens to Aunt Emily as she reminisces about a young poet from Powell Street who died in the camps, and an issei who gave his fortune and his mine to the government. She's walking down thorny pathways of the past, picking up forget-me-nots.

The chestnut tree is silhouetted against the night light. I watch the swaying branches as Aunt Emily talks on. In the end, she says, home is where our stories are, and that's not just a question of ethnicity or even country, though she passionately loves Canada. Home for her is where the struggle for justice takes place, and because that is happening in our backyard she has returned with a will.

We're pieces of a jigsaw puzzle, she says, scattered across the country. The scars, the marks of our separation, remain. But the picture grows clearer, our wholeness starts to form, when even a few of us, in our brokenness, come together.

28

OCTOBER 1983. THE GARLAND HOTEL.

Green carpet, cream walls, recessed lights in the ceiling of this basement conference room. A windowless cave.

I wasn't intending to come but Cedric said redress was important. "You bet it's important," Morty said. "Too important to be left up to one egotistical control freak."

"Maybe," I suggested, "she'll come to her senses after this weekend and start working with the president?"

"Dream on," Morty said.

To my relief, I found that Morty and I were able simply to walk in this morning. No questions asked. And there were chairs at the back for us.

About thirty delegates, largely gray-haired men in dark suits, are sitting in clumps beside cardboard place-names at long U-shaped tables. Victoria, Vancouver, Kamloops, Calgary, Lethbridge—from west to east, as far as Montreal, twelve centers are here. I don't recognize anyone except Nikki Kagami, her shoulder-length hair a curved black frame.

"What a movie star," Morty whispers behind his hand.

Anna scowls. "Who cares what she looks like."

Morty and Anna are on either side of me in the front row of observers. Dan, Aunt Emily, Ken, Marion—about twenty of us are clustered here at the back.

The purpose of the gathering, Nikki has been saying repeatedly, is to finalize plans for a November conference. "The Minister of Multiculturalism has already agreed to attend," she says crisply for the third time, as if that were ultimately the most important consideration.

Beside Nikki at the head table, a plain woman takes minutes. The national president, an eager-faced deferential man with wide-set eyes, is to Nikki's left. Nikki's chin tilts upward as she slowly surveys the rather drab older men at the tables. She's in charge. She has an undeniable presence in her dark suit and her blood-red scarf. Something about her reminds me of Anita. The way she holds her head, maybe. A cocky kind of confidence.

A jovial man from Ottawa has his hand up. "You know," he says, waving his plump hand in our direction, "we should all be working together. Why is Emily Kato back there? And isn't that you, Dan?"

Nikki looks flustered. She wants no challengers, no rivals, no interference with her plans. The pattern is set, the cloth cut and all that's left is the hem. She doesn't want to unravel the whole dress. "Let me remind you," she says, "Toronto League is hosting this meeting and . . ."

"But the founders of the League should be at this table," the man interrupts. "I want to make a motion."

Morty turns around and gives Dan and Aunt Emily a thumbs-up. What an unexpected turn of events! Instead of observing a bunch of strangers, we see Dan nodding to his friends from across the country, and Aunt Emily waving to our enthusiastic applause as she and Dan make their way to the table.

A youngish man from Edmonton in a yellow sweater reaches out to shake Dan's hand as he passes. Then it's back to business. "Your conference, Nikki, your November deadline, is premature. And can you call it a national conference?" Clearly he's saying there need to be more measurements if the garment is to fit.

Nikki cuts him off quickly. "It *is* a national conference. You're all part of it."

Morty nudges me with his elbow. "Oh sure," he whispers sarcastically.

"I want to discuss the matter of questionnaires," one man says. "Some folks—"

"I want you people to understand," Nikki interrupts, "that things are at a crucial point. We have a sympathetic Liberal government right now and there's no guarantee they'll be in power tomorrow." She lifts both hands for emphasis. "The minister, as I've been telling you, is prepared now—right now—to give us an apology. We've waited forty years. If you want more time, more consultations, questionnaires—I'm telling you, you'll just open up a can of worms and everything will be dropped."

What can of worms, I wonder, is there to worry about? I don't in fact mind those pink squiggly, least threatening of all creatures. If we did drop some here and there, they would do the soil some good. We're probably a can of worms ourselves in this basement room, squishing and squirming about.

The young man in the yellow sweater has his hand up again, but Nikki is ignoring him. She stands, steps behind her chair and straightens her shoulders aggressively. She's no longer at a meeting of adults. She's a schoolteacher in a classroom of children. The head worm.

"When none of you were interested," she says imperiously, scanning the upturned faces, "my team in Toronto got things moving. We've been working a long time to get here." She points her finger at the Edmonton contingent. "Are you telling me you want everything to fall through? I know I speak for ninety-nine point nine percent of Japanese Canadians when I say the last thing we want is to rouse the rabble and stir up the past. Ottawa knows this. That's why they're prepared to act now, quickly and smoothly. I'm a hundred percent sure nobody wants to reopen old wounds. Nobody."

She must be correct on that point at least. Who in their right mind would want to waken the Ollie Olivers of Canada? Now, that would open a can—not of worms, but of vipers, rattlesnakes, deep bitterness.

Nikki wants to tiptoe round the fitfully dozing monster of racism. But the young man from Edmonton says we've been tiptoeing long enough. The monster is not sleeping. Ask the native peoples. Ask anyone with dark skin. We need to be linked arm in arm across the country and to march upon the beast.

Some of the people at the table are looking around in confusion. A woman from B.C. says in a hesitating voice, "We should thank Nikki for everything she did for us. She worked so hard." There's a murmur of agreement from some of the delegates.

Several hands are raised and the president points his pencil at each one. "Hamilton, Dan, Edmonton, then Vancouver."

A largish man with thick glasses leans on one elbow and says, "If Ottawa's ready to act, we don't want to hold things up. But we—all of us here, all Japanese Canadians—need to be part of what's going on."

"Exactly," Morty says between his teeth.

The desire for participation is burning like a slow coal fire in the whole room. For this entire year, the Thursday night Democracy group has been trying to be "part of what's going on." It seems that some people in the national body have been equally frustrated.

Dan is next and he's like a log thrown into the heat. His words flame with purpose. "I'd like to propose," he says carefully, "that those of you here who are official representatives of your local leagues form a new structure—become a national council—and be party to redress discussions."

Morty does a little jump off his seat and taps his knuckles on his knees. "Perfect!" he whispers. "That's perfect, Dan."

"And Nikki," Dan continues, "must be accountable to the council and, through the council, to all Japanese Canadians."

Ah. All Japanese Canadians. The dream of touching every single one of us wherever we were flung. This is the hope of the Thursday night Democracy group. I can see how Dan's proposed structure might work. Instead of redress being Nikki's rocket ship to the stars, redress could itself become the star, a movement bursting in all directions. The sparks would leap and glow, leap and ignite the people, "my people," across the country. This dream I begin to see is one I could share with Morty and Anna and everyone.

Nikki, who has been glancing from face to face, now stops and stares down at the table. Then she flings her red scarf back aggressively and glares at Dan. "You talk about me being accountable to you. I want to ask you, who are you accountable to?"

I take a deep breath and sit back in my chair. "There's got to be accountability," Morty says loud enough to be heard. "Thousands of people are involved." He's halfway off his seat and ready to stand up and give a speech. Trust Morty to be as indelicate as Aunt Emily. They're both graduates of the "get-the-work-done-and-let-'em-howl" school, which earns respect but not much love.

If the older niseis at the tables are perplexed by the tensions in the room, they aren't revealing their emotions. The faces are largely impassive, eyes downcast. Like their issei parents, these niseis have learned restraint.

The delegate from Montreal, a puffy-faced man, raises his hand. "Accountability is a loaded word," he says in a high thin voice. "Nikki should know we don't mistrust her."

"We do mistrust her," Morty hisses.

"Let's hear the motion again," the Edmonton man says and Dan states, "Moved that all official delegates representing League centers across Canada be formed into a national council to be the final authority of the National Japanese Canadian League. All committees shall be accountable to the National Council."

The debate on the motion begins. "A council isn't necessary at this stage. We need to make decisions about the conference," Nikki says. Marion, sitting behind me, pokes me nervously as Nikki, shaking the agenda sheet, declares the motion to be out of order. But Dan and Aunt Emily are eloquent in their call for structure, openness and greater grass roots involvement.

After an impassioned speech from the Edmonton delegate, the president ends the discussion and the vote is called. All the delegates except one bewildered man and those sitting with Nikki raise their hands. An overwhelming majority has chosen a new structure of involvement and accountability.

Morty jumps off his chair as the observers' section erupts in a burst of applause. "Do you realize what this means?" He lifts his arms in a funnel to the ceiling. "Political will!"

"I can't believe it," Anna cries. "We're involved, Naomi!"

I drink in the excited faces around me. We all know that something significant has just happened. A tiny green political shoot has nudged its way through a long winter's sleep. And in the wall of our community's long silence, a faint crack has appeared. A thin spear of light leaps toward us.

Nikki rubs a finger across the ends of her mouth and bites her fingertip delicately as she watches the jubilation. She seems to be considering what to do. Then she gathers her papers, stands and walks out of the room.

29

"National Council formed to conduct redress discussions."

Brian's short item appears next morning on the front page of *The Globe and Mail*. It's unbelievable but we've become national news. I feel a kind of awe now when I see Brian. There's power in print and there's power in the hand of the man who brings forth the print.

Nikki has reacted instantly and with outrage. "The council is illegal," she told Brian's editor. "Delegates were invited specifically to plan a conference. They were not, I repeat, not, there to organize themselves into a council." Nikki's version of events is published in an Ottawa paper. "Redress plans fail. Hopes dashed for Japanese."

"Let them be dashed for the Japanese," Morty scoffs. "They're not dashed for us."

Our Democracy group is amazed that Nikki credits us with masterminding a national conspiracy. "The takeover ploy was orchestrated by a young militant pressure group," she writes in the community papers, under the heading "Redress threatened by radicals."

The following week, an anonymous letter appears in which *Bridge* magazine is accused of being a "lair of traitors, full of unethical, power-hungry Johnny-come-latelys." And right there in the second paragraph is my insignificant naked little name in print beside Morty Mukai. My name!

Strange how that shadow slinking across the path in the forest of my childhood has found its way indoors. Once it spat the single word "Jap." Now, week after week, words, words, wounding words, venomous words, slither through the mail slot. *The New Canadian,* which used to be such a friendly paper, has overnight become a thing of dread.

Nikki's proposed November conference fails to materialize as the community's leaders call out for more time. And then one day we read that Nikki has received the Badge of Merit from the federal government's Race Relations Board and she's been appointed a board member.

"Nikki? The Badge of Merit?" Morty cries in disgust.

I'm cowed by all this. I was drifting gladly along in the redress river but I'm with the others in white water now, paddling madly, organizing information meetings, trying to avoid the rocks. And all the time, I'm looking over my shoulders, though the rapids are not a place for looking back.

"After the froth and the spray," Eugenia says, "we'll come to the calm."

Aunt Emily says we'll survive. The hailstorms teach us to fret less about the rain.

Once in Cecil, I remember, a hailstorm came up so fast there was barely time to get home. A luminous dark whiteness fell upon us and chunks of ice the size of golf balls crashed down. Only a couple of farms escaped. Windows were smashed and the car was pelted so badly it lost its sheen and was instantly aged.

Sometimes these days I wake up with a start. Some long-ago cry fills the air. One night I dream about eggshells so soft I can't pick up the eggs.

When I talk about these things to Marion, she says, "Love is the answer, Naomi," but I have no idea what that means. At church a man told Aunt Emily that she should love more and that redress was about vengeance, not love. Cedric was as impatient as I've ever seen him. "Without justice, love is a mockery," he said. He put his arm around Aunt Emily's shoulder, saying, "I'm with my friends for the long haul."

I wouldn't at all mind, I was thinking, if he'd make such a statement to me.

We've been on several hikes, Cedric and I, since our first walk in the woods of the Laurentian Shield. Once down into the snowy ravine near the St. Clair subway, twice along the Bruce Trail. He's called me each time early in the morning and each time we've walked mostly in silence. I don't know what the holding means. At times his angelic smile seems demonic. There's a certain lift, as of wings, at the ends of his eyebrows.

In dreams I am never safe. I run and run. A potted plant marks the place where I live. Beneath the soft soil lies a flat green flower. If you press with fingertips on the earth, the flower quivers greenly into view.

Some flowers live in the mist but wither and die in the sun. Some questions remain in the shade. If I had the courage, I would ask outright, "Cedric, who am I to you?" But the sea that we enter is empty of speech and there is no map. He alone is amphibious. He moves with confidence through laws that are written in water. Could it be, I wonder, that he simply feels pity for a lonely and tongue-tied shadow?

On Monday mornings, we're back in our regular wordy world where we nod and pass. "Good morning," we say cheerily in our *Bridge* office voices. There's a solidity here and only the rattle drum on my desk signifies the mist.

DECEMBER 1983.

It's a snow-melting day. All afternoon, swatches of slush have been sliding—kathunk and ploop—off the roof and onto the sidewalk. A series of mini midwinter avalanches.

Out of Cedric's big front window I can see Nikki with Dr. Stinson as he backs his car into a parking spot across the street. This morning, Dr. Stinson, who recently became a member of a Special Committee on Visible Minorities, was at the hearings. Nikki must have been there as well.

They're heading this way. Their heads barely miss a freak icicle that's dying as it dangles on the scraggly tree branch by the side window. Even in summer, that branch is leafless and sends its sharp curved end, like an eagle's talon, to scratch at the glass.

Dr. Stinson arranges one of his mirthless smiles as he ushers Nikki in and closes the door neatly behind him like a pocketknife.

Seeing Nikki this close, I can't help noticing the great deal of makeup she wears. Her beauty, I think, is in spite of herself. She reminds me of geishas with their white white masks and red arrow lips. Her thick powder doesn't quite cover a birthmark, and her face is immobile, as if the least expression might create cracks. Perhaps she's older than I first thought.

Dr. Stinson appears to have a cold and wipes the end of his twitching nose rapidly with his handkerchief. "I can say this, Cedric," he says between sniffs, "as a member of the Special Committee, I found Nikki's presentation to be excellent."

Nikki's been hard at work representing our "visible minority."

She nods to me without expression and sits on the chair that Cedric offers, feet and knees pressed tightly together, back straight.

"I'm recommending that Government continue in discussions with her."

"Discussions with Nikki?" Cedric asks.

"Yes."

"Not with the president? Not with the National Council?"

These questions are coming from Nikki's "lair of traitors." Her eyes are wide and aggressively alert.

"It's my understanding," Dr. Stinson says, "that there were some irregularities regarding the so-called council.

I must say I agree completely with Nikki's concerns—both about the council and about *Bridge* magazine." He peers into Morty's office. "Is Morton here?"

He isn't. This is one of his teaching days.

"A pity. I do think, Cedric, that we must, as Nikki puts it, 'keep a lid on the radical element.' We did agree, did we not, that we should strive for a balanced approach in *Bridge*. . . ."

Cedric picks up a copy of the latest *Bridge* from the worktable and hands it to Nikki. "You find this unbalanced?" His smile is almost mirthful and his thick eyebrows are raised in friendly inquiry.

"Well, how shall I say this," Nikki begins. One hand caresses her throat. She looks through me blankly as if I'm part of the office furniture. She knows through her pores and her nisei antennae that I'm not ever going to cause trouble for her. I'm the un-at-home, ultra-quiet, predictably compliant Japanese Canadian that she knows so well.

Cedric is grinning at me as if to say that I am quite clearly not furniture at all. And in some hindquarter of our brains we are all conversing loudly. Recognition breeds recognition. Nikki notices Cedric's smile and her eyes dart rapidly between us.

"I know Emily means well . . ." She pauses and takes her hand from her throat, then turns directly to me. "But in these sensitive—these delicate redress discussions . . . I mean, you know her better than I do. She must run you ragged." She chuckles lightly.

When the shape in the forest chuckles, I'm thinking, one hears it as a hiss. I look down at the floor. This must be the way it is with Min—mistrust, suspiciousness, his eyes steadily on his boots.

"Let's be clear about one thing," Dr. Stinson cuts in. "I've warned Morton, and I would warn him again if he were here, that St. John's College will not have *Bridge* magazine used to foment discord."

"Foment discord!" Cedric looks as if he's trying not to laugh out loud.

"What we really need to ask," Nikki says to Cedric, "is what redress is all about. It's about dignity. Not money. Personally, I don't care if I never see a single cent out of all this."

Cedric looks a little surprised and the glance between us asks, "Yes? And the twenty-five million?"

"Money moves in its mysterious ways," he says softly, "its wonders to perform."

Especially, I'm thinking, in the snake pit. There's something murky in the mix of politics and money. "The love of money is the root of all evil," Pastor Jim used to say and I believed it. I still do. Nikki's statement may well be her truth, but from everything I've ever been taught, Mammon is a demon, stalking us all. When it catches our eyes it lures us into the pit and all our fine and noble truths are enmeshed in its snares.

"St. John's has its integrity to maintain," Dr. Stinson is saying. "And *Bridge* must not be accused of partisan politics, especially community politics. May I suggest, Cedric—surely there should be no difficulty with this— but shouldn't *Bridge* have Nikki's judgment on matters affecting Japanese Canadians?"

I can't see Nikki's face at the moment but I can feel her desire to control, almost like a breath on the back of my neck.

"I'd be quite happy to help, Cedric, in any way." She emphasizes the "any," clasping her hands together as if for prayer. She crosses and uncrosses her legs and leans toward him, blocking his face from my view. I'm in the coolness of Nikki's shadow and I feel the tiniest chill.

"*Bridge* could use a moderating influence," Dr. Stinson suggests. "Do you not agree, Cedric?"

Cedric's chair makes a scraping sound as he pushes back slightly. He's still friendly, shrugging his shoulders. "I trust our editors," he says simply. He leans over to catch my eye and grins and the chill vanishes. Sunshine once more. Snow melting. How very changeable the weather is these days.

Nikki's thumbing through *Bridge* and finds Aunt Emily's editorial. " 'Over the years, the Japanese Canadian community went into hiding and became silent as rape victims.' " Her dark red fingernails tap the words as she points them out. "Rape victims?" She turns to Cedric with earnestness. "We aren't rape victims, for heaven's sake. Emily should know better than to take her cues from young radicals like Morty. He's deliberately inciting unrest. And why?" She rolls the magazine into a cylindrical rod and punctuates the air. "I hate to say this, but it's money. Pure and simple. Individual compensation is what the young radicals are after. But Canada can't afford that kind of nonsense. The approach is wrong. What we need in this country right now is cooperation. Not greed."

"I totally agree," Dr. Stinson adds quickly. "Rape victims, indeed! Hardly descriptive of a highly successful community."

Dr. Stinson and Nikki share a view which is hard to dispute. Japanese Canadians are indeed not needy. We're middle-class, law-abiding, good Canadian citizens. A model minority. If Morty were here, he'd be doing battle —definition against definition.

According to Cedric's riddle, definitions are weary-making places to begin. Far from filling the world with wonder, they too often are words for war. Greed? Rape victims? Half-truths struggle with half-truths and together are slain.

It's the early morning dew that is the dryad's drink. Cool water in the dawn's green light. What would a dryad do if she were trapped in a battle of words? Would she transform herself into a tree, perhaps, or a snowdrop? Or a small white stone?

Cedric stands up and paces. "We can only—each of us—do what we believe is right," he says quietly. "After that? It's not in our control, is it? We plant, we water. God gives the increase." He's gazing up at the dead tree branch. The icicle, I notice, has dropped clean away.

30

"Why don't they damn well get rid of her?" Morty

asks.

It's a dull drizzly day. Cedric, Eugenia, Morty, Aunt

Emily and I are making our way down through the back

alley heading toward a Chinese restaurant for noodles.

We're dodging the winter's debris, the flattened foam

cups, the dog droppings that are suddenly visible in the

new season's slush. Gutter weather.

"They can't get rid of her. They're niseis. It's harmony

first, harmony last, harmony above all. They'll keep
her in the council even if she takes herself to the
moon."

Aunt Emily has just come back from a council meeting in Calgary. "Compromise! Compromise! It drives me
crazy. The issei's legacy, the nisei's muzzle."

"But she gets to keep all five Toronto votes! All five!
All to her slimeball self!"

It seems that Toronto, which has the largest number
of Japanese Canadians, has five votes on the National
Council. Vancouver has four. Edmonton and Victoria
have fewer, and so on.

"She's the official council delegate," Aunt Emily says,
shrugging. "She's made the Toronto rules. But the really
bad news, folks, is really bad. Government, after all our
excitement—our elections, our new president—Government is completely ignoring us."

"They can't do that! How can they do that?"

"They can do whatever they want. They've got their
puppet."

"Terrific," Morty says.

Morty's two huge dogs are with him today, one on
each side. They've been to obedience school and are
shambling along through the puddles of rain worms
without swerving to the right or to the left. The shaggy
dogs are quite unlike Alex's "beri good" Dog who followed his nose. If Dog were here, he'd have been up and
down the alley several times by now, marking the posts,
checking out the garbage, chasing the pigeons that flut-
ter about. I wonder if Morty's dogs could unlearn their
mindlessness if they suddenly found themselves in the
wild.

"I think she doesn't realize it," Aunt Emily says, "but

she's still doing the nisei thing—trying to appease. At some level she's being sacrificial."

"Sacrificial! You've got to be kidding."

"But all her talk about being cooperative with the government. She really means it," Aunt Emily says.

"What!" Morty's high shout is a yelp. He kicks a crumpled can so hard it ricochets off a fence and bounces back at us. The dogs are startled and break their stride, looking up at him reproachfully. "She's as cooperative as a crocodile," he says. "Look at her teeth next time she opens her mouth."

"Her teeth?" Cedric laughs. "I didn't notice."

Aunt Emily says the ones who have the biggest teeth are people of privilege. They define and control. And Nikki is being used by the powerful to define us to their advantage.

"You mean she's the smile on the crocodile," Morty says. "If she can't get twenty-five million, five will do. And they'll all smile, smile, smile. Those B.C. senators and all those dudes who got rich off my granddad's land."

Here we are talking about money again. Morty's grandfather owned part of what is now Vancouver's British Properties. Morty would have been a millionaire several times over.

The power of Mammon is a great mystery to me. I don't know how it touches my life. Maybe it's buried too deep to reach.

It's hard to hear what anyone's saying over the sudden sound of a jackhammer rat-tat-tatting its way over the changing neighborhood face. Something, a sidewalk or a foundation, is being broken up. To our right is a partially demolished row of old rooming houses. The building where Min lives is also, as Morty puts it, "on the urban hit list."

It must be Mammon again that is destroying this old neighborhood, as it destroyed our communities in the past. It's trampling the whole world. We cannot, I suspect, fight it directly, or alone. I have no idea how to begin. I only know that the more I stare at it, the deeper the pit grows, and the dew on the morning leaves is more distant than before.

We're passing a section of wreckage where an entire wall has come down, exposing a bathroom with toilet, bathtub and lopsided sink. An unexpected and sudden intimacy overhead. Someone has written in red lipstick, "Owner cuts water" on the pink-flowered wallpaper. And the graffiti on the fence says, "Kill! Kill! Kill!"

It's a message to Cinderella—a clamoring message I have chosen to dismiss. There is, after all, as I said to the dream, enough death in the world as it is.

Cedric and I are walking together, as we seem to do most of the time these days. I don't know if my relationship with him is headed anywhere, but our connectedness is uncanny at times. Just this morning, a song was in my mind and he whistled the exact ending at the exact moment. It made my hair stand on end.

What we do when we're alone is of little interest, I'm sure, to anyone—except, that is, to the gossipers in my inner world. They wink and giggle about the slow-going romance between the spinster and the priest. "C'mon," they snigger. "Get on with it." If there's any killing to be done, I'll silence them. My Granton ghoulies.

Morty's murderings are more visible than mine. He's

choking the life out of his fingertips as he wrings his hands. "Okay, Em," he's saying. "So what's the solution?"

"We build the League, Morty, with every bit of mortar we can find. It's our only hope. We write. We phone. We visit. We hold meetings. We inform. And we rally everyone. Especially those who've climbed out of the gutter." She turns to me. "Where's Stephen, Nomi? Call him. If you don't, I will."

Call Stephen? I hesitate a step and fall back. She doesn't understand. She never will.

People keep asking me how Stephen is and I reply, "Fine, I guess." But who knows if he is? I stopped trying to reach him a long time ago and he, it's obvious, is not trying to reach me. I can think of a few things to say but I don't.

"He'd know some powerful people," Morty says.

"True," Aunt Emily says. "Stephen has connections. But no connections are more powerful than Min's."

"Now that's a statement worth pondering," Eugenia says cheerfully.

"He's got the power to wake you at midnight, uh?" Cedric asks. "Good connections." He points upward.

"Min is everyone I ever knew and lost who's still there just around the corner."

Ever since the day she saw Min, Aunt Emily looks at people more carefully. So do I. Every unkempt old man shuffling about on the streets in Chinatown could be someone we once knew. Some niseis, she said, tried to pass as Chinese and have lived here since the forties.

The little restaurant we frequent on the edge of Chinatown is tucked between the skeleton of one building going up and another coming down. It survives un-

changed, seemingly unaware of the neighborhood writh-
ings of birth, restoration, destruction and decay. Morty
parks his dogs and leads the way through the back entrance, past the crates of vegetables and the steaming
kitchen to the corner where our round "table for five"
waits for us.

The waiter, who is sometimes the cook, signals with
one hand raised, his fingers spread widely. "Noodle? Fie?
Chicken?" he asks, and we nod. Pidgin English is so efficient. It conserves air space. It's absurd that Stephen
associates the broken English of the issei with a lack of
intelligence.

Eugenia fills our chunky blue-and-white cups with
tea and Morty lifts his, saying wryly, "Cooperation."

"In the struggle for justice," Aunt Emily says.

"To the struggle," Cedric says and squeezes my hand.

We clunk our cups.

"Here's mud in your eye."

31

True to her energetic word, Aunt Emily has reached my

unreachable brother, and here we are in his expensive

hotel restaurant, Anna, me and Aunt Emily, with Ste-

phen, his streak of white hair wider than before. He's

put on some weight. His voice is still the rich baritone of

a singer.

"Well, h'lo."

To most people our lack of expressiveness would

seem peculiar. This is my one and only brother whom I

haven't seen in over a decade and all I do is say "hello"

and sit down. No hugs, no kisses, not even a handshake. We come from the territory of stone.

"So, Nome. Long time no see, eh?" He's in Toronto to judge a Mozart competition.

"How's Claudine? Are you still with her?"

"We survive."

I'm wondering as I sit here, opposite him at this square table, whether my heart has turned to stone, lava stone, rage grown cold. I'm Naomi Watcher Nakane to-night, hovering somewhere in the air, observing as I eat in this public place that my abdomen is in discomfort. I have a vague and general discomfort about everything and my appetite is dull.

What a long, long way we are from Granton, from Slocan, from the woods in the mountains and the sugar-beet fields. I glance at his face and find no clue to the pathway home. Stephen the celebrity beckons to waiters, orders wines. And there's not one pebble on the forest floor to guide us out of these woods. He'll be the guest adjudicator tomorrow for the piano sonatas and then he'll be gone.

I'm more at home in Chinatown than in this glitzy candlelit room of pink cloth napkins and waiters in bow ties. We've had crab and avocado appetizers, cold creamy soup. Next the entrées. Too much food. What must life be like for Stephen, who lives in hotels much of the time and eats like this often? No wonder he's put on weight.

There's a pianist playing light classics. Stephen says she's terrible. Some sort of business convention is on. We're surrounded by dark pinstripe three-piece suits, these suits of success, suits of armor, that declare down to the shiny shoes that here are today's knights, fighting the windy ways of Mammon with their ledger sheets and their wits.

Aunt Emily's mission tonight is clear. We need Stephen for the League. Whether he likes it or not, he's getting a short course on Japanese Canadian politics. It's like the old days in Granton when Aunt Emily would visit and they'd sit at the table arguing into the night. Stephen's been trying to change the subject.

"Really, your career is more important than all this redress stuff. Think about your future, Anna."

"Get thee behind me, Satan," Anna says and I smile, remembering her as a little girl defending Gaby and shaking her finger at Dog as she chanted the magic words.

"You can take the girl out of Granton," Stephen grins, "but you can't take Granton out of the girl."

"And you?" I ask. "Is Granton still in your veins too?"

"Not a drop." He flicks a non-existent piece of lint off his jacket.

When Stephen left Granton, he left. But his leaving goes with him. He's in perpetual flight. His eyes, even now, are wandering around the room.

For just an instant when I first caught a glimpse of him waiting in the lobby, I felt a flicker of something. I hardly know what the feeling was. But the sensation disappeared as swiftly as it arrived.

Neither Stephen nor I is fully here. He's walled away from Aunt Emily's insistent agenda, and I've fallen through my trapdoor into a room beneath the room where we sit. A bulletproof space.

Aunt Emily is intent on getting through to Stephen and she's being as patient and self-controlled as I've ever seen her.

"Tell me, Stephen," she says, "you surely do not agree with the prime minister. Tell me that you don't agree."

The prime minister's latest remarks have left people nonplussed. He, the man who speaks of "justice in our time," has dismissed our community, saying the "descendants of dead ancestors" are not deserving of either compensation or apology.

"Who's a dead ancestor?" Marion wanted to know. Ken said not only are we alive, but so are the perpetrators. And Sumi, smiling gracious Sumi who adores the prime minister, sat with her hands folded in her lap, saying nothing.

"So what do we expect of a man who thinks we're Japanese?" Anna asked.

It rankles people that the prime minister apologized to the Japanese in Japan for what Canada did to us Canadians. "Can you see him going to France to try to make amends to French Canadians?"

The report from Ottawa is that Government is prepared to offer its regrets, but there can be no further acknowledgment of the actions taken against us. The leaders of the past acted legitimately and their names are not to be tarnished today by an apology for their deeds.

"The Bundestag is supreme," Anna says. "We've got our Eichmanns in Ottawa, still defending the old laws of the land, and nobody twitches in bed."

Stephen recoils. "That's pretty offensive, Baby Anna."

"But don't you see her point, Stephen? If we're going to get anywhere with this obtuse government, we've got to pull together. We need our high-profile people."

"Look at it this way," Anna says. "What if one person from that elitist school, Upper Canada College—say

Robertson Davies—what if the government took his house? See what I mean?"

"I get so tired of being used."

"Used?" Aunt Emily is getting fed up with the patient approach. "Used? The League doesn't use us! We use it!"

"Well . . ." Stephen looks away. "I've got better things to do. There's a broader picture out there."

"Good grief, Stephen!" Aunt Emily's voice is shrill.

The men at the next table glance our way. I nudge Aunt Emily to calm down, but she's getting geared up and nothing I know can stop Hurricane Em when she gets going. I can hear Stephen thinking, "Well, she certainly hasn't changed." He's embarrassed, but Anna's eyes are fixed on Aunt Emily in fierce identification.

"You can neutralize anything with the 'broader picture.' " Aunt Emily clutches his arm so that he's forced to look at her. "Listen to me. People need mud in order to see. You're living proof of that. If you don't get your hands in the mud, you won't get the eyes you need to see what to do about the broader picture."

In times like these, she says, a pristine name is like a lake killed by acid rain—beautiful but dead. He must, he must come down and join the struggle, because we, his family, his community, will never be at home, in this country or anywhere, unless we first achieve redress. This we must do for our psychic survival. This first, this basic thing. What heals people is the transforming power of mutuality. Mutual vulnerability. Mutual strength.

This is Aunt Emily of the Japanese Canadian Redress Crusade, reaching out to Stephen the Infidel. But he's not being persuaded. He pours wine into our glasses and sounds offhanded as he says we aren't realistic if we think we can attain mutuality. "Look at the facts," he says. He picks up a crumb from the edge of the bread basket. "Japanese Canadians count less than *this* in Parliament. You haven't a hope."

"You're wrong," Aunt Emily says. Her voice has quietened to the dead calm of conviction. "We're human, we're equal and we're coming through." She leans toward him and raps the table with her knuckles so hard the candle flame flickers. "Nothing in heaven or on earth can stop the labor of the heart, Stephen." She's preaching the Gospel according to Aunt Emily. The heart's power is greater than any power known.

Redress, she says, is a Canadian liberation movement. We're fighting the oppression of an entire Canadian minority.

"Oppression, now that's an abused word." Stephen hunches forward, leaning on his forearms. "You've got it all wrong. We're not oppressed. There comes a time when you've got to stand up and recognize that things have changed. Redress? Come on! The way everyone loves to play the victim. My God! Think what Japanese Canadian redress sounds like to the rest of the world. Can't you hear the false note in it?" He shakes his finger at us. "You're all suffering from a North American pathology. Do something useful, why don't you. Something for others."

Something for others! Has Stephen ever thought of anyone but himself? This is the man who never once condescended to visit and comfort the old woman who worshiped him. This is the man who will not stoop and lend his name to help his community. And he is blind to the fact that some of us do not feel as privileged as he now does.

"Your so-called little liberation movement . . ." He

waves his hand, dismissing us. "A bunch of myopic crybabies."

Aunt Emily is taken aback for a moment, but she will not be dismissed by her nephew. "What an outsider's point of view that is. I'm telling you, Stephen, whether it's in suburbia or Ethiopia, when we fight oppression, we're fighting with the oppressed." She's carrying on doggedly, but I can see she cannot win. He's made his position totally clear. He won't be involved. Somewhere in all these truths lies a failure of love.

"I'm a minstrel," he says and shrugs. "I'll put the story to music if you want. Don't expect anything else from me."

He may well write a ballad, but the tune will be wrong. Stories without love are words without song.

32

SUMMER 1984.

Phone ringing as I walk through the door. "Good morning. *Bridge* magazine."

It's Anna asking breathlessly if Aunt Emily is here. She isn't, although she's expected any moment.

Anna says Brian down at the paper just got wind of an ethnocultural breakfast the Minister of Multiculturalism is holding downtown. Good old Brian, scouting through the woods for us, relaying news. There's some urgency surrounding the prime minister's plans to retire. He says Nikki is bound to be there. "There's bad stuff going on, Naomi. I'm calling the Rainbow Coalition. Can you make it?" Anna names the hotel.

"Who? Me?" I sound like Min Kawai.

Cedric chimes in that he's always prepared to join his friends as a breakfast gate-crasher. He admires the Rainbow Coalition—a group of lawyers, all women of color, who have joined forces to fight racism.

Morty prances about, jiggling his keys as is his habit. He's ready to leave for the hotel the instant Aunt Emily gets here.

"I'd like to ask that senior representative of the crown why he refuses to consult with our president," Morty says.

From all Aunt Emily's reports, Mick Hayashi, our new JCL president, is perfect for us. "He's a genuine community person. Open. Unflappable. It's a democratic miracle," she said buoyantly. But he's been scorned by Ottawa. The minister told a columnist that Mick Hayashi was "a featherweight who has trouble expressing himself."

By the time Aunt Emily arrives, I'm feeling trepidation. I'm not sure about going to a breakfast where we aren't invited and I suggest they go ahead without me. But Eugenia gives me the boot and Cedric, Aunt Emily and I take off with Morty in his hairy old car. In damp weather, it smells like a kennel.

"Hope there's food left," Morty says.

Last night I dreamt of being poor and needing to feed people and carving a huge roast out of my abdomen.

We inch along in the car-clogged streets to the hotel, go up a winding staircase and enter a plush area with chandeliers and thick red carpets outside a banquet room. What pomp and circumstance! Scarlett O'Hara could come sweeping by.

A small group of smokers is standing outside the giant floor-to-ceiling doors and no one is checking for invitations. Inside, hundreds of people in clusters of ten or so sit at round tables. Several tables at the edges are empty. A buffet still has some leftover sausages and scrambled eggs. We stand at the back.

A stocky dark-skinned woman with black wavy hair is speaking at the floor microphone in the middle of the room. At the front, on a platform, is the bald and portly Minister of Multiculturalism, feet astride, arms folded.

I locate Nikki sharing a table with half a dozen other Japanese Canadians. Anna, her back to us, is seated near the mike with a racially mixed group of flamboyantly dressed women. The Rainbow Coalition. They're as swift and organized as a SWAT team. Here they are, seated at a table together, and one of them is commanding the mike.

The woman, hands on hips, fist full of papers, is speaking in a throaty voice heavy with denunciation. "And you say you understand us because you're an immigrant too? Well, Mr. Minister, I'm no immigrant. My family have been in this country three generations and you're an adopted son who has received more privilege, and yes, I'm making personal remarks. This is all very personal to me. . . ."

"Just in time for the fireworks, eh?" Morty whispers, his hand shielding his mouth. "What is this? A venting session of the 'restless minorities management bureau'?"

At Anna's table, a young dark-eyed woman in a fringed jacket is chanting in a loud voice, "Talk about it, sister, talk about it."

"What I want to say is that when you leap in with your white voice to usurp the voice of a person of color, when you equate your lack of privilege as an immigrant with centuries of racial oppression, you trivialize our suffering, and that's racism."

Some of the people in the room are glaring at the woman. Some are glancing nervously at the minister. He frowns and is about to respond but she shakes her papers and goes on. "By everything that's measurable, by income, status and power, we blacks are the fleas, you whites are the elephants. Yet just let us get a little too close—let us stub our toes on the line of privilege—and then watch the reaction from even your most liberal do-gooders. If we don't get our facts exactly right, you whites say, 'Look, look, she made a mistake on the third line.' You look for errors in our remarks rather than for the truth beyond our errors. And that too is racism. We're all trapped in it." She includes the whole room in the sweep of her arm. "Every one of us lives and breathes in structures of racism from the moment we're born. We're caged in standards controlled by people of privilege—standards of truth and goodness, standards of excellence, standards of beauty which are standards of privilege through and through, and those are the bars that deny our specific realities and lock us out of even your most anti-racist institutions."

A large white woman at Anna's table applauds and the speaker carries on. "I want to call out to the rebel that lurks in the heart of every person of privilege. 'Come out! Come out!' "

"Hear hear!" the large woman shouts and bangs a fist on her table. But others are fidgeting uncomfortably.

A tall white-haired man in a gray suit gets up to

speak, but the woman is not finished. Maybe she'll never be finished. The minister's lips are tightly pursed as she carries on.

"Some of us of the rainbow persuasion are here today in solidarity with each other, and we're saying, along with Anna Makino and Japanese Canadians, we don't need you to foist the leadership of your choice on our communities. Speak to properly elected leaders. Not the self-appointed. Speak to the president of their national organization."

Anna applauds wildly. So do Morty, Cedric and Aunt Emily. I realize, with a little surprise, that I feel less like fleeing than I would have a year ago. Perhaps Nikki is wanting to flee. Her head is bowed.

"Stop the policies that promote rivalries. Stop tossing crumbs that make us fight each other like dogs. Stop the divide and conquer."

The man standing behind the woman has pushed ahead to the mike and in a heavy European accent he says he came this morning not to complain but to have breakfast. There is a light sprinkle of laughter, but the woman is neither joining in nor leaving her post. The man thanks the minister effusively, declaring that in the country he fled, any criticism of Government would have been severely punished, and that he's sure others in the room feel, as he does, a great sense of gratitude for the wonders of this wonderland, Canada.

The minister signals appreciation with a genial wave.

"Of all countries," the man says passionately, "is no place so good. Here, paradise. No diktat. No diktat."

There's a smattering of applause as he steps aside, giving a peremptory nod to the woman.

It's a Rashomon reality wherever one goes. There are

so many truths. His view of the woman's "complaint" is probably, like Stephen's, that she's a spoiled child, ignorant of "real" oppression, whereas she would see him as blinkered by the color and gender of privilege. If Aunt Emily is right about the ripple effect of liberation struggles, both their tales of suffering should be their bond.

The woman takes back her place at the microphone. "I want to say one more thing," she says, her voice rising over the growing murmur of reproach from the crowd. "Of course it's a great country. That's why we're committed to it. This country, my country, your country, is one country where the great wide Technicolor dream can come true. We can stamp out racism and show the world how it's done. Not by homogenization. We know that a homogenized mind-set is ecologically unsound. But by real plurality. And I'm not talking about ethnic folk dancing. I'm talking about access to power. I'm talking about distinctness and mutuality, collaborative politics at every level. Not tolerance of difference, but celebration. . . ."

Anna has spotted our little group by the door and is making her way between the tables toward us in quick little sideways hops. She beckons us into the lobby outside and there's tension and urgency in her breathless whispering.

Her news is paralyzing. Everything is happening in a great rush because the prime minister, having announced his retirement, is stepping down, and we're an unpalatable bit of leftover grit on his plate. They want us removed, right away. This Wednesday, she says, Government is making a public statement of regrets to us. But there will be no negotiations, no compensation, no redress, no apology. They'll announce a general fund to combat racism. It's a complete whitewash. She doesn't think they're even going to use the word "injustice." She is so agitated she's shaking.

"They're going to do an end run."

The bewilderment is in all our faces. "Wait a minute," Morty says. "Slow down, Anna."

The plan is to wrap everything up before the prime minister leaves office and that's why they're going to go ahead this week. This very minute, Government is preparing to pull the rug out from under the redress movement.

"How can this be? Does the council know? Have you called the president?" Aunt Emily stares at Anna in disbelief.

"She's got to be stopped. This has to be stopped," Morty says.

"Wait—that's not all," Anna says. "Isseis are supposed to be there to applaud and there's going to be a press conference afterward. It's their quiet little deal. They're going to pull it off with Nikki and that's it. Finis." Anna looks at us helplessly.

Aunt Emily is grim as she turns abruptly and marches to the nearest phone.

Morty, Cedric, Anna and I are left standing in the plush red-carpeted concourse with the constant glittering crystalline chandeliers that make night and day interchangeable and irrelevant. Cedric shakes his head sadly. " 'They have healed the wound of my people lightly, saying, "Peace, peace," where there is no peace,' " he says under his breath. It's the words of the prophet Jeremiah.

33

June 1984. Sunday afternoon. An emergency long-distance teleconference of the National Council.

We are the fishes in the deep blue sea and we are the fisherfolk standing on the shore. We have been hoping against hope that Nikki would swim with us. Now we see she is not swimming at all. She has been hooked by a shining lure and is being pulled as a lure herself. Uncertain of nets and snares, we are peering into the waters and the fish darting here, there, seeking safety, seeking each other.

If Nikki forms a breakaway group today, she will go

in triumph to Ottawa on Wednesday. Our history, made trivial and palatable, will be offered to the public in bite-sized regrets, and in that moment the movement for redress will be swallowed alive. The League will be dead dead dead once more.

Dan and Aunt Emily, two of Toronto's council members, are standing by, ready to cast their lines. The rest of us, Brian and Anna, Sumi, Morty, Cedric and I, are waiting anxiously on the shore, hoping the council will pass safely through this test and continue on course.

I'm thinking of the schools of little gray fish moving like shadows in a stream in Slocan. As a child, I stood on the bridge and watched them, and here we are now, forty years later at *Bridge,* watching the shadowy council struggling through the murky waters of Canadian politics.

Aunt Emily is in Morty's crowded cubbyhole, phone gripped in one hand, her other fist gouging a hollow in her cheek. Dan is at Cedric's desk. The rest of us are going to listen in on Eugenia's line and mine.

I'm curled up on my chair, chin in my hands, trying to calm myself. I'm connected viscerally to what's at stake.

Morty is bouncing on his toes, shifting his weight from one foot to the other, tying, untying his shoelaces. He's the only person I know who wears out his laces every few months. Anna is pacing. We're all waiting waiting for the Bell operator to signal the go-ahead. Sumi, bolt upright on the couch, says she can't think of any isseis who would go to Ottawa with Nikki. Not if they knew the League was opposed. Brian, reporter that he is, is writing the names of all the delegates. Which ones are with Nikki? What chance that she'll succeed in hijacking the others? It's going to be a battle for leadership this afternoon. That much we know.

Groups like ours must be in offices and homes across the time zones. The NJCL now has fifteen centers. Nikki is in another part of Toronto, we don't know where.

Through Cedric's window, I see Ken Suzuki hurrying across the road, a cardboard box in his hands. Marion is close behind. They've come from church and are in their Sunday clothes.

"Has it started?"

"Not yet."

Morty and Brian crowd around as Ken, fumbling in his haste, installs a speakerphone on Eugenia's desk. The moment he turns up the volume, Mick Hayashi's mellow voice comes through from Winnipeg. "All right, everyone's on the line." The conference was to begin at 2 o'clock sharp. It's now 2:09.

"Let me begin right away." Mick Hayashi begins by explaining the crisis. Nikki has called certain council members, ignoring the president, ignoring the council's decisions, and asking them to go to Ottawa. "I think this is a serious matter."

"What an understatement," Morty mutters.

"Sh."

"Mick, before you go on," Nikki's voice cuts through, "this whole thing is very, very simple." She's cajoling him and reminding everyone that last fall she championed the Japanese Canadian cause in front of the Special Committee on Visible Minorities. That was the day she and Dr. Stinson came here. "And now we've simply been invited to go and listen to Government's response. That's all. There's nothing to get excited about." Skip, skip. The words dance lightly over the waves in a singsong. "If the council represented all Japanese Canadians, of course I would have contacted all of you, but there's a segment of the population that is not, I repeat not, listened to, and of course I have obligations to them."

"The gall," Anna whispers.

Nikki's self-justifying remarks will either repel or capture her listeners. I'm picturing her as she stood last year in front of these same delegates from across the country, her red scarf flung dramatically across her shoulder. Now, from her corner of the country, she's addressing them again with the same confidence, her voice rising as she accuses the president of failure to communicate with her. "And so I submit to you council members," she says finally, her words measured and deliberate, "I submit to you that we be prepared to move a vote of non-confidence in the president."

There's an audible gasp in the room. Sumi bounces forward and grasps Marion's hand tightly. We're all hooked to the long-distance telephone line and can feel the sudden yank. This is the move we've been dreading. Cedric, arms folded, looks grim.

The president sounds as polite as if he's just heard a personal compliment rather than a call to mutiny. "Okay. Fine. Thank you, Nikki." In a steady even-tempered voice he says, "What we're concerned with today is Government's proposal."

"It's no secret," Nikki says. "We've known about their response."

That's true. Both Government's sentiments and the League's resistance are common knowledge. What wasn't known until three days ago was Nikki's double-dealing.

"Recently, Nikki," the president says, "you called

some council members to go to Ottawa. I'd like to ask council members whether you think Nikki's action was meant to involve the League or not. Our organization knew nothing about it."

"I don't agree with you at all," Nikki interrupts haughtily. "*The Toronto Star* called and told me you knew what Government was going to do, at which point I contacted Government. Now, what did you tell the *Star?*"

"A trial balloon," Brian says. He's told us before that Government regularly leaks its news to gauge reactions.

"I think we're getting out of hand," the president says coolly. He never ever seems to raise his voice. "I'd like to ask council members if they're prepared to tell us. . . ."

Nikki interrupts again. "Mick, I'd like . . ."

A high-pitched voice interjects. "What's your question, Mick?"

"The question," the president says, "is, which council members were contacted by Nikki to go to Ottawa and what was their understanding of why they would be going."

"Before you ask that," Nikki says, "I'd like to know what you told *The Toronto Star,* Mick."

"Can we get Mick's question answered?" a new voice asks. "After all, we're all on the phone." And another voice adds, "Ask each one whether they got contacted."

"Okay." It's the president again. "I'll go through and maybe we can get a yes or no. Victoria. Were you contacted?"

Victoria comes through. "No."

"Vancouver?"

"No."

"Kamloops, were you contacted?"

"Never."

The roll call proceeds from west to east, into Calgary, Lethbridge, Edmonton, Regina, Winnipeg, Ontario and Quebec.

Morty is scratching his wrists, sitting down, standing up, leaning into the speakerphone. Cedric is gripping the edge of the desk as if to make sure he's connected on this ledge of suspense. My amphibious friend who is at home in the sea or in the air is clinging to the cliff with the rest of us.

Four centers were contacted by Nikki. But no one seemed to realize that their attendance in Ottawa would be misrepresented as support for a statement that the League has already rejected.

"How can they be so dumb?" Morty mumbles.

"They're not dumb," Anna says sharply. "They're just decent."

"There's such a thing as too much decency," Brian ventures.

Morty paces rapidly from one office to the next, urging Aunt Emily and Dan to move that Nikki be removed. "Get going. Get a motion going." Thus far, the only word we've heard from this huddle has been Dan's voice answering "no" to the question about whether he'd been contacted by Nikki.

Nikki is on the line again, questioning the president about *The Toronto Star*.

"It was just a journalist's trick," a voice says. "There's no sense . . ."

And another voice speaks. "Victoria here. We're prepared to make a motion to dissolve Nikki's committee. . . ."

Morty bites his knuckles. "Go, Victoria! Go!"

"The first thing we have to establish here is some bottom line," the speaker from Victoria begins. "We've got to speak with one voice. It's obvious Nikki isn't going to work with the president. We all agreed the president should always be the first to be informed about anything to do with Government. So I feel very strongly and I move that Nikki's team should be dissolved immediately."

"And we should let Ottawa know right away."

"I agree with that."

Morty shouts, "Second that motion, Dan." But Kamloops has already seconded it and the president has asked for an exact wording. The motion is open for discussion.

Hardly anyone is breathing as a slowly paced roll call begins again and each representative has a say. The president urges careful consideration, saying it's a major motion and therefore a sixty percent majority is required.

A man on Nikki's line interrupts to declare that Nikki has done all the redress groundwork to date. "A decision of this kind can't be made by phone." A woman from B.C. says, "We should be loving one another." Another speaker fears the president is too burdened to take on the work that Nikki has been doing and that only Nikki knows the people in Ottawa.

Dan finally comes on the line. "I think it's imperative that this motion be passed." He's formal, clear, calm. "Otherwise we're going to have disruptions without cease. And I would ask council members to allow Emily Kato and me as Toronto delegates to have one vote each, since we are council members, so that Toronto may have a more representative voice."

A hushed cheer goes up from our office, but is immediately quashed as voice after voice comes on to declare that the council will have no part in deciding how Toronto's allocated votes are divided.

"That's Toronto's problem," each center declares, and we shudder. Nikki has been maintaining that as representative of the Toronto League she has the support of twenty-four affiliated organizations and the entire Toronto Japanese Canadian community. She therefore should control all the Toronto votes. But as everyone here knows, Nikki has not ever called a general meeting on redress, and a Toronto League election is long overdue.

"Tell them about our public meetings," Morty says. "People in Toronto deserve a voice."

"They're just going to tell us to get it together with Nikki," Anna says.

"She's got no rules," Morty cries. "How the hell can you . . . ?" He stops short as Ken raises the volume of the speakerphone and we are frozen.

The vote is being called. "Moved that Nikki Kagami's committee be dissolved." One by one we hear the slow count.

"Victoria. Two votes. Yes."

"Vancouver. Four. Yes."

"Kamloops. Yes."

And on and on across the country. From somewhere within our disbelief and relief we hear the president conclude, "Motion carried." Nikki has been cut loose. And I, the most non-hugging woman in the world, am tripping over the wastebasket to embrace my friends.

34

SUMMER 1984–SPRING 1985.

"President must resign, charges rival."

"Militant faction overthrows moderates."

Media focus is fast and furious these days. I've become a newspaper addict, getting my fix before work every morning. Certain things have been clarified. Certain things are muddier than before. Government, fortunately, fails in its plan for a quickie little statement of the country's regrets.

"It's difficult," the minister says, "to have to deal with a community that keeps changing its representatives."

The country, we note, changes its representatives more often than we do, as the Liberals are defeated, the Tories arrive and we have a new prime minister, Mr. Brian Mulroney.

Meanwhile, Nikki has launched a fresh assault on the leadership of the National Japanese Canadian League. And whom does she place in the front lines of her war? It's the issei generation. The ones who, in her own words, "don't have a clue."

"She's sold out her soul," Anna says. "She came to the crossroads and took the wrong turn."

Nikki holds press conferences throughout the summer and fall, declaring that the silent majority of Japanese Canadians, particularly the elderly issei, reject the greed of the young militant radical League. And the new minister, a Tory, is prompted to declare, "I won't insult Japanese Canadians by offering compensation."

"Insult us! Please insult us!" Morty says and slaps the newspaper shut in disgust.

"Government is so smart it's uncanny," Anna says. "If they can't get Nikki to deliver us, they'll use her to divide us."

And "a divided community" is the phrase the minister uses now in his statements dismissing the League.

I am wretched with sadness when I see the wide-eyed worry in Mrs. Makino's little wrinkled face. "Annu-san and Marion make mistake," Nikki's mother told her. "They want fight Government. No no. Don't ask money. Better do Nikki way. Maybe lose pension." After not seeing each other for forty years, they're no longer seeing each other again.

"Mata itsuka . . . ," Mrs. Makino says to comfort herself. Someday, someday, the better time will come.

Elsewhere in the grass roots, we are toiling night and day. A sense of rightness nurtures confidence, confidence sparks activity, activity kindles more confidence and the movement spreads. House meetings, fund-raisings, public forums increase. A brief is being prepared. Much of the work spills over into the *Bridge* office and Dan, our candyman, comes by with his gifts. A computer. Another computer. A printer.

As I sit in on our meetings, I feel two engines, love and anger, one in front and one behind, pushing and pulling the train as it chugs up a steep hill. There is love for the community and anger toward anything that would deny its rebirth. When love grows weary, some new outrage by Nikki or Government fuels the rear engine into a forward thrust and the slow-moving train keeps climbing.

Meanwhile, in the passenger cars, perceptions of reality are surreal. It's right, it's wrong, to be humble. It's wrong, it's right, to speak up. Truth is dismissed by those who must win and the timid are blown away in the dust. Although, as we all know, we must speak with one voice, there is more than one view. From within the turmoil, it's commitment that's being formed. We're no longer on the sidelines watching others. Japanese Canadians are in the spotlight's glare.

Government's intention is that we should harmonize in perfect Government-approved song. But no matter how ardently the choirmaster flails his arms, we sing out of tune. It's a cacophonous choir, howling its way through the redress blues. I expect that at any moment the curtain will thud at our feet. But some people, having discovered their voices, will no longer be still.

Each time there's a report that Nikki represents the

silent majority, derisive cries fill the air. Letters pleading for sanity and loyalty appear in the community papers. A few voices soar into prayer.

One anonymous writer, like a rabid dog with its teeth in the laundry, foams his vitriolic abuse, attacking Mick Hayashi, attacking council members. From out of one person's poisoned pen there flows a steady stream of hurtfulness, and people who read the papers are dazed with embarrassment.

It's the personal attacks against Aunt Emily I find unbearable. "Bet she's writing about all this. Yeah, anything for her own glory." We're accosted on the street by a woman who says, "Why are you bringing the past back again?"

"It's the workings of a culture of oppression," Aunt Emily says wearily, the darkening bags under her eyes showing her fatigue. "We've got to have a public meeting."

And the largest public meeting on redress to date gets under way at Harbord Collegiate.

NOVEMBER 1984.

The event tells me that more things are wrought by passion than this world dreams of. You don't need hired staff or gobs of money. All you need is belief and a handful of people phoning, running around putting up posters, delivering press releases.

There's a quiet undertone of excitement in the crowded auditorium. Not since childhood, not since Vancouver or Slocan, have I seen so many Japanese Canadians. Mostly niseis. The hall's capacity is six hundred and every seat is taken. "Where do they come from?" Anna keeps asking. Min looks completely dazed, standing against the wall at the side, rocking back and forth, back and forth. A couple of men peer at him, but they don't approach. Morty is in great form, trotting up and down the long aisles, getting press kits to the media.

People have come out from their suburban homes, their white neighborhoods, their high rises and, like Min, their little rooms. They've come stumbling out of the highways and byways, the dusty attics and the railway stations of the mind, eager to hear the latest word. A sense of mission fills the hall. We all know we are a people who were wronged. It's time to stand up. It's time.

Following the meeting, hundreds of petitions are sent to Ottawa. Hundreds of small signatures swim hopefully upstream, only to fall through the sluice gates of bureaucracy. "We respectfully request Government to recognize the National Japanese Canadian League, and our president, Mickey Hayashi," we say. And in the newspapers, the reporters write, "Japanese Canadians assail Ottawa."

The statement that comes back to us is the minister's standard line. "Japanese Canadians are a divided community." Nikki, we assume, is spreading her word.

"You're working too hard, my dear," Eugenia says to Aunt Emily. "I do worry about your heart."

"My heart's okay," Aunt Emily says. "It was built in the past."

"Your heart's from the past, your head's from the future. And your body's in the battlefield, eh?" Morty gives her a military salute. "See you in the war zone, Sarge."

The war zone is a stormy zone and we're all in the weather together. Across the country, here and there, little gray-haired niseis with their fiercely determined hearts are huddling together for warmth. "It's winter's feeble stand," they say. "The ice will disappear."

And within our cocoons, new life is being formed. One by one, we are coming forth with dewy fresh wings. The more meetings we attend, the more we need to attend. We're learning how to fly by stuffing envelopes.

35

Some days, weary with labor, I crave the wide sky solitude I used to have in Cecil. No Japanese Canadians in sight.

"Let's wing it out of here," Cedric says, and from time to time we sneak away like fugitives.

This afternoon, he rolls himself out of his office and stops with a clank of his metal chair legs against my wastepaper basket. "Toronto Island?" he asks.

"Why not?" We've been working late as usual, but it's still bright with the summer's light. I switch off the computer, grab my jacket, and we're about to go out the door when we collide with Aunt Emily. She looks exhausted and sinks into the old couch without even a rudimentary "Hi."

Cedric asks her to join us but she looks at us as if we're out of our minds. "Who's got the time?" she asks, shaking her head. Aunt Emily can be like a dog with an old shoe, her mind stuffed with worry as she shakes her problems to tatters.

Walking is one of the things that keeps us from going out of our minds. But no one I know has ever been able to slow Aunt Emily down.

"What can we say to the war vets?" she asks. "Imagine mounting a campaign against us." The Ontario Legion has been vocally opposing Japanese Canadian redress. They seem to share Ollie Oliver's view that we belong to a foreign country.

"Come away with us and rest your mind," Cedric urges again. But she won't. She's putting out brush fires one by one. Meanwhile the forest is blazing with indifference. "That's the deadliest fire of all," Cedric says as we walk Aunt Emily to her car.

The rush-hour traffic has abated and the rays of the early evening sun are slanting horizontally, glinting dark gold in the top windows of the high-rise towers on Bay Street. We wave Aunt Emily on and turn south, arm in arm, down Spadina Avenue. Min is standing around outside a Chinese restaurant, looking scruffy as usual, but here, who cares. This corner of the city with its funny-looking belongingness has its liberating aspects. We call out to him but he's ignoring us in his unpredictable way.

Our northern walks have evolved this year into these after-work strolls. In spite of the traffic, we enter our own bubble. No typing. No phones.

Normally we make our way up Philosophers' Walk. In the sweltering days of summer, we'll join students on the lawn in the shade of the trees. Cedric says we have so much to learn from trees. They are the signs of an active mercy. Year after year, they give us the breath of life.

Marion said the other day, she wondered if we were wrong in seeking justice when we were so caught up in our community's wars. "It's human to want justice and it's human to wage war," she said. "But if we can't be merciful, don't you think justice is wasted on us?"

Anna said mercy was wasted on people unaware of doing wrong. "Therefore justice before mercy. Therefore name the crimes."

It's a relief to get away from redress discussions now and then. We have our favorite bookstores on Bloor Street. And the ice-cream store. If Cedric picks up a paper, I prepare myself for the ambush of print. Any speck of news about Japanese Canadians and demons leap off the page. Out come our quarters for phone calls. I'm glad we're off to Toronto Island today.

By the time we get to the dock, have a supper snack and take the ferry across to the island, the light is almost gone. We make our way down to the beach in the twilight.

I don't know how it happens, but sometimes as we walk together there's a burst of silence so filled with a wild unspoken sound that it's more eloquent than anything we could say.

Last month, while tromping through the trees on the edge of a northern lake, we heard a quivering wail and there, far off in the middle of the lake, was the sleek shape of a loon. Then suddenly, behind it, another loon.

I was mesmerized by the wavery cries. From elsewhere on the other side of the lake came the noise of humanity. A motorboat with its guttural roar raced about.

In the early evening, we sat by the water in the stillness, our fingers touching, our toes making circles, and he asked me, gently, tentatively, if we might be together through the night. I looked down into the water, at the trees reflected there, the ripples shimmering, and nodded yes.

It was a cool and extraordinarily calm evening. We swam, we lay in our blankets, we traced the flight of an owl across the sky and drank the wilderness into our lungs. And as casually as breath, we held each other, and safely, softly, we descended, down and trembling down, to the shuddering cry of the loons.

Later, in the evening's faint light, we shared our tales. Petal by petal and shard by shard we unfolded the patterns of our hopes and fears. At this season of our lives we are neither of us old nor are we young. Our journeys are more than halfway done. I don't know whether our days now will be more interlocked. It hardly matters. I only know that I have walked a narrow and barren path all my dusty long life. And that I sit now in the shelter of a kindly tree. When I look up into the branches, there are pathways of leaves. And singing.

Here once again, this early evening, we have the cool sand under our feet, the grass tufts. There are light watery sounds. This is what I have come to love. An outdoor meditation. A satsang in a breeze-filled temple where the music is the sound of waves, the incense is the green scent of growing things.

We are here with our love, our hands resting from labor, and suddenly, pouncing upon us from out of the bushes, is a patchy white-and-fawn-colored blue-eyed puppy, foxy-faced and playful, its head bobbing down to its forelegs, its rear holding up a proud little flag of a tail. Wag wag. Cedric calls, slapping his thighs, and off they go, the sky-eyed puppy and the man with earth-colored hair, frolicking over the sand, both their heads cocked in the language of dogs.

I sit on a log, take off my shoes, and it's childhood again as the lights of the skyline sparkle across the waters.

The fact of flesh is new in my life. A simple fact, as commonplace as pebbles on a beach. But I'm a pebble that was lost. Now I've been found. I'm held in a hand that's as warm as song.

I watch them as they play and he is no longer Buck Rogers from another galaxy and we are not on a spaceship headed for outer space. I'm glad enough to see twinkly reflections in the waters of Lake Ontario.

36

SUMMER 1985.

The waters of Lake Ontario do twinkle indeed, but the fish that swim there are diseased and dying. That too is what one knows as one sits on the shore.

"It's redress redress everywhere," Aunt Emily says, "and not a drop to drink."

Cedric's presence in my life is what makes me see the lights in the night—the cruising ships, the stars. But there are unexpected squalls that come up, churning the lake into a frothing rage. In the dizzying darkness, life rafts are lowered. Some float to safety. Others fail.

Anna and Brian have been lobbying friends at Toronto City Hall. It's in the wild and windy world of friends that dreams are born. And drowned. Nikki too has allies—in the Liberal Party, in the Multiculturalism Directorate, at the CBC and here and there. Friends, and friends of friends, and friends of friends of friends, are linked in a shimmering weave of schemes.

"Great news!" Anna announces one day. "City Hall is giving the League a grant!"

But a few weeks later, we hear the funds are being held up. Nikki, all on her own, has gone marching down to the mayor's office. "I represent Toronto's Japanese Canadian community," Nikki declared, "and twenty-four organizations here. We do not support the position of the National Japanese Canadian League. Redress is a painfully divisive community matter. The federal government is wisely avoiding it. Toronto should do likewise. Moreover," she adds, as a final condemnatory note, "those NJCL people are militant left-wingers—they all support the New Democrats."

Anna flings her head back and laughs aloud when she hears of this crowning accusation. "NDP supporters! Is that the worst thing she can say about us? Little does she know how radical some of them are at City Hall."

Morty is tired of being called a militant radical and has been making efforts to look respectable these days. He's shaved off his wispy beard—"the ultimate sacrifice."

Morty, Anna, Dan and Aunt Emily hold a council of war. "Twenty-four organizations support Nikki?" they ask. "Well, let's just find out." And from door to door, swift as a prairie fire, questionnaires spread.

We're astonished as the results come in. There's almost total solidarity with the National JC League. Com-

munity leaders, lawyers, clergy and executives of organizations sign statements and write letters completely
repudiating Nikki's claims. Not only do people disap-
prove of her actions, they are appalled that she purports
to represent them.

"Well, so much for the divided community," Brian
says as we heave with sighs of satisfaction and leaf
through the pile of documents. "Here's all the hard facts
we'll ever need."

"And just think about it," Morty says as he slaps the
evidence with the back of his hand in triumph and disgust, "Nikki and her buddies haven't held an election
since 1980. They have no credibility. None. Zero. It's
over, Nikki." He dares anyone to say we're a divided
community.

But now, this very morning, less than ten days after
Toronto City Hall gives the NJCL its grant, that is exactly what's being said by the most powerful and credible
voices in Canada—the major media.

If it were just a question of one step forward and two
steps backward, we would still be doing a recognizable
dance with Government. But this morning's step is a
plunge off the deck. The biggest shock wave thus far has
hit our ship.

Anna comes dashing in to *Bridge* and collapses into
our arms. "They've done it. They've pulled it off." She's
fighting back her tears.

The event was just a blip on national television's
noon news but the message is a full-bodied frontal assault on the NJCL. We've been riveted to Morty's radio
since we first heard.

It happened at ten o'clock this morning. Nikki and a
handful of elderly Japanese Canadians, plus government

officials and members of Parliament from all three parties, the Conservatives, the Liberals and the NDP, staged a media event proving that two separate national organizations, in open rivalry with each other, claim to represent our community.

"Two national bodies? National!"

One, the new "Moderate Majority of Japanese Canadians," belongs to Nikki. The other, the "young militant radical NJCL," is ours.

Whom did Nikki enlist for the press conference? Her mother? The bowling group? Aunt Emily must know every issei in Toronto and she can't think who would go. Perhaps the rabid-dog writer with his disgusting prose was there.

Nikki stood in front of the TV cameras and proclaimed to all of Canada, not only that her brand-new Moderate Majority organization exists, but that it's already meeting with the minister. "We're on the same wavelength as Government," Nikki said, "but this is not a happy day for us because it shows we're a divided community." The minister was standing solemnly beside Nikki and added, "I'm reluctant to try to resolve the situation until the Japanese Canadian community speaks with one voice."

"It's grotesque," Aunt Emily whispered.

I can't bear the thought of the shock and unhappiness across the country among all the people who have been laboring all this time for the sake of our "one voice." But there's no question about it now. We've lost. It isn't only the League's actual unity that matters. It's the perception of unity that counts. And the perception is lost. How do we fight the authority of national media? How do we fight the Government of Canada and all three parties? How has Nikki managed this spectacular lie? We heard she hired a media strategist. They must have planned this surprise announcement months ago. Our "hard facts" in Toronto, our signed statements, our questionnaires, our public meetings, all our labor is in vain.

Morty is looking vulnerable as he squats in front of his radio, scanning for more news. He's hardly said a word since Anna arrived.

Brian rushed down to the paper the instant he heard, to see what further shock wave would be coming across the wires. "If all the major TV was there, so was the press," he told Anna. He'll phone us here the moment he picks anything up.

Aunt Emily's hands are folded over her abdomen and she's sitting in Morty's chair, rocking lightly.

It's long past lunchtime but no one's hungry. Morty is at the worktable and is trying to carry on with *Bridge* work, but he can't. His head is down on his arms. Aunt Emily, at Morty's phone, has been calling but not reaching MPs in Ottawa, calling the League president, calling the press and media. She's going the step beyond the finish line, believing we've lost the race, believing that Government's effort to dismiss us has now been accomplished, believing that her calls will likely be heard as simply more proof of divisiveness and rancor. This is Aunt Emily's last battle in Canada. She's lost all her wars thus far.

Her voice is deadly straight as she talks to the news desk of the CBC. She's an ancient warrior, still carrying the shield of faith and the sword of our truth, both now obsolete in this high-tech war. She's saying the media's

been duped by a bogus organization with no membership. "I've got documentation."

Next she calls the politician priest from our church,
telling him that the League will be holding press conferences to refute Nikki's claims. The NJCL across the
country is contacting allies in the media. "We're not finished yet," she says.

At three o'clock, Brian calls. We rush into Cedric's
office and breathe down Anna's neck as she relays the
news. A Canadian Press report from Ottawa has come
in. We want the exact words.

Her rapid scrawl covers four pages and we are as-
saulted by every damning word. "Ottawa — MPs were
lobbied Tuesday by a group of Japanese Canadians . . ."
It's all just as we've been hearing. Nikki's "breakaway
group, comprised of older people, has a position similar
to that of the Progressive Conservative government,
which is that there should be group, rather than individual, compensation in the form of a Japanese Canadian
memorial foundation."

"Money talks," Morty says.

Anna holds up her hand for quiet as she listens to
what's been happening down at the paper. Brian stopped
the report from spreading further, she says. He ran with
it to a senior editor and the two of them dashed down
the length of the newsroom to kill the story. We can,
Brian assures us, at least breathe on this one count.
Nikki's new "organization" won't hit print in *The Globe
and Mail*.

37

Nothing is going to stop Nikki. And nothing is going to stop the NJCL. Nothing, I suspect, will ever stop either. We're going to go on and on forever on our chosen paths to oblivion. And when we get there, I imagine we'll look at each other and wonder what on earth we were trying to accomplish back in our little lives.

Here in the mid-1980s, we're still hacking our way through the wild woods, struggling to better the human condition, or whatever it is we tell ourselves we're doing.

The Tory government in its wisdom appoints its second, and rougher, tougher Minister of Multiculturalism. He's forthright in his favoring of Nikki and his opposition to us. For its part, the NJCL is carrying on. An economic-losses study is under way. A national questionnaire reveals overwhelming support for individual compensation. As for Nikki, I have no idea what she's about. She must surely believe that she's doing the right, the necessary, the sacrificial thing and that history is on her side. Why else would she go on?

Aunt Emily has been obsessed with trying to reach her. Once she stood for an hour in the lobby of Nikki's apartment building. And now here we are this afternoon, trotting along Bloor Street on our way back from the printers, when lo, there's Nikki in the flesh, sitting at a booth in a brightly lit café having coffee with Dr. Clive Stinson.

Aunt Emily charges in instantly and plunks herself down. What can they say? Nikki is startled and not at all pleased to see us. I stand somewhat embarrassedly to the side. I haven't seen Dr. Stinson for a while but he hasn't changed. Same thin rigid neck. Same dark suit and tie.

The café walls are a scissoring pattern of splinter-shaped mirrors. Booths, dishes, windows, people, all are reflected in bits and fragments, and the waiters walking past can be seen simultaneously coming and going.

Aunt Emily gestures impatiently for me to sit. "I must have called you fifty times," she says to Nikki.

At least fifty. I watched her once punching the automatic redial button. She said that, like Churchill, she would never give up.

Nikki lights a cigarette and eyes her warily. Her elbow rests on the edge of a large pot overflowing with a luxurious fern and her wrist and fingers with their long red pointed nails are perched against the green, like a bird of paradise.

"We must talk, Nikki. Things can't go on this way. Your claim to represent all the seniors right across Canada . . ." Aunt Emily throws up her hands. "It really is too much."

Nikki glances uneasily at Dr. Stinson and blows a whoosh of smoke out of the side of her mouth. He's frowning with disapproval at Aunt Emily.

"A divided community. Is that what you think the issei want?" Aunt Emily has had her questions bottled up for so long they're about to spew themselves out all over the shiny black table.

Nikki draws back. She's taking a second to compose herself. Then she clears her throat and taps her cigarette in the square glass ashtray. "The issei don't want the community to fight with Government," she begins, her voice tight, restrained. "They want redress to go away. Just to go away! You people won't accept an apology unless there's cash. It's disgusting. It truly is. It's blackmail."

"The council doesn't want a meaningless apology, Nikki, they . . ."

Nikki's reaction is swift, her glare as aggressive as her sharp fingernails. "Who are the council? There are thousands of us who want nothing to do with them."

"In a democratic society . . ."

"In a democratic society," Nikki pounces, "the majority's wishes are done. I know the majority doesn't want what you want."

Aunt Emily is not flinching. "And this is what you've been telling the minister. A quiet deal between you and Ottawa. You really think that's what the majority wants?"

We're in danger of becoming a public spectacle. I know Aunt Emily is capable of losing control. She's stomping hard. If politics is the art of watching toes, Nikki's superior. She's a toreador with a raging bull.

"People want to be cooperative." Nikki is suddenly smooth. "They want peace. They want forgiveness." She quivers her cape, then steps swiftly aside as Aunt Emily lunges. Then up with the cape again. She's talking about "the punks, like Morty and Anna," and Aunt Emily roars.

"Punks! The brightest lights in our community!"

From Nikki's point of view, the NJCL is indeed dominated by "young militant radical punks" who are "crass and barbaric." She says promoting the idea of individual compensation is the real sellout. It's spreading false expectations. And it's ridiculous as an idea. Equal chunks of money to each of us have nothing to do with individual losses. "And here's something else Clive pointed out. Canada has always put the group ahead of the individual. We're not Americans. We don't have to mimic them."

Nikki's idea of group compensation, I'm thinking, might have been acceptable to the council if she'd been willing to be accountable.

"So you'd like to eliminate the individual component of a group package. What was it, Nikki? Why didn't you stay and argue your case? Couldn't you have been the loyal opposition, as we all are from time to time?"

"And work with those thugs?" Nikki laughs thinly. "Impossible. I mean, ask Clive. He knows Morty. He knows what they're like."

Dr. Stinson has been watching the match with little amusement. He turns slightly now to face Aunt Emily.

"I would say the League isn't so much undemocratic

as impractical. No government is going to consider individual compensation. We'd go bankrupt. The Chinese.
Ukrainians. The Germans."

"People are really getting hurt by this, Emily." Nikki
is solidly alongside Dr. Stinson. "It's immoral to make
people think they might get money. Government won't
set a precedent."

"That's exactly correct," Dr. Stinson nods rapidly.
"Government is not prepared to consider it."

"You mean we should let the precedent for wrong
stand, but not set a precedent for doing right?"

"Emily, you simply don't understand Government."
Nikki taps the table for emphasis. "You're not realistic.
All you people jumping on board—just because you
smell money. . . . Oh! The greed!"

"Oh yes, there is greed involved," Dr. Stinson adds
quickly. "Unquestionably."

"Greed?" Aunt Emily jabs her finger at Dr. Stinson.
"You're saying *we're* greedy?"

The waiter, a thin young man, walks past with fresh
coffee and Nikki pushes her cup forward to have it filled.

"Well now, I suppose in these matters the truth is a
question of perspective." Dr. Stinson smiles his quick
mirthless smile as he makes his pronouncements from
on high. "I would say that a cooperative attitude is what's
called for here. That's what really matters."

"We should cooperate, right or wrong." Aunt Emily is
not disguising her sarcasm.

"I happen to believe Government is right and this
issue is not as all-important as you, perhaps naturally,
Emily, feel it to be." Sarcasm is being countered by condescension. "There are others in Canada besides your
people. Nikki has pointed out, quite rightly, that if you'd

been in a different country you might all be dead. After all, it was a war."

"A war!" Aunt Emily cries. "It was racism! Racism, Stinson!" She brings her fist down on the table. "Racism!" She's prepared to say the same thing a hundred thousand times to a hundred thousand people.

Nothing will dislodge Dr. Stinson from his position. He's a statue, a permanent monument to the war. "Well, what had to be done had to be done. You must admit, it was relatively humane. If we'd had Germans on the east coast, the same thing would have happened." Nikki nods as he speaks. "There was a report circulating at the time. And a genuine fear of spies. The Japanese government was out to recruit anyone they could."

Sitting this close to Aunt Emily, I can almost feel her rise in temperature. Her body heaves with a deep sigh. "There was a report circulating," she says, looking at him as if he weren't here.

I've seen a copy of the secret report somewhere in her files. What was it called? "Japanese Activities in British Columbia"? Something like that. It's a ludicrous portrait of our "dangerous" community. Some of our most outstanding community leaders were listed and labeled as subversive, suspicious, potentially traitorous. The good, the innocent, the passionately loyal were viewed with fear. Dan was on that list. An aura of mysterious power and evil surrounded the most innocent acts. Two men were seen discussing the news and were overheard speaking in Japanese. A pretty woman was particularly suspect because she associated too much with white people. A First World War vet was dangerous because he said of the conditions in Hastings Park, where we were kept like cattle, "Food no good. Government bad. God damn." Neither speech nor silence nor acts of friendship were viewed as anything but treacherous. And nothing, not anything, was able to transform that perception.

Aunt Emily looks tired as she turns away from Dr. Stinson. "All I want to know, Nikki, is, what about the community? You know and I know and the Gallup poll knows we just can't guess at what a community is or wants or feels. We have to have a process. Democracy. It's not perfect, but the League is the only national body we've got and you know this very very well. Forget Government for a moment. . . ."

"Well. . . ." Nikki rubs the back of her neck and smiles fraternally at Dr. Stinson. "I certainly can't leave Clive out of this. . . ."

"But the community, Nikki." Aunt Emily is pleading now. "You're part of us. We agree on basic issues. What Government did was a serious serious crime."

Nikki lights another cigarette and pauses as she inhales thoughtfully.

"There are many Canadians," Dr. Stinson interjects in her stead, "—and I have had conversations with a number of them—there are many who would object to that statement. It wasn't a crime. Nothing illegal was done by Government."

"True. It was legal." Aunt Emily turns back to him reluctantly. "That's what makes it worse. It wasn't just Government-sanctioned, it was Government-initiated. It was wrong wrong wrong. Let that be stated and let right be done."

"It *was* done." Dr. Stinson is secure in his conviction and defending history against the falsifier. "The leadership did what it had to do. I'm not saying it was pleasant for you, but there's no question—if Japanese troops had landed, your community would have turned against Canada."

"That's a lie."

Dr. Stinson has spoken the unendurable word. He is calling us traitors. This is the still smoldering war to which Dan and Aunt Emily have given their days and nights, their hearts, their minds and their lives. Dr. Stinson's perception is the ghost against whom we fight.

"But come now, Emily. Every political party agreed to the safety measures—the churches—everyone agreed. We can't pass judgment in hindsight on men of good will. They felt the threat. That was reason enough. And you know, I've talked with a number of your people— people Nikki knows—and they tell me it was a good thing. Fundamentally, it was right. We protected your people. You can't rewrite history and make something a crime that never was."

Aunt Emily is staring right through Dr. Stinson. "Not everyone agreed it was a good thing. I didn't. Putting victims in jail to protect them isn't the kind of protection you can call 'good.'" She slaps the table wearily. "For forty years we've been silent. Nothing in the schools. What you're saying is, you want to keep it that way. Silence makes for good government."

Dr. Stinson draws back stiffly. "Let's not misunderstand each other, Emily. I know innocent people suffered. That's what war's all about. Even today Government expropriates land. But that isn't the point. What you need to understand is that justice isn't served by special-interest groups making history up for their own selfish ends. It's not justice you're after. It's advantage over other groups. It's political privilege. So I say the redress movement is wrong. You're abusing the political process."

"If you're saying, Clive, that we're seeking privilege and not justice, you're conveniently forgetting where privilege really lies."

Dr. Stinson crosses and uncrosses his long thin legs uncomfortably. There isn't enough room in this booth for all of us. "But your community doesn't need money. If you were sincerely interested in justice, you'd concern yourselves with the genuinely disadvantaged."

"Clive's right." Nikki reenters the fray with this latest shot. "And most NJCL people aren't really interested in this community either. They weren't even involved with other Japanese Canadians before money got in the picture."

Is she thinking of people like me, who weren't involved with the community before? But it isn't money that drew me. What would Nikki think if she knew I'd only become involved because of Cedric? And Cedric was drawn by Aunt Emily, who was drawn by Min. It's probably true that it's love, not money, that makes the world go round.

"Try to understand, Nikki," Aunt Emily says, "our community seeks a genuine relationship. We have to use appropriate symbols. That's all money means to us."

"If symbolism was all that mattered," Dr. Stinson shoots back, "you'd have accepted a token amount. Government made a significant offer. No, the League is after more money, there's no question whatsoever on that score. But it's too late. You should have dealt with the issue within, say, something like five years. Forty years after the event, you can't expect taxpayers to foot the bill. If I was swindled out of my life savings forty years ago, should I expect taxpayers to compensate me today?"

Perhaps it's Aunt Emily's tiredness that's making her voice sound so empty. "First," she says, with her hands covering her eyes, "stolen money doesn't belong in the national pie. Secondly, yes, Government's offer was significant. It signified that seven lost years amounted to one pair of shoes each. Thirdly, the process was wrong. Unilateral proposals don't work. And finally, as to yourself—if Government swindled you for no other reason than that you're English—if you and all your English Canadian cousins were denied your rights for seven years and you had no access to the courts and no vote, if all English people in this country were scattered and Englishness was so despised that you had to hide everything English about yourself—yes—if after forty years your English leadership was trying for the first time to be heard—yes, you should fight. You'd never regain the inheritance you could have passed on to your children— which has now been handed on to some other racial group—but yes, you should strive to reveal that evil for what it is."

Dr. Stinson draws back. "Well, Emily, let's be realistic. I can tell you there's not enough money to go around." He lowers his gaze. "And you should understand this—your movement is headed for quite a backlash. If it was ever revealed—if what Nikki tells me is right—now, I personally believe the majority of you were loyal Canadians, but there was a sizable number—Nikki says it was a majority—that were loyal to the enemy. . . ."

There is a shocked silence as I glance at Aunt Emily

and catch her eyes. A majority of Japanese Canadians loyal to the enemy? A majority?

"We wouldn't want that word to get out to the public, would we?" Dr. Stinson continues. "Just think for a moment. There was a good reason the whole thing happened."

Aunt Emily doesn't say a word but I know what she's thinking. The lie is alive in the world. It was there in Nazi Germany. It's in South Africa. In Latin America. In every country in the world. This is why redress matters. Because there are many many people intent on defending the oppressor's rights no matter what the truth, and they are in places of power. Not one of us, not a single one of us, was ever found guilty of a disloyal act against Canada. But the accusation remains.

I can feel Aunt Emily's deep despair as she faces Nikki. "So, the majority of Japanese Canadians were disloyal to Canada," she says quietly.

Nikki is squirming and tapping her cigarette nervously, her red fingernails clicking. She gulps the last bit of coffee. "Whatever you're thinking," she says, "I can tell you the NJCL will go down in history as a bunch of opportunists and vultures who tried to blackmail the community and the government for a few dollars."

Dr. Stinson is looking satisfied as he agrees. He says offhandedly, as an additional shot, that acquiescing to the clamor of minorities leads to anarchy and the rule of chaos. Aunt Emily, I know, believes that empowering the oppressed leads to a new day of peace where the moral law is written within. Dr. Stinson has faith in government and in the rightness of order and might. Aunt Emily has faith in the educated heart and the still small voice that wakens her at night.

She and Nikki are staring blankly at each other, two Japanese Canadian women, one glamorous, one dumpy, one middle-aged, one old, and this is where they meet, as opponents in a ring. In our corner the NJCL cheers and shouts. I can't see who fills the rest of the hall, nor can I see any referees. But right or wrong, wrong or right, Nikki sides with Clive Stinson, I side with my aunt, Dr. Stinson sides with the minister and the people in the government. Somewhere in our journeys, our paths may meet again. And somewhere at some cross-roads we may face a judge.

38

SUNDAY AFTERNOON, JULY 1986.

I'm late. There was an accident on the subway line.

Couldn't get a cab. I ran into Min shambling along in

the opposite direction. I was in such a hurry I didn't

stop. "Coming?" I called. Min had a wild look in his

eyes.

There must be well over two hundred people in this

church basement. Nikki, in a cool green dress, sits be-

hind a long table on a stage beside another woman and a

man. Some Sunday school banners are stacked behind

them and one shows the wing of a dove, with the letters "od Is Love" in wavery black letters beneath.

If I weren't here in the doorway, slightly out of breath, my black shoulder purse against my hip, I don't think I would believe it's actually happening.

It's been six years since the last election. One was due in 1982, but no one was interested. In 1984 people began agitating and by 1985 there was enough foam and froth to plug up the city drains. Now today, in the heat of a midsummer afternoon, finally finally, a Toronto JC League election is taking place. We'll know, at last, if Nikki has any support at all.

I was lost a few minutes ago, bumbling around the basement hallway maze. It was so quiet I didn't know I was in the right place till I spotted the two demure nisei women at a table. Things look organized. There's a tray of sheets and red, blue and yellow slips of paper. I sign in. Pick up the agenda. One of the women whispers, "That's all you have to do."

Anna, close to the entrance, gestures me to a seat beside her.

The impatience is visible as the treasurer's report drones on. People sit with arms folded, hands aggressively on knees. Several women fan themselves. There's an unusual level of fidgeting. It's been a long wait for this day. "Morty moved that we go straight to nominations," Anna whispers. "No luck."

I know that "our gang" has a full slate ready to present. Morty and Anna both said they would run.

Marion, Aunt Emily and Ken are a few rows ahead of us. I saw Dan in an aisle seat near the middle of the room. Morty is dead center at the front. Everyone I have ever met at Anna's house is here, plus artists and entertainers who over the years have helped to raise funds. Most would probably vote for our candidates, though one never knows. Here and there people hold various colored slips of paper. "Those are for proxy votes," Anna whispers, and shrugs. She points out one of Dan's war vet friends who hasn't been to a meeting in thirty years. The row opposite us is half full of issei men.

People are so anxious to move to the elections, no one questions any of the reports. As soon as one ends, someone moves that it be accepted. Then, at twenty-three minutes after four, the election begins and Nikki announces a single slate of candidates.

Dan has his hand up. "Madame Chairperson," he says, standing, "your announcement in last week's paper said that you would accept written nominations till Friday and that there would be no nominations from the floor." Trust Dan to get to the point clearly, in his grammatically perfect way. He always sounds as if he's reading from a written text. "Accordingly we drove that evening to your apartment and placed a list of candidates under your door. What I would like to know now is, where is that list? If we're to have an election, Madame Chairperson, let's have an election."

One gray-haired man in the front row turns around in surprise. "What do you mean, no nominations from the floor?"

Nikki hands the microphone to the thin timid-looking woman beside her. "I'm the person who was supposed to get all the lists and I didn't get one from you, Dan," she says in a squeaky little-girl voice.

Dan holds up a sheaf of papers. "I can distribute the

list right now," he says, beginning to walk down the aisle toward the stage. Hands are outstretched and Morty, who also has some sheets, stands and holds them up.

"Hey, this is the League, isn't it?" a man in a dark suit calls out. "What's the reason for not having nominations right here?" He has his hand out and Dan gives him a bundle. The papers are being moved rapidly and somewhat erratically about the room.

"Yeah, we always had nominations from the floor before."

The war vet who hasn't been to a meeting in thirty years has his hand up. "I've driven over three hundred miles to this election and I want to nominate Emily Kato. . . ."

The two women at the entrance table are looking alarmed, their eyes darting back and forth from the stage to the audience. Nikki holds her hand up for attention as a growing rumble begins to take over. "There are a number of people who aren't here," Nikki begins. "We've assigned proxy votes to certain people. . . ."

A man waves a yellow slip of paper about. Morty jumps to his feet and shouts, "That's crazy." Nikki points at Morty and commands, "You're going to have to sit down." She's in command here. She intends to have order. She brings the microphone back close to her mouth and her voice blasts through the loudspeaker. "Only card-carrying members can vote at this election, and if you haven't got this green card . . . ," she says, holding one up high.

"What green card?" Anna asks.

"Most of you people here," Nikki calls out, "are not paid-up members for this year. . . ."

There's an instant murmur from the floor. Several people have their hands up. One man holds an open wallet. A man who is handing out sheets shouts, "I object. I'm a lifetime member. I'm a former president. Those are not the rules."

Nikki interrupts and asks him to sit down. Dan's deep voice shouts. "Let him speak." Diplomatic Dan, driven to shouting.

"You never told me about a green-card membership!" Morty shouts. "I'm a lifetime member. You can't disenfranchise me!"

Nikki's voice through the loudspeaker is slow and deliberate. "We have the right . . . ," she repeats several times, drowning out a woman who is telling her to sit down sit down. "We're going to proceed to voting on the candidates."

Half a dozen people have their hands up but Nikki is ignoring them. Morty, who is standing, raises both arms. "This is outrageous!"

One man gets up and pulls his cap down hard. "Stupid. Stupid," he mutters as he walks out of the room. "I've never seen anything so stupid."

"We're not accepting new memberships today." Nikki's voice takes on her familiar singsong quality.

Morty has moved to the foot of the stage with both arms still raised. "I was at the last election in 1980," he's shouting.

"You're out of order!" Nikki shouts back. "I'm asking you to take your seat right now!"

"And there's been no general meeting since then," Morty continues.

"The mike!" one man calls out. "Morty, get the mike!"

The health-care people are looking on wide-eyed, one of the men clutching his head in both hands.

"The Japanese Canadian League," Morty shouts, and the room is attentive in spite of Nikki. "The Japanese Canadian League has never before, never before, in all its history, denied the vote to Japanese Canadians or refused nominations from the floor, paid membership or no paid membership. Its mandate, its sole reason for existence, is to serve—not to bully—Japanese Canadians. . . ." A burst of applause. "We have the right of membership," Morty goes on, "because we are Japanese Canadians. That's all that matters here. This is our organization and every single one of us belongs to it. No one interested enough to show up to a meeting has ever been denied a vote. And I demand that we have a free and democratic election here today." There's a passionate clap of applause and several hands are up to speak.

Morty isn't finished. "People like Emily and Dan were founding members back in the forties, and you can't tell me they can't vote in 1986 because someone suddenly dreamt up some secret green card." He's drowned out by another thunderclap. "And not only that, not only that, but the executives' terms expired four years ago. . . ." More applause.

Nikki has one hand on her hip, one hand over her mouth as she waits for the applause to die down, then her voice speaks confidently and calmly through the loudspeaker. "My lawyers tell me we can hold this election according to any rules we want. We don't have a constitution and . . ." I can barely make out what she's saying through the chorus of groans.

"Shame on you. Shame on you," one old woman is interjecting in a high voice.

Some people are glancing about nervously. Others are grimly clutching their colored slips of paper and looking dead ahead. A few professional people, a doctor, a professor, are glancing at one another and shaking their heads. I can't guess which people here are Nikki's supporters, except that I imagine the people with colored slips of paper must be.

Nikki is ignoring everyone. "We don't have a constitution," she repeats, "and the National JCL does whatever it wants. We can do whatever we want. We have the right to oppose the NJCL and all you NJCL people can go and hold your own elections. And right now I'm going to ask voting members to raise their cards if they are in favor of electing the slate of candidates."

There's pandemonium at the registration table. A young woman has jumped up and grabbed a bunch of colored slips. A man is wrestling them out of her hands. Morty rushes over and a shoving match is under way. It's bedlam. Nikki speaks into the microphone. "Hold up your cards so we can count them. Hold them up if you're in favor of the candidates."

The issei men opposite us look frightened and confused. Three of them hold up their yellow slips timidly. The man who is struggling with Morty stops and moves down the aisles, pointing as he counts. Dan and Morty are also counting. At the most, it looks as if twenty or so hands are up holding various colored slips.

"Okay, we got the count. Those opposed." A dense forest of hands leaps up. These include a handful of people holding colored cards. A number of people, notably the health-care group, have not voted at all but are frowning, staring at the confusion. Many are simply aghast. Nikki is looking around the room as though she's counting.

"Don't count those. Not this row. Not that one," I can hear the official counter saying as he and a woman walk past ignoring Anna's hand and mine.

Nikki leans down from the stage to consult with the counters, then holds up her hand for attention. The room quietens. Her voice is expressionless as she declares the results. "Without taking into account the unlimited proxy votes assigned to the secretary, the candidates have been elected by a majority count of sixty-eight for and twenty-three against."

There's an instant gasp from the crowd. Anna and I stare at one another, more amazed than appalled. This is Nikki's election victory. How will she describe it? Will she say she had to endure an attempt to overthrow her by ruffians who packed the meeting? Will she say she's been able to preserve the "cooperative" voice of Japanese Canadians?

One man stands and shouts, "Outrageous," as Nikki walks rapidly to the door. But others are too incredulous to do much more than stare blankly at one another in this tiny imperfect corner of the democratic world.

39

Morty is beside himself for weeks after "that revolting display of demagoguery." He wants to organize a proper election. So does Anna. But Ken says the Toronto JCL is so discredited now that it's pointless. "And anyway, it's not going to make any difference to Government."

The most recent Minister of Multiculturalism, our fourth so far, has said he wants to consult and find out for himself what's involved. We're having to start all over again, as we do with every new minister, sending letters, petitions, asking for meetings, declaring that the NJCL is our only legitimate and democratically elected national body. When will we be believed? In 1984, the Liberal minister simply ignored us. The next, a Tory, dismissed us. The last one opposed us. What will this new one be like? Wearily wearily we straggle on, disappointment having become a way of life, as this minister, too, holds meetings with Nikki.

Only the hard-core, the bloody-minded, now remain in the redress toil. It's a desperate yet strangely exhilarating sensation, running with the dwindling pack. If we weren't before, we certainly are now, militantly, indelibly NJCL. We're probably radioactive and glow in the dark. We hear the League in Vancouver is also, like us, wretched with labor, still holding meetings, still rallying the disheartened community.

Morty wants to march on Ottawa. He wants to take his grandfather in his wheelchair and his two dogs. But there isn't a person around who thinks we can stage it. We're not the marching kind.

In July 1987, after talks break down again, Morty publishes the NJCL's official litany.

November 21, 1984. Government petitioned for redress.

December 1984–June 1985. Intermittent talks with multicultural ministry. Results: negotiations denied, restitution denied.

June 5, 1985. Second minister offers to memorialize Japanese Canadian experience. NJCL asks for apology and negotiations on restitution.

August 1985–May 1986. Talks with third minister. Results: negotiations denied, restitution denied.

May 9, 1986. Income and property losses set at "not less than $443 million" in 1986 dollars. NJCL asks for repeal of War Measures Act, acknowledgment of injustices and restitution.

May 28, 1986. Minister terminates all discussion on redress.

July 1986–July 1987. Talks with fourth minister. Results: negotiations denied, restitution denied.

July 11, 1987. Minister offers apology and $12 million community fund. NJCL asks for negotiations on restitution. Minister terminates all discussion on redress.

We're back to square one again. Have we ever been anywhere else? Almost mechanically, we accept this latest defeat. Our leaders, we now know, will withstand Government's will to crush them. Whatever storms rage above, or whatever floods of futility devastate us here below, they will endure with their dreams undimmed—a community made strong, and the forces of racism cowed.

But the cost to us, their supporters, is heavy. The laws of oppression are at work, as failure in the public realm is translated into blame close at hand. We hear the disturbing news that someone wants to oust the president, and we catch that slightly nauseating scent of something raw. A type of blood lust is taking hold.

Here in Toronto, people are visibly stressed. Ken looks thoroughly depressed. Thin Marion is losing even more weight and her eyes are puffy from sleeplessness. And now Min too has disappeared.

The Clarke Institute of Psychiatry.

Trot trot through the lobby, past the receptionist, up the elevator to the ninth floor, and what a long time it's been since I visited a hospital. Aunt Emily is walking ahead of Cedric and me.

We've reached the end of a long corridor. There's a plumpish young woman with raggedy hair glowering at us as we walk toward her. Near the middle of the next hall, a young man, gazing blankly, stands by a telephone, dialing and dialing compulsively. We pass a TV room. A woman inside looks utterly forlorn. A little match girl. The last waif in the orphanage.

We pass more doors, turn another corner and come to a room with two people and three beds, and there he is, sitting on the farthest bed, his face barely recognizable. He looks up at us as we stand in the doorway. Beneath the brown irises, the whites of his eyes show. His head is lowered and he watches us as if through the top of his head. He has an expression of great mistrust, or as if he is at the bottom of a well and cannot see. I almost recoil.

Aunt Emily approaches him. This stranger. Cedric goes halfway into the room, his hands raised in a gesture of welcome or inquiry. I wait in the doorway.

So this is where Min lands when he drops from view.

All those weeks when he wasn't around, I assumed he'd withdrawn like a sensible soul. But he's been here—in and out as a patient at the Clarke.

Min rubs a hand rapidly over his head. His eyes are fixed on an empty chair in the hall. He leans forward staring intently. Then, abruptly, he stands and puts his mouth to Aunt Emily's ear. One hand grips her shoulder convulsively. Her arms encircle him and Min clings as if he's drowning. Cedric approaches, putting his arms around them both gently.

How much more accurate it is to address a person by touch than by words. The spontaneous warmth is there, unedited in the body's parchment. Better the instant language of limbs than the stilted messages we form and reform with the tongue.

Min steps back and looks over at me. His feet march up down, up down on the spot like a small child's.

There's an elderly man sitting on the bed near the door. He stares through us, eyebrows lifted high, eyes wide. White tufts of hair stick out from the sides of his head like wings. White hair, white bed, white walls.

Cedric beckons to me as Min sits down on his bed. Aunt Emily pulls up a chair. Such suspicion and tension in Min's face. Cedric takes Min's hand and I join them and Min grips mine tightly as I sit on his other side on the bed. I'm aware of a gnawing within. Some ratlike activity. Something unpermitted within needs to weep.

Someone in the hall coughs loudly. A staff person strides briskly into the room and briskly out again. A siren screams down Spadina Avenue. Min's breathing becomes rapid and uneven for a few moments as he rocks unrhythmically, and then he becomes rigid, his hand even tighter.

Peace. Grant us peace.

The traffic sounds are the city's murmurings and from out of its depths Friendship comes by. We have come to the harbor—from Powell Street, from the B.C. camp, from Granton and from Gary's Hideaway. And we sit together here. It may be ten minutes. Or five. Or more.

I think of Min cut off from his family, his family cut off from the community, the community cut off from the whole country. He's walked so much on the edges of worlds, he lives now in this desperate fragility. What betrayals he has known—Min the young criminal from Powell Street, whose one crime was to try to go home. It was in the winter of 1943 that he walked out of the camp one afternoon. He was carrying some paintings wrapped in Christmas paper. He trudged through the snow. He was caught before he reached home. He was jailed for a year.

Was it the snow that he was unable to overcome? The overwhelming avalanche of whiteness within and without—the shame, the suffocating rage, the white whiteness everywhere. Stealthy and persistent as a shadow, it stalked and pursued him.

He was released after a year, broken and without tools. He rejected the world of art. And he's walked, like many of us, for forty years in a white white world.

The snow has grown old and bored over time. It invites him, it invites us all to a party. There's a multicultural event in the foyer of the Arts Center where we sing pretty songs. Lullay thou little tiny child. We tell people we're integrated here and get along in our neighborhoods. Then we step from the stage and disappear while the snow carries on. And on and on. One does not inconvenience the everywhere softly—the everywhere such lightness falling. The snow is a spell.

We hardly know what the choices are as we walk under the overcast sky. We long to belong. We cry out our names and the air everywhere absorbs the sounds. We shout and snow falls from our lungs. Like a cloud in winter unburdening itself, we seek to shake free of the heavy cold weight, but there, lurking in the shadows, in the everywhere snow, is someone we trust. The snow enters us through someone we trust. Our memories disappear.

"Lots of visitors today?" the nurse asks cheerfully as she walks in with her trayful of pills. She waits as Min drinks from a tiny paper cup.

This is the place where hope comes in the form of a pill, or a white powder, or a liquid potion that plunges into your body and declares itself your savior. This is where your sovereign, who dwells within, lies bound and gagged and waits without sleep for a rescuer. This is where you are homeless and you no longer dream of the home that no longer is.

And this is where Min sits on his white bed, unkempt and small. Min of the interiority, of the too much seen and unseen. Min, the painter of a translucent bird. He does not sing. He is hidden on this island, in this foraging rain. And all the while, unknown to us all, his canvas teems with invisible wings.

"Where's Min?" we ask in passing.

40

Somewhere along our windswept journeyings, we come to a place where the wells have gone dry. There are no maps, roads, explanations.

I never thought I'd see Aunt Emily turning into a brooder, but that's what is happening. The little red hen has become a brooding hen. She sits and stares. She's venturing more and more into inner space. "Where are you, Min?" she'll suddenly ask. "Where's ground control?"

The League too is in some darker region of the universe these days, on a cold inner planet. It's being ambushed, Aunt Emily says, by a thousand betrayals—political betrayals, personal betrayals, betrayals of values—from the top down, from the bottom up, from the outside and from within. She's trying to place her turmoil into some larger grid of understanding—to label and so to contain it. She says she's seen the way it happens all over the world. People are sold out by the false kiss of friendship—by governments, by community leaders. The Great Pretense takes hold. Strategies focus on manipulations for the sake of appearance.

Nikki, after all, is only a mirror, no more or less deluded than are we all in our vain imaginings. Together, we are the weak and the strong, living by the sword and perishing by it. We claw one another, desperate to be right, to be victors, to be cooperative, to belong. And all the while we betray the weak, we betray one another, we betray the truth in ourselves and we hardly know that we do.

I've been up to Aunt Emily's apartment with groceries recently. Mostly Japanese food. She hasn't been well. Today, Anna, Mrs. Makino and I are bringing her a jar of umeboshi, red salty plums, and some shiso flakes to have with her hot tea and rice.

"I'm probably contagious," her gravelly voice says on the intercom.

"Who cares," Anna says, and we go up.

Aunt Emily looks alarmingly pale to me, bundled up in her old robe, staring like a trapped animal. She says she's having stomach flu.

"Nutrients for old roots," Anna says, offering the food.

We go to sit out on the sky-high balcony, though it's not that warm this afternoon. Mrs. Makino says we should eat Japanese food when we're not feeling well, because our bodies are Japanese. She puts her perfect mind/body hand on Aunt Emily's back, massaging it with her firm, knowing touch.

The small balcony barely holds the four of us, Anna and I on kitchen stools, Aunt Emily and Mrs. Makino on the patio lounges.

"Fighting fighting, too much fight fight, no good redress," Mrs. Makino suggests. "Better more peace. Better not get sick, Emiri-san."

Time has gone backward, Aunt Emily says. We're in the forties, lost in bewilderments again. People are long past hoping that anything will be done by Government. Not after such prolonged, such intense efforts. And paranoia is an epidemic. The mistrust has spread to our vital internal organs.

"Could Emily be talking to Ottawa?" Dan was asked. Government knows our strategy even as it's being discussed. Spies must be everywhere.

No matter what fingers are pointing her way, Aunt Emily remains firmly wedded to the League. When it's wounded, she's wounded. If it died, I think she'd die.

Anna says Aunt Emily should write the "real" story of redress. But Aunt Emily says there is no such thing. There are as many stories as there are individuals. And there's nothing all that special about the Japanese Canadian community either.

"Do you think Japanese Americans are having the same trouble we are?" Anna asks.

"No doubt," Aunt Emily says. "Magnified by a factor of ten."

But the Japanese American campaign is light-years ahead of ours. They have a formidable team of World

War Two veterans in high places. Just a few days ago, on
September 17, the American House of Representatives
passed a bill proposing $1.2 billion in reparations.

"It sticks in my craw," Anna says, "that Canada's
been worse on this issue."

Japanese American families, I've heard, were kept in-
tact, and their internment was canceled before the end
of the war. Their property was not seized by their government. Nor were there policies of dispersal and exile.

"Still, I'd rather be a Canadian," Anna says.

Aunt Emily is staring at the clouds as Anna talks.
There's a cluster above that looks like a turtle. It's rapidly
losing its legs and will soon be part of a larger cloud.

"Bit by bit we're being eaten up—as a community, as
a country—because others define us," Aunt Emily says,
"with their movies, their realities, their news. We can
hardly know ourselves." She looks so tired lying in her
lounge chair, her head rolling wearily on a cushion. "Our
story is about how our stories disappear."

Anna says of all the horror stories our community has
lived through, it's the betrayal of the issei in these, their
very last days, that is the worst. Some of the strongest,
the most politically conscious, are bowed down by a
sense of shame. Their deepest belief in harmony has
been completely distorted. Nikki's effort to organize people in their eighties and nineties, and to separate them
out of the community, is unforgivable.

I remember Nakayama-sensei saying that issei immigrants were the people of sacrifice. They came to the
new land only to perish in the culture clash. They offered their lives for the young. "Itsuka," he'd say, "your
sacrifice will be known. On that day, we will rejoice. The
children will return. But if they do not—and if you can-

not leap to where they are—my friends, have faith. Love leaps where we cannot. Trust then, always, that Love."

The sermon was on a tape that Mrs. Makino used to bring on Sundays, and she and Obasan would sit and listen while they sewed.

I know that what the issei wanted above all, wanted more than life, was to give good gifts to the young. Beneath all the community turmoil, beneath the bafflegab about cooperation, beneath the weariness and the paranoia, I have heard many an issei say quietly, "A good name—that is only treasure. That is only issei want give children. To future."

The good name of the issei is their legacy to us. Though they lacked political power, their spiritual powers remain—their steadfast rock-hard endurance, their determination, dignity, graciousness, loyalty, modesty, resourcefulness, reliability, industry, generosity, their reverence for nature, their respect for education, their amazing tenderness toward the young, their intense passion for us to be worth something. But first and foremost was their arigatai, their gratitude, the underground stream which nourished their deepest roots. Because of it, they endured. They endured for the sake of the long-term good, for the well-being of the whole. They endured for a future that only the children will know. Their endurance is their act of faith and of love. What they offer to the future are their keys to the safekeeping of the soul.

Mrs. Makino fills our empty rice bowls, scooping the cold rice from the pot with the flat rice paddle. There's a big thermos on the floor. The round lid acts as a pump and hot water steams out of the spout as she presses it with the palm of her hand.

41

It's one week later. We've dropped in to check on Aunt Emily again. She's not getting any better. I suggest that she see a doctor, but she ignores me.

Anna's in the kitchen making tea and the electric kettle is whistling away when the phone rings. It's Marion, Anna calls out, telling us to put the TV on quick.

"Stephen's on," she says.

Anna's reaction is faster than anyone's. She hops to the messy coffee table and grabs the remote control. A couple of channel switches. A toothpaste advertisement.

Switch again, and there's an eerie sound, with a face I recognize.

What a strange sensation. Here's a virtuoso in a black jacket, with his wide streak of white hair, his violin bow singing, wailing, and it's my brother on an empty stage, in Aunt Emily's little TV.

Amnesia must be like this. You know you're supposed to feel something, but a connection is missing. It's not as if the nerve ends have been cauterized or somehow destroyed. It's that the nerves aren't there. Something has been excised. All that registers is a television screen, a piece of glass masquerading as flesh, making these outer-space sounds.

"Wow, isn't he amazing." Anna's eyes are bright with excitement.

"Shh." Aunt Emily sits with her elbows on her knees, leaning forward as if that will bring her closer to the stage. She is captured by the magic bow. I am not, and I say with a light ungenuine voice, "Imagine that. He's national news."

"They'll see him in Granton," Anna says.

"He's wonderful. Wonderful," Aunt Emily whispers.

God help us. Obasan's last words. "Rippa. Rippa." Both my aunts, praising Stephen all the day long.

"My sister's genius kid. Nomi, aren't you proud?"

If I were back in my little apartment, I'd step into my thongs, run down the stairs, out the side door, into the alley. I'd look to see if the car was there, and if it was I'd go up. And Cedric would know and nod and not need to ask and, yes, that's what I would do.

Such loneliness, Stephen. The chaotic sound of much rushing—a weeping of winds. I can no more attend his voice than he can heed mine.

All these years I've been living his absence, and here he is, a ghost in a box. A demented leap of chords. Then finally, the bow suspended, the last plucked string plinks a dissonant twang. There's a full close-up of his face as the camera angle changes and suddenly he is gone again. The announcer is telling about an award he won in Berlin and she says that, in a moment, she will be back.

Anna, Aunt Emily and Mrs. Makino applaud. I go to the kitchen to plug the kettle back in. I wish Aunt Emily would make some comment of irritation, like "He could have let us know," but she doesn't.

So what if he never ever calls his only living relatives. There are other things on his mind, no doubt, like television appearances, concert tours, recording sessions. It has always been so, my dear aunt. His muse is his queen, his one true love, and he's her devoted slave. I wonder if he has been corrupted by fame with so many people fawning at his feet.

There's another advertisement and perhaps Aunt Emily too would like to turn the TV off. There's no frown or searching in her eyes to signal the slightest distress. Makino-obasan looks sad as she says, "Such happiness. Such satisfaction for your father, Naomi-san, receiving such a great son."

Aunt Emily has picked up the phone. She's trying to reach Stephen in Montreal. I fervently hope she doesn't succeed.

None of us has heard from him since our supper in his hotel two years ago. The two times I saw him before that were in southern Alberta, in 1972 at Uncle's funeral, then at Obasan's. It was the same both times. He was a showman passing through. And the show had to go on. His show. In Paris. In England. He wasn't booked in

Granton. His face was turned toward the city lights. He sought a different sun.

For Obasan's funeral in Coaldale, he and Claudine arrived an hour before, stayed for the tea in the hall and left immediately after. I never saw him alone.

Aunt Emily, I have such a need to turn this off.

The drive to the cemetery took place the following day but they'd already gone. When her coffin was lowered into the space beside Uncle's, I picked up some earth for him and said his goodbyes. He never heard of her last words.

The Christmas following her death, he and Claudine sent a circular letter describing their drive to the airport on the day of the funeral. They saw the biggest, most brilliant rainbow, they said. They drove toward it down the highway, then straight into the golden glow.

Everything about that Christmas made me weep. I kept thinking of Obasan and her long long wait. "Merry Christmasu ni." I was angry when I read the letter. And envious. When Obasan died, I saw yellow flowers. He saw a rainbow. I wanted the sky's light and the golden road.

I hardly felt anything when I saw him two years ago. And I don't know what I'm feeling right now, except perhaps that the dust in my attic is being disturbed and I need to shelter my eyes.

Stephen, dear Stephen, we have lost each other. How shall we now depart in peace?

42

Art, Aunt Emily says after the program is over, after the news is over, is the arena of the artful dodger, of the shadow boxer, of the soft shoe. Stephen's strategy is to be evasive—neither to flee nor to parry, but to be there like the air. If Min had stayed invisible, he too might have survived.

Anna and Mrs. Makino have gone home and Aunt Emily is talking to herself. She seems to be changing her mind about Stephen. Two years ago she told him that artistic excellence, like every other form of excellence, must not exclude the heart, and that Japanese Canadian artists who stood aloof from the community needed to have their hearts examined.

Stephen's so aloof that he's vaporized himself onto a glass screen and at the flick of a switch he vanishes. He's turned himself into one of those unreal TV people. There he was, like so many of them, wearing a decapitated rose on the lapel of his jacket. No stem. No thorn. No roots.

"So you don't think he's fiddling while Rome burns?"

Aunt Emily turns and faces me, her whole body pivoting because her neck's been sore these last few days. "The thing about his talent, Nomi, is that he's powerful enough to draw people. When you're that good, you're not aloof."

His music is inspired, she says, and he fulfills his responsibility to his community by being true to his art. And who's his community? It's whoever is inspiring to him. If it's not us, it's not us. "Of the two of you," Aunt Emily says, "I'd say you're more aloof than he is."

Stab. Of all the unfair comments. Who's the one who brings her food and buys her the right shampoo? Thankless old mop. Tactful she's not. But she's all I've got and I'll forgive—not that she's asking. The one thing I will not do for her is call Stephen. That I will not, will not do. I choose not to be the big bad wolf, huffing and puffing, puffing and huffing, blowing his walls down. Anyway, it's Claudine who answers the phone, and she's his solid brick house.

People who have no vision, Aunt Emily says, devour their artists, envy their achievements and denounce them when they withdraw. If our artists leave us, we have no one to blame but ourselves.

There's been no leaving the community for Aunt Emily. When she wakens in the night, there's no escape for her except work and more work. It's Labor that comes to her at midnight, carrying redress petitions.

At times, Aunt Emily says, an artist must choose between people and the muse, between the voice at hand and the voice from the stars. If someone's drowning nearby, the muse must wait. At least momentarily. In politics we sacrifice the voice from the stars. It's a sacrifice she makes, she says, but people like Stephen are barely of the earth.

What an irritating comment. Of course he's from earth. If he got hit by a truck, he'd be as dead as anyone else, whether he drove up a rainbow or not.

I only wish Aunt Emily would get back to her own writing. At least at the end of it she'd have something tangible. At the end of the community's labor—well, for one thing, there is no end. And the forces of oppression continue no matter what she does.

When I told her this, she said that out of the tasks of the hands would come the words for the pen—in their appointed time.

A few months ago, she came down to the office and heaved her armful of writing into a box. "Stay," she said as if to a dog. And there the papers still are.

Morty said he would feed the dog but he couldn't promise to take it for runs. Eugenia said that as long as Aunt Emily knew she was listening to the right voice, that was all that mattered. And Cedric said love's voice was always the best guiding voice. According to him, it's love's voice that comes from the stars, whether they are from the Milky Way or from the twinkly reflections in the lake. When we follow the light, we extinguish the night, and we do this through politics as much as through art.

Stephen, Aunt Emily says, is declaring his heart's land. A dark land. He is calling for the sun. He's a politician of space.

I've a mild feeling of unreality as I listen to her.

A storm that was brewing all day has come and gone without fuss. A few rain plops. No great lightning bolts. No tears streaking down the windows. The city from Aunt Emily's apartment looks vaguely brown, with smog filtering the evening sun. The air has turned to rust.

It's time to be off. I've done the dishes, taken the garbage out to the chute. I've even watered that dried-out old plant Aunt Emily insists on keeping. It's a sickly thing, hanging in the window. She hasn't had time to take care of it, yet she can't bring herself to throw it out. All the leaves closest to the root keep turning brown and the leafless stem gets longer and longer, but then there are always new green leaves moving out from the tips. Once she dug up the roots to see how they were, and they looked rotten all right. She stuck the healthy-looking tips in water, then potted them again, but the new cuttings were soon like the old. She lets the thing grow on and on in its diseased way. "Looks awful, I know," she says, "but I've had it so long."

Maybe it has a fungus. Or bugs. Or too little water. Or too much sun. Neither of us knows much about plants.

My footsteps speed to a trot as I leave the glittering apartment complex. It's a skeletal building that clanks as you go. I feel a bit like a skeleton myself tonight. Walk walk down the tunnel, through the doorway, large square

doorknob, and into the shopping center, pink plastic
lights in restaurant window, down wide stairs and along
the ramp to the subway.

On the way up here today, the subway trains were
delayed. Aunt Emily told me that suicide attempts happen sometimes. People jump. They don't publicize these
things for fear of creating an epidemic.

This is the way things are here. Strangers commit
suicide. People with glassy eyes walk out of glassy buildings. Sirens scream. My closest living relative is a ghost.
We're all such ghosts here, avoiding one another as we
stand on our shadowless platforms, waiting for our
trains.

All the way from Aunt Emily's apartment through
subterranean mall to College Street, we are inside the
city's skin. People can spend days without ever going
outside.

The last time Cedric and I were in the northern
woods it was early evening, and as we saw the first star in
the blue-black sky he talked about a time, centuries ago,
when his mentor walked upon the sea, among the stars
reflected in the waters. Those who travel by starlight, he
said, are drawn by a light that is a memory of a light.

Nakayama-sensei used to say things like that. However distant or faint the memory, he said, we travel by it
still.

The trouble is our mock stars that shine in the city's
sky—our neon lights, our flashing bulbs, our countless
baby moons. The trouble is the subway and people
speeding by.

43

Can't sleep. Can't decode the body/mind's distress. Call

off the war, my Sovereign. This is your servant calling. I

had not intended to dwell in a land too deformed, too

unpleasant. I had intended a peaceable life. Send peace.

Send down, I pray, no rockets to this field where I toil.

Grant me this night sweet rest. Grant peace.

Stephen!

I will not call him. I will not shape his absence power

into armaments against myself. I will turn from all this

and waken a sleeping friend.

"Oui? Ah. Naomi."

"My brother—"

"Stephen?"

"He was on TV. He won an award."

"Ah."

It's long past midnight. The dog next door is growling at the footsteps. I go to the door on tiptoe, and he is here. "Sh." He is warm. He wraps me round like a comforter.

"It's so late, Cedric, but I—"

He nuzzles my neck and I can feel the late-night bristles on his 2 A.M. face, the soft wool of the sweater I gave him last Christmas. We pull the other foam pad beside my bed and behold, there is no stranger anywhere in sight and I am not in a beet field trying to escape.

Stephen is there. He is still in the field with Uncle, hoeing the beets. He moves in his lopsided way down the row, the long unending sugar-beet row, humming his tunes. I can hear him. But I am here in this little Toronto room. I am watching him as he runs to his music, escaping the field, the heat, the drudgery. And it's my turn now. I am abandoning him there as he abandoned me. It's time to leave the beet field and the clay mud, the dry wind, the nausea. It's time to leave the home that is not a home and the stranger who lurks there.

My overburdened conscience is the God who makes ill. It's the fundamentalist's God who lurks in the field. And where is the truth that makes free?

From where Cedric and I are lying on the foam, we can see the branches of the chestnut tree and one bright star. One bright distant untouchable speck of light. Stephen is out there somewhere in some world of otherness, orbiting the muse of music with all his heart and soul and mind, attending and attending and oblivious of all else.

"I had a choice between calling you or Stephen."

He chuckles.

"Will you stay?"

He will. He sighs and he is weary but he is here and he is whispering to me. See? Up there? Love is watching us through the branches of the tree. Love watches the spaces between people, while they are absent from each other. He says that in all our hands are many wounds, and in the wounds Love toils and strives with us.

And I am striving now, within my body, that I may be free. I am burrowing into the coils within, challenging the old rage, the fears and the old griefs, the old old sadness, the envy, the loneliness and other still militant demons that ravage my flesh and encase it in disease.

He is soothing as friendship. He cradles me as a mother holds her child, with care and confidence. He is as gentle as the smallest waves from the sea where the rainbow is moored and he does not, he does not invade. With my eyes half closed, I drift in the slipstream of my half-moon thoughts.

These bodies that we are inhabiting are light specks —infinitesimal colored things in a golden road, in a blip of time, dreaming we live and breathe and have our being. We are gliding into the world by rainlight, down the highways of the mind, the backwoods, the trailways, by word, by flesh. We are here to tread this dreaming earth, its surfaces, its winding private ways, by foot, by limbs, by eyes, by touch. We are moving past closed doors of houses whose closets and attics I cannot see, past mountain camps and northern lakes with ghosts hiding among trees, into villages where lights have yet to be installed, and we enter the city by way of its skyline and the smoke and smog that surround it. We carry no weapons. We are looking for home.

"What is home for you, Cedric?"

"This. This is home enough. That you trust me. That we so much trust each other."

And with fingertip and tongue and tangled hair, through the falling air, through starlight, into stone, into stone become flesh, into the ancient myths of birth and rebirth and the joyful rhythms of earth, we are journeying home.

44

And when the body is not well? When the body betrays us? Where then is home?

I can't bear this place. This house of sickness. A new hour of waiting. The hospital corridor again. I can't sit with the others in the lounge at the end of the hall. Can't keep still in the chair in her room. I'm sick of hospitals.

Let calmness descend. Time is a friend. Take time, take time. I'll walk to the end of the corridor and back. The air is teeming—believe it—is teeming with peace. Seek peace and pursue it.

I don't know what's going on in the operating room. Maybe she's holding a mask up to her stubby nose. Maybe the knife is poised. Or they're sewing her back up. What if, God forbid, they find the trouble the doctor suspects? Anything's possible in the ganglia of one's abdominal walls.

Her faithful little car broke down last week. That was ominous.

Where in the air is peace? In which drawer can I find it?

"The tests," the doctor said, "show some suspicious cells. You must be prepared. . . ."

Aunt Emily doesn't believe anything can be seriously wrong. "I've got too much work to do," she says. My demented aunt.

I was doing her laundry last month and found bloodstains on her sheets. She wouldn't go to the doctor till I made the appointment. She had to see a gastrointestinal specialist. There were enemas and laxatives, Agarol, X-prep, magnesium citrate, then X rays, a sigmoidoscopy, a colonoscopy and suddenly this wretched hour.

It was heartbreaking to see her so submissive last night. "The bod is odd," she said to Anna and me. She was trying to reassure us that things would be all right. "Anyway, the grave is the most common doorway there is. Just think of the billions who've gone through before." And she changed the subject back to redress.

Wherever her body may be, her soul is still engaged in labor. Her mind has been constantly on the planning of an Ottawa rally to be held this month. It doesn't occur to her that she may be forced to rest. It's a kind of madness. I can imagine her on the operating table right now, fretting about the rally as she's counting backward, or whatever anesthetists ask you to do these days.

There are so many problems with the rally, but what on earth is the point in worrying, Aunt Em? Government will simply do what Government will do. Last week we held a huge public meeting at the St. Lawrence Center. We had five seats for the speakers but one remained empty because Government stayed away, claiming "the community is divided." In 1988, they're still saying that. Let them say their empty words from their empty seat.

The last Minister of Multiculturalism said there would never be individual compensation and he didn't think the American government would compensate Japanese Americans. Does it so much matter? Aunt Emily, when you fight the good fight and your body caves in, it's time to let go. It's beyond me how she can care more about redress than about her own health.

This morning, as she waited for her operation, she was reading a newspaper item and commenting that media coverage has been shifting. Criticism of NJCL and its "young turks" has appeared from a previously supportive journalist. The latest poll shows an almost even split in the country. About forty and forty, for and against compensation.

She handed me a work list and her briefcase with toothbrush, hairbrush, files and folders. There was just a moment's startle in her eyes when a gurney was wheeled into the room and out again.

It's the stress of these years and the constant disappointment that have, I'm convinced, affected her health. I've heard that some people become victims of cancer about six months after a serious emotional crisis. What about after five years of heartbreak?

She long ago stopped believing that there's any good will in the Cabinet toward us. There's been no shift in Government's fundamental trivialization of our cause. She's been resigned for some time to fighting a battle that will not be won in her lifetime.

So many have dropped out. In Toronto it isn't, for the most part, a young person's cause. Brian wants Anna to cut down, but Anna won't. She's in the early stages of pregnancy with what Brian calls "our Jewpy." Other sansei professionals who flipped into the movement in 1983 have long since flapped back out of the community coop, pursuing careers and the glitz at the end of a different rainbow. One with a monochromatic color scheme.

"They're not going to keep me down at the farm," one sansei told Anna. "I've got a life to live."

It's the gray-haired niseis across Canada who have been perishing in their trenches in this quiet little war. Some never gave up, to the very last gasp. We know of those who died, as they say, with their boots on.

We all do what we can do, we stand by each other, though it's not because we will win. Everyone, from time to time, is fed up with it all—the hair shirt of ethnicity we all must wear. But by now we know that, however much we may wish to flee, our ethnicity will thud after us. That's the way things are in this country.

The sudden decision by the strategy team to have us rally on Parliament Hill this month has seemed to many of us to be the most desperate and foolish effort to date. The futility of it. Getting our exhausted people to march is like forcing a corpse to twitch, Marion says. The idea was just suddenly sprung on us and there's hardly been time to organize. It's the unthinkable thing Morty proposed a year ago.

The decorous and polite are aghast. March on Ottawa? An unspeakable embarrassment! Completely out of character! Japanese Canadians will never be so garish as to stand around in front of people and hold signs, they say. The League has got to be crazy. We are not a vulgar community. We will not put on a circus. Not us. Moreover, Government doesn't change its mind just because people show up on the Hill. Even among the most stalwart, a few more have dropped away.

Aunt Emily, whatever her doubts, has been dancing like a puppet on a string. Her body is her puppet. Her commitment to the League is the puppeteer. She's handed out hundreds of petitions in schools, in basement halls, at supper parties. She's pushed herself beyond herself. It's so pathetic.

"We must never give up. Never, never," she said, just before the orderly came to wheel her away.

The last I saw of her was the back of her head as the gurney turned the corner of the corridor, her hair a gray mop on the flat pillow. She's always had such healthy hair.

The thought of chemotherapy and baldness slips like a ghost through the walls of my mind. Resist these thoughts. Resist, resist. It's Fear, the old beast, wanting to dance.

She's written a work list for me on the back of a blank check. New names for the National Coalition, our support network. Morty says that every single name on the coalition is music to his ears.

It's been almost an hour. Maybe the anesthetist is checking her pulse. The operation is a complete success, the doctor is saying, is he not, and there were a few non-malignant polyps. O Lord, that it may be so.

Eugenia sent flowers this morning. So did Anna.

"Ridiculous," Aunt Emily said in appreciation. "I'll be out of here this afternoon."

One never knows about these operations. If they find something more, they'll keep going. And if it spreads? I've heard of people who've died almost immediately after an operation.

Where into the mind does one go for ease?

Where into her mind has she gone? I can imagine her drifting through an anesthetic cloud, preaching to the cloud lumps as she goes. If Justice flees, I can hear her say, we must pursue. If Justice sleeps, we dare not rest. We will go to the attic, dig through the dust, shake her awake.

I'm leaning against Aunt Emily's bed, staring up at the ceiling made of white speckled rectangles divided by white metal strips. In the corner of the room, there's a gleaming white sink with its gleaming chrome plumbing, and there's a white two-drawered side table beside the bed on which sits a white phone. Over the bed there's a neon light, and on the wall a glass bottle with plastic tubing and a circular gauge. I'm cataloguing the room to order the world, but it will not stay still. There's a cool gray shadow filling the air. It rests on the metal lever-handle of the door. It waits, as I do, for the verdict.

I can't imagine life without Aunt Emily. My telephone would hardly ring. Her body would shrink to a photograph. I'd have to look for her in the world of dreams.

Outside the window of this time-heavy day are the screaming towers, the afternoon smog, the few brave trees below. We can bring health back, ah, we can bring health back, sing the tiny flowers here and in their boxes outside. And across the street the rectangle of grass strives for breath in the traffic and the dusty air.

Since year upon year it rains too much, since rust rains down like a river, we must dig up determined fistfuls of roots and tamp them into the eroding soil. We must plead for kinder weather.

Here in this high room by her empty bed I'm listening for the underground voice. I'm no longer trusting the lighthearted words. I'm bringing my petition and offering it here to the Spirit that moves through the deep. For Aunt Emily, for her lost labor, for the sake of her dream. To plead that there may be breath at the end of this present journeying.

45

When she wakes up from the anesthetic, the nurse is gently tapping her on the cheeks. "I'm going to the rally," she says. Those are her first words. She looks as if all the blood has been drained from her body.

"If you're going to the rally, I'm going to the moon," the doctor says.

It's such a relief when Cedric comes by after work. He brings some magazines—not *Bridge*—and we read and play Scrabble and drink tea while she sleeps.

She's allowed to go home under strict conditions. I

move back in with her. But last night she ordered me to join the great trek to Ottawa.

APRIL 14, 1988.

In spite of all the trepidation and countless minor catastrophes, the unimaginable is happening. Rally day dawns in cloud and faith.

A large square room in the West Block is packed with all generations of Japanese Canadians from across the country. The community that is known to be "largely reserved" has come forth. And there are fifteen thousand others with us, who have signed our bright yellow cards. There's a huge full mailbag that's going to be taken over to the prime minister's office after this.

From where I'm standing with Morty and Anna, somewhere in the middle of this dense crowd, I can barely see the speakers. Only a few rows of chairs have been put out to seat the older people. Anna should be sitting. She's been having morning sickness and almost didn't make it. She made sure her mother got a seat. Mrs. Makino is talking with an issei couple from Montreal whom she hasn't seen since 1942.

A white-haired man directly beside me has grabbed the sleeve of someone ahead and is exclaiming, "Yosh! That you? What're you doing here?"

"Well, I'll be damned. Is that Tom? Whaddya mean, what'm I doing here? What're you doing here? Haven't seen you since road camp."

Earlier on the Hill, beneath the patchwork of umbrellas, I saw Sumi beaming, clutching the arm of another older woman I didn't recognize. Sumi, with her tweedy coat and her bubbly infectious chuckle, waved and said, "Guess what? I found Keiko. We're the Kaslo contingent."

That's the way it's been with this mist of a presence on Parliament Hill. People, some nervously, some boldly, climbed off buses and found old friends from Powell Street, from New Denver, from Slocan and Tashme. It's a rally and a reunion and a brave little dream. An artist from B.C. found Min and they walked together in silence.

We've come here. We've marched, smiling politely to the cameras, up the wide semicircular walk to the Center Block, down the middle of the Hill to the Centennial flame, carrying our banners, our huge black-and-white now familiar photographs, a sea of confiscated boats, truckloads of people in Slocan. We carried our slogans—"Justice for Canadian Citizens," "An 'Enemy' of Canada at Age Four," "Guilty Without Trial," "This Happened in Canada." A group of our soldiers in their berets marched under their sign, "WW II Vets for Redress." There are a few hundred of us, plus a warm assortment of friends from here and there and from our church.

I was part of the group that carried bright yellow cascades of streamers, our "ribbons of hope" with names of those who contributed but could not attend. I held Aunt Emily's name out to the side for a photographer as I marched along.

People keep asking me where she is, or, oh they heard she was in the hospital, was it serious? Must be, if she's not here.

She would have come, I reply, she would have.

Everyone has sent cards or phoned or they've visited.

It turns out—it's no great surprise—that my fierce aunt is fiercely loved.

Stephen walked into the hospital room one afternoon and I thought, this is the way it is, after all, I suppose. He'll come to my bedside if I'm critically ill. I'll go to his. After all the estrangement and the numbness, he is still my brother.

He went up to the bed and leaned over to look at her sleeping face. He didn't stay long. I didn't expect him to. I didn't ask about Claudine and I didn't ask if he would come back. I let him go. I was the tree. He was the leaf. He seemed like a little boy.

It was disquieting, when it came right down to it, that I didn't—or couldn't—care that he was there. I felt for one instant the potential for the old raging storms of my Cecil nights. But like a passing breeze, the moment was gone. This time, I wouldn't be screaming, "She needs you." His arrival and his departure slipped past as unmomentously as they did two years ago. He was Stephen. That was all. A stranger that I love. Stephen, the deaf brother of Naomi the dumb. We're two missing babies in the midnight woods. And is God the woodsman who will someday bring us home?

It would take a miracle, I think, to bridge the distance between us now. It's as impossible for me to reach him as it is for the NJCL to reach Nikki, or for the entire Japanese Canadian community to reach Government. Still—who knows. Maybe someday—itsuka, itsuka, perhaps—via music, via letter. Meanwhile, there is work to be done. This is Aunt Emily's way. And Stephen's, no doubt, as well. It's the way of those who are granted no rest till they've given themselves to the one who calls. And my calling may well be to serve my dear aunt.

In this last month I've learned that gray hair can turn white in weeks; that plastic colostomy bags can leak and stain bedsheets and the smell is horrible; that the area surrounding the little opening, the stoma to the left just below the waist, can be red and sore. You can say all you want that the Queen Mother also has a colostomy but that's not going to help a great deal.

"You're a fighter," the doctor said. "This may just be temporary, Emily. A lot of people with half your guts recover quite easily."

"Half my guts?" Aunt Emily asked weakly and managed a sort of snort.

Her bathroom has a powerful deodorant smell and I've tacked a mirror up at waist level so she can see what she's doing with her bag. The doctor says her general health is improving. She's at least getting some nutrition now. In due course, he should be able to put her back together again. She has a temporary double-barreled colostomy and twice a day she has to irrigate it with a saline solution to get the mucus out. She has to eat and rest and rest and rest. The doctor introduced her to one of his colostomy patients who lives in the same building as Aunt Emily and has something called Crohn's disease. The woman is in a life-threatening depression. She's about ten years younger than Aunt Emily and views her body as her enemy, refusing to change her bag alone, refusing to leave her apartment, becoming dependent as an infant. I've been spending a fair amount of time doing chores for both of them. I told Aunt Emily I shouldn't go to the rally, but the suggestion enraged her. She wouldn't let Eugenia stay with her either and said we all belonged in Ottawa.

We closed the office for the day. Cedric and Eugenia

are somewhere in this quiet crowd. I saw Sumi earlier introducing them to some older women who said they never dreamed they would ever do such an embarrassing crazy thing as come to a rally.

The speeches have begun. Cool water for the thirsting crowd. There are church leaders, members of Parliament, and another brand-new Minister of Multiculturalism sitting in the front of the room at a long table. The former minister said before he broke off talks last year that at least Government now recognized the NJCL as our official organization. After five years of non-stop labor, that's as far as we've got.

Alan Borovoy, the lawyer from the Canadian Civil Liberties Association, is just beginning. He's standing at the lectern to the left. He speaks so distinctly and slowly that every word drops like a jewel of clarity.

"In May of 1984," he begins, "the then Opposition leader, Brian Mulroney, said that he felt strongly about compensation for Japanese Canadians."

He pauses. "Don't laugh," he says, as his eyes sweep across us all. "Be grateful. Imagine how long you'd have to wait if he didn't feel strongly."

There's a rather gentle roll of laughter.

"I sometimes marvel at the priorities we have in this country. As I read the claims made by your community, in total they amount to less than five hundred million dollars. And this in response to one of the greatest outrages ever perpetrated by a Canadian government. And yet just a couple of years ago, a couple of banks went belly up out west and within weeks—you've been talking to Government for years—within weeks the government resolved to compensate the uninsured depositors to the tune of more than eight hundred million dollars. And what's interesting is that those depositors knowingly incurred the risk. The only risk Japanese Canadians knowingly incurred, indeed they did not knowingly incur it, the only risk was to be born Japanese Canadian. I'm not suggesting the government should not have compensated those people. Nor am I suggesting that the two situations are completely comparable. All I'm saying is that, if the government could be so quick and so generous with them, couldn't they be a little less slow and a little less stingy with you?"

One of the war vets in the middle of the crowd shouts out, "Right on!" and several people turn and stare at him. The woman standing in front of me puts her hand over her mouth and looks around aghast. These mostly older niseis are such shadow dwellers, but here they are, and here we all are, defying the giants of Parliament Hill.

"Japanese Canadians have been criticized for this campaign," Alan Borovoy continues. "You're told to put the past behind you. Live in the present. What about all the other injustices in our society? Don't be so provincial, you're told. Don't be so self-obsessed. These criticisms are profoundly wrong. They are profoundly wrong. By your campaign of seeking compensation, you are not living in the past, you are working for the future. You are helping to create a precedent from which future governments would find it very hard to retreat."

The man referred to as Yosh has stepped back and is standing beside Tom. They're shaking hands as they listen.

"View this campaign not as parochialism by Japanese Canadians, but as social justice for everybody. You are fighting not only for you but also for us. Instead of our criticisms, you deserve our commendations."

Yosh mutters to Tom, "This is a goddamn miracle—this rally."

"We know that we cannot adequately rectify yesterday," the speaker concludes, "and we cannot adequately guarantee tomorrow. But we want to do whatever we can do. That's why you have our support. Because it's the only way we know how to say to ourselves, to say to you, to say to each other, to say to posterity—'Never again! Never again! This will bloody well happen never again!' "

I'm applauding till my hands are red and sore, as I've been applauding every speech. Sister Mary Jo Leddy, another speaker and a friend of Aunt Emily, is cutting through the crowd toward us. As the applause dies down, she asks how Emily is and she says she has not in all her years of attending rallies been to one like this. The old ones sitting on the few seats in front are so gentle and so dignified.

"Their faces," she says. "Their faces. . . ."

Some people are seeing this event as evidence of the reawakening of a buried community. A coming of age. I'm thinking that whether we ever attain redress or not, whether Government ever does or does not make a formal acknowledgment of the injustices, we are at least making a statement today ourselves. The politicians may remain unimpressed and continue to see us as ghosts rattling chains, a militant unrepresentative nuisance, an echo from a distant past. But this gathering is alive. We have come from out of the shadows of Government past and the community that once was. And in the light above the shadows, the balance scale rests. Justice sits on the side of the oppressed.

46

"But all shall be well, and all shall be well, and all manner of thing shall be well."

That's the quote that's embroidered on the beautiful altar cloth at church. Waves of pastel colors flow into and around the graceful figure of a woman seated on the ground. One feels the benediction in her body, her right hand raised in greeting or in praise.

The doctor says Aunt Emily's progress has been wonderful after her second operation and he didn't expect a woman of her age to recover so quickly. I notice, though, that she's weaker than before.

"But all shall be well," I hear her saying from time to time. I'm not sure whether she's making a statement of faith or commanding her body.

The words come down to us from Julian of Norwich, a saintly woman who is said to have been granted a holy illness.

"Hard to think of illness as holy," Aunt Emily says. " 'Specially mine."

Aunt Emily, Eugenia and I are on cushions on the floor in a small attic room of the church office building. We used to meet with others about once a month but the three of us have been meeting more frequently since Aunt Emily's hospitalization. Eugenia mentioned the group to Anna but Anna said she's had so much fundamentalism in her time that she couldn't bear the idea.

Aunt Emily says that she prays out of the back of her head and that her faith grows by hindsight. She is confident she will learn whatever it is she's intended to know. "Whatever," she says, lifting both hands. In some ways, she is not unlike Pastor Jim. She walks down a road made narrow and straight by an unswerving heart.

When her test results first came in, Aunt Emily said she had a glimpse of the inevitable door but thought it was a mirage. Death wasn't really there. She found herself constructing absurd elaborate notions about the incompetence of doctors, errors in tests. People were surely lying. She even had a flickering thought about a certain lab technician in the hospital who didn't like her. She recognized paranoia in her mind's wild gyrations. It was the same phenomenon at work in the community. Stresses and fears send the mind rushing about looking for a way out. And the only non-circular route she could find was the way called prayer. She summoned prayer to her ocean of fears. Prayer walked the plank with her. She called Eugenia.

Prayer, Nakayama-sensei used to say, is a practice of trust. One practices trust through believing the report that God is Love.

I can hardly remember the last time I prayed a believer's cloudless prayer. I know there was once upon a time a kind of pure trust that I shared with Tina, filled with such certainty that even longing was absent. But these days I am full of longing—longing for Aunt Emily to be well—longing for the community's healing.

In Tina's last letter she wrote that she is "rejoicing mightily" to know Canadian Mennonites are supporting redress and have set up a scholarship.

We can hear footsteps on the stairs and Min comes in, followed by Cedric carrying a paper bag. "Lo the angels," Eugenia says. Aunt Emily chuckles and makes room for them. Eugenia places the tumbler-size candle in the center of our circle. Min grabs a cushion, scrunching it down into a pillow. He lies on his stomach, watching as Aunt Emily lights the wick. A small pearly glow. It's the signal for quietness.

There's a long intake of breath and peace on Aunt Emily's face—a letting go of the reins. She closes her eyes. I can feel the weary galloping of her horses slowing to a trot. I sink into the general sigh of relaxation. "But all shall be well and all shall be well. . . ." Breath in. Breath out.

Aunt Emily is smiling and Eugenia looks bemused as Min falls asleep and snores. Angels can fly, I've heard, because they take themselves lightly.

After a while, Min wakens and sits up. Cedric takes his hand. Aunt Emily takes mine. We are a circle of hands. Then, as randomly as leaves falling, words are addressed to the Presence. Gratitude for the moment and for the candle's small light. Gratitude for the mystery that leaps into our lives.

If politics is the sacrifice of the voice from the stars, this is the practice of the presence of angels.

"That which delivers us is here at work in us," Cedric says. He takes a cup, a flask of wine and a bun from his bag and begins a two-thousand-year-old ritual of memory.

Outside, the bonging of a clock marks the half hour and some young people are laughing uproariously. We huddle closer to the candle's soft glow.

Min hasn't spoken. Neither have I. Aunt Emily prays for redress and for the power of reconciliation to be released—a power, she says, that is greater than the atom bomb. Like "the importunate widow" of the biblical tale, she will ask for redress to the end of her days.

Just last week, August 10, we were holding our breath waiting to hear what was happening with our counterparts in the United States, when the word came down. It was done. President Reagan signed the Civil Liberties Act into law. Japanese American redress was a reality. Such a relief. But no one suggested it would make any difference to Ottawa. The only word we heard from government officials was that the American situation would have no bearing, none whatsoever, on the Canadian government.

Min is breathing in shallow gasps. It has to do with his medication, I'm told. He lies down on his side and in moments he is asleep again.

More random thoughts.

Aunt Emily says that in looking at Death's door recently, she felt it to be more porous than it seemed before. She now feels that everything is more porous—the seen, the unseen, moral and physical laws, the past, the present. Everything wends its way through everything.

"Through the living," Eugenia whispers, "and the dead."

Aunt Emily says a world of saints is with us—her parents, her sister, Uncle, Obasan, Min's devoted mother. She names friends who were with her in the forties, some who died in the camps, some who died in the midst of this latest struggle, old people, young ones, people in the prime of life. What a long time she has lived to have known so many. She is here with her thirst and she drinks from her memories, long and deep. It's almost like that day in Japan at the high hillside grave—this strange sense of approaching the dead.

I'm staring at the flickering light and thinking of Hawaii and the long white forever wave that is never the same and the dream I had. The conviction was so strong at the time—the dead as alive and somehow, in some actual way, living in the element of thought.

Aunt Emily comes to the end of her roll call and we're back to stillness. Rest. Peace. I'm sinking into the silence, into the sound of snow falling, and it's as if the snow is imprisoned within a precise band of temperature —not too hot, not too cold—and every thought is held— but briefly—because the snow dies in a moment, melts, evaporates and is gone forever—but in this brief hour comes my mother, my silent mother, in this flowing dot of breath. She breaks through to whisper, yes, she's here. It's just that it's a little hard to be heard, she says, because we're so deaf in this world, so unable to hear those who still love us. Oh yes, they do love, as fiercely as we in our fiercest loving moments do, and the labor of the dead is through our dreaming, through our unexpected sideways glancing when they break through at last.

They practice the cutting edge. They inhabit the spaces of easy believers. They are in the sound of snow falling, in an avalanche down every mountainous thought, scraping down the melting roof, an apostrophe, a period, a punctuation sound. They are at the juxtaposition of sound and thought. All we need do is listen. They have so very much to say. They require us not to neglect the earthy sounds of night, the fridge humming, the icicle melting, the traffic—every twig-snapping pen-scraping sound. Mostly the message is love and warning, love and telling us which path to follow. Love sees how blind we are.

We make tiny cracks in our minds when we pray, tiny check marks in the ceilings of our consciousness where Love breaks through. Love enters our busy walking days, our ceiling-staring moments, breaks into our smooth white painted thoughts. Love surprises us. In our dreams, in our prayers, Love declares to us that Love will guide us as we practice our trust, as we do not lose hope, as we keep dialing and dialing compulsively in the hallways at the Clarke, as we stretch out our timebound brittle arms. Love declares that Love is our safety net. This we will know in the snowflake moment of our flesh melting, and with utter joy we will enter the waiting arms. This is what I hear Love saying this August night.

Meanwhile the candle burns on and I surrender my thoughts.

Lead, kindly light.

47

Dreams dreams dreams.

It begins in earliest infancy, this journey through the world's many borderlands. It proceeds through the day of the odorless fawn, past summer, into the mustier season of leaves, orchards, the harvest with its memories and dance. To be without history is to be unlived crystal, unused flesh; is to live the life of the unborn.

What I've wakened to in this new autumn day is hunger. My eyes are hungry. The palms of my hands are hungry. And somewhere beneath my ribs. I'm hungry for this square inch of space we are inhabiting today. Our bite-sized moment of life. I'm as small and as hungry as a newborn sparrow.

SEPTEMBER 22, 1988. OTTAWA.

Perhaps it's in the scheme of things that when life is most bleak, miracles break through. It's such a mystery. And so completely unexpected. I first heard about it last night. Last night was another lifetime ago.

I was still at *Bridge* when Aunt Emily called around seven. Dan had just called her. She immediately called Anna and me. She couldn't call any others because it's still completely confidential. All she said was "Come over immediately. I can't tell you why." I rushed up to the apartment and found her looking around abstractedly. She packed in silence, mechanically. We tried to sleep. We were up before the alarm. Anna, looking like a blimp, came by with Brian at 5:30 A.M. and we set off along the 401. We're in a daze.

The strategy team, unlike most of us, had felt something would have to happen following the American resolution, but over the many years they'd grown wary of false optimism. They did not communicate a word of hope to the rank and file. There had been so much debility and loss of morale when repeatedly, after promises of negotiations, there'd be a collapse in talks. Then suddenly, three weeks ago, the team was called to a Montreal hotel, and after a weekend of non-stop negotiating the unbelievable happened. An agreement was reached. There's to be a full acknowledgment of the injustices, individual compensation of $21,000 each to those affected (the Americans are to receive $20,000), a community fund and a race-relations foundation. It's a $350,000,000 package.

"All that? Just like that? But—but was there no warning?"

The team was sworn to secrecy. They were told that if the news leaked out in any way, and if the Legion, for instance, objected, the whole thing could be jeopardized. Even now, everything could be stopped. Dan took his oath so seriously that he went north to an isolated cabin.

"It's a miracle. What happened, do you think?"

Brian thinks it's because it's election time. Plus they're copying the Americans, for sure. Maybe it's because of a few key people—like John Fraser, the Speaker of the House.

Young John Fraser, Aunt Emily tells us, was a child in Vancouver when we all disappeared. His father took him to the cenotaph in Stanley Park where Japanese Canadian veterans of the First World War were memorialized. "I fought beside those men," he told his son. John Fraser never forgot.

Whatever the reasons may or may not be, we're so used to pessimism that the fact of a settlement isn't really registering. Aunt Emily says she doesn't want to say another word until she's actually in the House and the papers are actually signed. Dan told her the whole thing is so precarious anything could still stop it.

"How do you think Nikki's going to react?" Anna asks.

"Publicly?" Aunt Emily says. "She'd be a fool to oppose it. And Nikki's no fool."

"Privately, she'll break out in a rash," Brian says.

Privately, I'm wondering if Nikki is still convinced the NJCL are greedy opportunists. Vultures, I think she called us. Could there be any truth in her statement that history will condemn us and vindicate her? That, I suppose, is something none of us can know. What we as a community decide to do from this day on will reveal who we are.

Brian is familiar with the route. We take a rest break at Tweed, get to Ottawa shortly after ten, check in to a friend's house, collapse for a second on our beds. And now here we are in this city, the country's capital, the four of us, walking up to Parliament Hill under the blue-white September sky.

I think of the years of labor, the rally half a year ago that Aunt Emily missed—how we walked along in the drizzle and how I wasn't feeling a whisper of hope even though I was carrying the yellow ribbons of hope, and suddenly this unbelievable, this most astonishing day.

If I were a watcher in the skies, I might notice small antlike groupings of people walking up Parliament Hill this morning, up past the Centennial flame, up the wide walk and the steps and into the lobby of the Center Block with its high vaulted ceiling. Dan flew up last night. Others from the strategy team are here, plus some people from the Ottawa community. Only a few passes have been arranged since it's all such a secret. We hand over our cameras and notebooks at a desk, go down the marble hall, enter the narrow gallery high above the House of Commons. The strategy team is on one side, we are on the other, and we look down on the people who lead our country. We can see the top of Prime Minister Mulroney's head from the back and, across from him, Mr. Broadbent, leader of the New Democratic Party. The leader of the Liberal Party is not present. To our right is the public gallery, without a single person in it. The huge chamber seems almost empty. A few members of Parliament. A handful from our community. So little flesh, but so many ghosts.

11 A.M.

The prime minister stands. The magic of speech begins—this ritual thing that humans do, the washing of stains through the speaking of words.

"Mr. Speaker," the prime minister begins. "Nearly half a century ago, in the crisis of wartime, the Government of Canada wrongfully incarcerated, seized the property of and disenfranchised thousands of citizens of Japanese ancestry. . . ." Even as I strain to hear and remember the many words, they are gone and speech is a trickster, slipping and sliding away.

"Most of us in our own lives," he is saying in his low voice, "have had occasion to regret certain things we have done. Error is an ingredient of humanity. So too is apology and forgiveness. We all have learned from personal experience that, as inadequate as apologies are, they are the only way we can cleanse the past so that we may, as best we can, in good conscience face the future. . . ."

In the future I know we will look back on this moment as we stand and applaud. We'll remember how Ed Broadbent crossed the floor to shake the prime minister's hand, and we'll see all this as a distant sun, a star, an asterisk in space to guide us through nights that yet must come. The children, the grandchildren, will know that certain things happened to their ancestors. And that these things were put right.

Sergio Marchi, the Liberal Party representative, is

commending our president and community "for their never-ending determination and deep belief in the cause that they carried so well for so long. Today's resolution, no doubt, is a tribute to their sense of purpose, but it is also an appropriate response to those who continue to question the legitimacy and motivation of the leadership. . . ."

I feel us wanting to jump up and cheer but we are contained. And as I look down I can see Mr. Broadbent, who was married to a nisei and knows our story from the inside. I'm glad to be on this side, facing him. He appears agitated, his hands shuffling papers, his eyes glancing up to where we sit. And then he rises and speaks and he's fighting to control his voice. "They, as Canadian citizens, had done no wrong," Mr. Broadbent says. "They had done no wrong. . . ."

This feast of words is too wonderful, too sad, too joyful. I'm numb. Aunt Emily too is listening from some great slow distance of time and space. We are seated at a banquet table that was a hope for people yesterday and will feed us with hope tomorrow. The power of this hour is being stored now in our hearts as a promise fulfilled, a vision realized, and the healing rises up to us, the healing falls about us, over the countryside, here and there, today and tomorrow, touching the upturned faces filled with the waiting and longing of all the wordless years.

The speeches end and it's all going by so fast, so fast, and we're back in the west hallway, in a room where a small throng is gathering. The signing of the agreement is happening here and I catch just a glimpse of the prime minister again, no more real than any other person as he steps into the room. The TV cameras are directed upon him and our president, smiling, shaking hands, then sitting at a table, the strategy team standing behind. A flashing of lights and cameras clicking. And it's done.

Then, like a gathering swarm of bees, politicians, staff members, the League vanguard in a block, TV crews and reporters all move down the hall, the wide stairs, back down the middle of the Hill to the press conference. Aunt Emily is sleepwalking.

We can't get into the room and go with the overflow, up the crowded elevator to a sixth-floor lounge and a television screen, then back down again into the world of microphones and cameras, and catch up with Dan and the others as they walk back up to the Parliament Buildings for a reception.

I want some way to slow down the day, but the waterfall refuses to be contained in a cup and we're swept along into a room with tables of food, glib words, glazed eyes, cameras flashing, and Aunt Emily is standing with Mr. Broadbent and she looks stunned and not altogether coherent.

"I feel I've just had a tumor removed," one of our friends from Ottawa says to me. "Can you believe it, Naomi?"

We're in a buzz of sounds whirring about.

"Let me congratulate you, Mick. I think you've created a vaccine."

"Yes?"

"Against fatigue. A vaccine against compassion fatigue."

Cedric, Morty, Marion and Ken have just flown up from Toronto and Cedric has the most joyful tearful smile I have ever seen. He comes rushing up to me and in all that crowd he takes me in his arms. "Watch out, world," he whispers. "The mouse has roared."

I laugh. I am whole. I am as complete as when I was a very young child. Marion puts her arms around us both. "God bless us every one," she says.

Aunt Emily and Dan are talking with a man from the Secretary of State who asks Aunt Emily, "How did you feel when you heard the apology?"

Aunt Emily is in a trance and can't reply. My aunt of the so many words. How does she feel as this day speeds by? How does the grass feel in the cool autumn air? How does the sky feel? And the community across the country as it hears the news today?

Ken says, "I finally feel that I'm a Canadian." You can hear the trembling in his voice.

Aunt Emily and I look at each other and smile. We've all said it over the years. "No, no, I'm Canadian. I'm a Canadian. A Canadian." Sometimes it's been a defiant statement, a demand, a proclamation of a right. And today, finally, finally, though we can hardly believe it, to be Canadian means what it hasn't meant before. Reconciliation. Liberation. Belongingness. Home.

Anna and Brian, Cedric, Morty, Aunt Emily and I walk to a friend's house. We let ourselves smile. "Well?" Aunt Emily asks, looking up at the sky. That's all she can say.

We have tea and catch the TV news on every channel we can find. We gasp when we see the official shots. By focusing on the prime minister and the MPs behind him, the camera makes the House seem packed, when in fact it certainly wasn't—not that it mattered. There's a brief report on the radio that Nikki was contacted in Toronto. She said she was very happy about the announcement. We all applaud and toast Nikki with our cups of tea.

The Vancouver contingent phones and we go off to

meet for supper. Someone is doing an interview with
Dan outside the restaurant. We go in. Wait. Dan arrives.
We eat. A few Ottawa people drop by. Then Cedric and I
excuse ourselves and leave, ducking past a man taking
pictures. We walk hand in hand out into the evening air,
up Elgin Street, along Rideau, where strangers are
standing at their bus stops, waiting for their many buses,
walk past and up to the grounds of Parliament Hill
again. We're walking off the stage of the day with its
hovering of well-wishers and the great happy crush of
the press—away from the speeches, the interviews, the
congratulations, the shaking of hands at the restaurant,
where some people are still looking at one another,
pinching themselves, asking if it's true.

We're taking time, taking time to quieten this day,
and to bring it back from its already past. We're stretching it out on the canvas of the night air, shaking it out
like a blanket to wear.

Oh Aunt Emily, Aunt Emily, is it not the happiest
day of your life? I want to remember everything. Savor it
all. Our frantic search for a safety pin for the tie on
Anna's skirt. The man who honked his horn on Rideau
Street and waved. The pattern of sand on the Center
Block steps. Our brave president, with a hand in his hip
pocket as he walked briskly ahead of us. I want to etch
the day onto the permanent airwaves of memory, replay
it over and over until it starts to seem real. Aunt Emily, I
want to be able to see you forever and ever the way you
were this morning, walking happily happily up the hill in
your brown trench coat and your good walking shoes, my
dear warrior aunt. I want to call all the ghosts back again
to share this day that none of us can believe is happening.

In my pocket, I have the folded piece of paper that contains the government's statement. I read the words again and I take them into my childhood home. I pile them like fire logs, one by one. I warm my limbs.

"As a people, Canadians commit themselves to the creation of a society that ensures equality and justice for all. . . ."

I hand the paper to Cedric and he reads it aloud as we stand, looking out over the shadowy trees and bushes on the slope, to the Ottawa River below. In a month's time the leaves of the trees will change color, and then they will fall as they've been falling forever, year after year, each leaf with its own tiny story twirling into every other ongoing tale.

This hill is not unlike the slope to the Old Man River near Granton, though it's steeper here and the river is more wide. Sixteen years ago I stood with my uncle on the Granton coulees in the coolness of a night like this, looking down at the ocean of grass, and he said, as he always did, "Umi no yo." It's like the sea.

It's like the sea tonight, Uncle. A busy bubbling trembling sea of the almost sighted and the sometimes blind, the swimmers, the drifters, and those who don't know how to swim. We are here together, and it's enough.

Sixteen years ago this month, my uncle died. And two years later, so did my Obasan. I'm thinking of them and of the rapids, the waterfalls, the eddies in the journey to the sea, and how today we've touched the sounds of the waves on the shore, the applause, the pulse of earth's heart still beating. And I'm thinking of Uncle's words and the words of an old man in Slocan.

"There is a time for crying," they said. "But itsuka, someday, the time for laughter will come."

This is the time, dear Uncle, dear Ojisan. The dramatics, the tears and cheers, have arrived in their own way in their own time. We have come to the hour when the telling leaps over the barricades and the dream enters day.

I can hear the waves from childhood rippling outward to touch other children who wait for their lives. I can hear the voices, faint as the faraway sound of a distant, almost inaudible wind. It's the sound of the underground stream. It speaks through memory, through dream, through our hands, our words, our arms, our trusting. I can hear the sound of the voice that frees, a light, steady, endless breath. I can hear the breath of life.

Thank you for this.

ACKNOWLEDGMENT

As a people, Canadians commit themselves to the creation of a society that ensures equality and justice for all regardless of race or ethnic origin.

During and after World War II, Canadians of Japanese ancestry, the majority of whom were citizens, suffered unprecedented actions taken by the Government of Canada against their community.

Despite perceived military necessities at the time, the forced removal and internment of Japanese Canadians during World War II and their deportation and expulsion following the war was unjust. In retrospect, government policies of disenfranchisement, detention, confiscation and sale of private and community property, expulsion, deportation and restriction of movement, which continued after the war, were influenced by discriminatory attitudes. Japanese Canadians who were interned had their property liquidated and the proceeds of sale were used to pay for their own internment.

The acknowledgment of these injustices serves notice

to all Canadians that the excesses of the past are condemned and that the principles of justice and equality in Canada are reaffirmed.

Therefore, the Government of Canada, on behalf of all Canadians, does hereby:

1) acknowledge that the treatment of Japanese Canadians during and after World War II was unjust and violated principles of human rights as they are understood today;

2) pledge to ensure, to the full extent that its powers allow, that such events will not happen again; and

3) recognize, with great respect, the fortitude and determination of Japanese Canadians who, despite great stress and hardship, retain their commitment and loyalty to Canada and contribute so richly to the development of the Canadian nation.

If you enjoyed reading ITSUKA, *Anchor Books also pub-lishes Joy Kogawa's first novel,* OBASAN, *which tells the story of Naomi's childhood experiences during the Japa-nese Canadian relocation and internment. The following is an excerpt from that novel.*

The bantam rooster's early morning crow is more a choked chirp than the full-throated call of the regular rooster.

It is early autumn in 1945, several months after the evening of the late-night bath. I waken suddenly, before the regular summons of the rooster, to the soft steady steam of rain and fog and a grayness thicker than sleep. Something has touched me but I do not know what it is. Something not human, not animal, that masquerades the way a tree in the night takes on the contours of hair and fingers and arms.

Only my eyes move, searching the shelf ceiling above my bunk. Stephen in the bunk below is asleep, his mouth squashed open on his pillow.

She is here. She is not here. She is reaching out to me with a touch deceptive as down, with hands and fingers that wave like grass around my feet, and her hair falls and falls and falls from her head like streamers of paper rain. She is a maypole woman to whose apron-string streamers I cling and around whose skirts I dance. She is a ship leaving the harbor, tied to me by colored paper streamers that break and fall into a swirling wake. The wake is a thin black pencil line that deepens and widens and fills with a grayness that reaches out with tentacles to embrace me. I leap and wake.

Something is happening but I do not know what it is. I listen intently, all my senses alert.

Yesterday Stephen came running back from town shouting that the war was over and we had won. "We won, we won, we won!" he cried, running through the yard with both hands raised and his fingers in the V-for-Victory sign. The bantam rooster that roams freely in the yard squawked and flew away to a branch in the apple tree, from which it stared down fluffing its brown and red feathers till it looked twice its size.

After Stephen calmed down, he climbed the woodshed and hopped to the roof of the house, carrying a hammer and nails and a flagpole with a well-worn Union Jack.

This morning there is no shouting, only the familiar soft thudding of a log dropping into the wood stove and the clank of the stove grate being pushed back into place. Obasan is up and there is the plip noise of the dipper entering the bucket of water and—splash—the kettle filling, once, twice, three times, then the lid of the kettle, clink, the shuffle to the stove, the slide of the kettle, and the hiss of the water turning to steam where it spills on the hot surface.

The grayness moves aside, then returns, separates, but returns confident as breath.

Obasan's feet are treading a faster rhythm than normal.

I turn my head and peer down into the kitchen. The coal-oil lamp on the table is lit, the wick turned just high enough that there is no smoke going up the glass chimney. On the window ledge by the cactus plants is the bowl of water with the three black hairs that Stephen has been watching for days. Miss Pye, Stephen's music teacher in Vancouver, wrote him that black hairs turn into water snakes.

"How long does it take?" I asked Stephen a few days ago.

Stephen shrugged as he stared into the bowl and pushed the hairs with his forefinger. However long the hair stays hair, Stephen swears Miss Pye never tells lies. Somewhere between her words and his watching is a world of water snakes he cannot find.

Uncle is up and sitting at the table, stretching his arms.

"Sa!" he says, punctuating his stretch as if he has come to the end of his thoughts. Obasan turns the toast on the wire grill and pours tea into one of the large flat-bottomed mugs.

I curl up under my covers again and close my eyes. The weight of the nightmare is as persistent as rain, a shape that falls and evaporates, rises up from the earth and disappears again.

"Stephen," I whisper, leaning over the side of the bunk and blowing at his face. I push aside the heavy futon with my foot and feel for the ladder rung with my toes. "Wake up," I say as I step onto his bed.

The bantam rooster has started a gurgle of croaks as if he is trying to outdo the proper rooster.

"So early?" Uncle asks as I appear.

"Sleep some more," Obasan whispers.

They are both still in their nemaki and Obasan's long braid of hair dangles down her back.

I stumble out to the outhouse. The sharp air of the mountain morning cuts through my fog. When I come back Obasan hands me a square of toast.

I glance at the water snake bowl to see if the hairs have changed, but nothing has happened. And then, as I finish my toast, I see through the doorway that Uncle's and Obasan's room is different. The cupboard bookshelf Uncle made which stood along the wall is no longer there and instead I can see the end of Nomura-obasan's cot. I stand up to see better and Obasan gestures me to silence.

"Quietly," she whispers.

"Who's here?" I ask, tiptoeing into the room. Has Nomura-obasan come back?

On the side of the room in front of the narrow bed and the piano, and all over the rest of the room, there are piles of empty boxes. Someone is in the bed, an arm crooked above the pillow. The sleeves of the nemaki cover the head.

The arms move then, and I see the familiar head, the smooth face, the high cheekbones, the black hair straight back over his head as if it had just been combed.

Without moving from the spot, my body leaps. My hands, palms open, fall to my thighs.

Without turning his head to look at me, he beckons, and I see the same hand, the long thin fingers that I have watched moving with confidence over the keyboard.

"Good morning, Naomi-chan." He is talking to me. How does he know it is me? He has not moved. His back is toward me.

He turns then and smiles and I scrape my knees on the cupboard as I fling myself onto the bed. He sits up and gathers me into his serious smile. His forehead is wrinkled with new puzzle lines as if he has been asking questions all the time.

We do not talk. His hands cup my face. I wrap my arms around his neck. The button of his pajama top presses into my cheek. I can feel his heart's steady thump thump thump. I am Minnie and Winnie in a sea-shell, resting on a calm seashore. I am Goldilocks, I am Momotaro returning. I am leaf in the wind restored to its branch, child of my father come home. The world is safe once more and Chicken Little is wrong. The sky is not falling down after all.

There is no sound in the house except the satisfied "Aah" that Uncle makes after he has swallowed a hot drink, and the scrape scrape of Obasan's knife buttering the toast. In the chicken house outside the rooster is still crowing and the neighbor's dog barks three short excited blasts.

The laughter in my arms is quiet as the moon, quiet as snow falling, quiet as the white light from the stars. Into this I fall and fall and fall, swaying safe as a feather through all my waiting hours and silent night watchings, past the everyday walk through the woods and the noisy school grounds, down past the Slocan City stores and the sawmill whine and Rough Lock Bill's cabin, back along the train journey and the mountain ridges and the train station in Vancouver with all the people and the luggage and missionaries and women trotting here and there, carrying babies and boxes. Back up the long bus ride to Marpole and our house and the hedge around the yard and the peach tree outside my window and the goldfish bowl in the music room and I am in my father's arms again my father's arms.

When I move my head finally, the words rush around stumbling to form questions, but there are no questions and I do not understand how he has found us or when we will return home. But he is here now and his hand strokes my sleep-tangled hair.

Then suddenly Stephen is in the room, barefoot, with his nemaki open to his belly and the sash half undone. He has his flutes in his hand as he usually does.

Father nods as Stephen stands there staring, wiping the sleep from his eyes. "Good morning," Father says.

"Dad!" Stephen is upon us with a howl.

Father releases me and takes a flute, his wide-set eyes delighted. For a moment, the lines disappear from his brow and he is exactly as he used to be. "These?" Father turns the instrument around, fondling it with his fingertips.

Uncle grins and squeezes into the room. He sits on the edge of the cot, pushing the wooden boxes aside.

Deftly, Father places the pads of his fingertips on the holes and, holding the mouthpiece flat against his lower lip, he plays arpeggios rapidly. Then, with a light legato, he opens with the first few notes of "The White Cliffs of

Dover." Stephen picks up the tune immediately and Father's flute dips and trills birdlike notes in and around the tune. Without a break, Father leads into "Waltzing Matilda," and Stephen improvises harmonies. Their heads nod in time to the music and their elbows sway like airborne birds as the clear notes bounce off the walls and the cow-dung ceiling. Stephen's head is angled up like the rooster when it crows and flaps its wings sending out its call.

The music goes on and on from song to song. Uncle taps with spoons on his knees. "Whoo," Father says finally, and shakes his head approvingly. "Not bad," he says and Stephen is on center stage, beaming.

"Not bad," Uncle says.

Obasan turns down the coal-oil lamp and, cupping her hand behind the chimney, she blows out the night's light. She hands us all pieces of toast.

Joy Kogawa was born in Vancouver in 1935. Like other Japanese Canadians, she and her family were interned and persecuted during the Second World War.

She is the author of two novels, *Obasan* and *Itsuka*. She has also written four volumes of poetry: *The Splintered Moon, A Choice of Dreams, Jericho Road,* and *Woman in the Woods.* She has received numerous awards and grants, and has contributed to many anthologies and periodicals; she has also worked as a schoolteacher, a writer for the Canadian Prime Minister's office, and is a member of the Order of Canada.